One of the most memor
about climate change I've
estranging and wonderfully .... *passion. The*
perfect blend of arctic mystery thriller, science fiction and post-
disaster apocalypse. You won't want to miss this one.
Adam Roberts, author of *The Thing Itself* and many more

Always North *is a book haunted by our present and by a future*
we are inexorably heading towards. It is funny, startling, uncanny
and beautifully written. A story with heart and determination
that will crawl inside your skull and nest there, staying with you
long after you've read the last page.
Ross McCleary, author of *Portrait of the Artist as a Viable*
Alternative to Death

Always North *confronts the oncoming future with power, wit and*
originality. Come for the intrigue of a mission into the changing
Arctic; stay for the ingenious shift to a Britain shattered by rising
water. It will mesmerise you.
M. T. Hill, author of *Zero Bomb* and *The Breach*

It hooks you in and draws you under right from the start. A
nightmare vision of the future from one of Scotland's finest
writers. An extraordinary achievement.
Pippa Goldschmidt, author of *The Falling Sky* and *The Need for*
Better Regulation of Outer Space

Vicki Jarrett is a tremendous talent and a writer fit for our
times. Always North *is packed with startling prose, sublime*
humour and prodigious heart. It is a hell of a story, one in
the great tradition of Atwood and Le Guin: terrifying in its
plausibility, provocative in its challenges, and above all massively
entertaining.
Iain Maloney, author of *The Waves Burn Bright* and *The Only*
Gaijin in the Village.

Also available from Unsung Stories

ALWAYS NORTH

VICKI JARRETT

UNSUNG
STORIES

Published by Unsung Stories

43 Mornington Road, Chingford
London E4 7DT, United Kingdom

www.unsungstories.co.uk

First edition published in 2019
First impression

Paperback ISBN: 978-1-912658-03-9
ePub ISBN: 978-1-912658-04-6

Edited by George Sandison
Proofreading by Dan Coxon

Cover Artwork © Caleigh Illerbrum 2019

Cover design by Vince Haig
Text design by Cox Design Limited
Typesetting by George Sandison

Printed in the UK by TJ International

FOR HEATHER AND ANDREW

First is a stillness, a breath-held moment of the kind that precedes thunder. The stomach-dropping certainty that, whatever is coming next, there is no stopping it and this present moment is the last that can ever exist before this new thing, this irredeemable thing, happens.

It is physical. A compression at the back of the throat, a tug of weight behind the eyeballs, pressure around the heart, a shift in the ears' understanding of balance. Something in the fit of the bones.

Then, only then, comes the sound. From the north, it starts and it grows, cleaving this moment from everything that went before, opening up endless oceans between one second and the next, moving towards us.

PART ONE

78.1323° N, 15.3736° E

1ST JUNE 2025

'You have a gun?' the owner asks, matter of fact.

Grant and I exchange a look. The tourist brochures we read on the flight from Tromsø were full of warnings about carrying firearms for self-protection, but we'd assumed they didn't apply to us. We're not planning any picnics.

'You must have a gun. Because of the bears.' He sighs and looks at us like we're children. 'You cannot be outside without one. A bear can appear anywhere, anytime, and they are fast. You must be able to defend yourself.' He adjusts the strap of the hunting rifle slung casually over his shoulder.

I glance around, scan the spaces between the cabins. A line of them finished in pale wood cladding, blackened and warped at the corners, faces north across the fjord. Beyond the water, mountains mass on the opposite shore.

The owner reaches into the pocket of his anorak, pulls out a ring of silver keys and prises two off. 'You have numbers five and six, at the end there. The heating is already switched on and you can have hot water in an hour by immersion switch next to the sink.'

I take the keys. 'We're only staying the one night.'

He shakes his head disapprovingly and works two more smaller keys loose from the ring. 'These are for the flare gun boxes in each cabin. A single overhead shot is enough to scare off most bears. But if not… Well.' He smiles without warmth. 'Best not go outside unless you really have to. Yes?'

We watch his pickup truck rumble out of the yard on its huge snow tyres and take the road towards the clustered timber-frame buildings of Longyearbyen, leaving a greasy cloud of diesel hanging in the air. I stamp my feet, cup my hands and blow into them. Behind the town, more mountains rise austerely, dark flanks marbled with snow. The longer I look at them, the more they appear tinged with something unsettling, a disturbing truth being slowly revealed. Like gazing at a beautiful human face before realising the exquisite bone structure is about to split the skin.

'You going to give me a hand?' says Grant, already hefting the equipment towards the end cabin.

I grab a couple of boxes and follow him, shaking off the niggling sense of unease. We lug everything inside as fast as we can. I take cabin number five, Grant and the gear take number six.

> • <

My cabin is small and panelled ceiling-to-floor with pine boards giving it the look, if not the temperature, of a sauna, sparsely furnished with a folding table, two chairs and a low bed with wrinkled mauve sheets. My skin feels thin and grimy. I flick the switch for hot water and stretch out on the bed to wait. We've been travelling since early morning – the flight from Edinburgh to Tromsø, then an ancient 737 into Svalbard, its single runway stretched across the ragged lip of a fjord. In the morning we have one more short flight, north to Ny Ålesund where the *Polar Horizon* is docked.

By the time I feel clean enough to get out of the shower, condensation is running down the walls of the tiny bathroom. There's a small frameless mirror screwed onto the wall, a crack forking across it diagonally from top to bottom. The line is so sharp and black, the shape of it so like a bolt of lightning, I run my hand across the mirror's surface, wondering if it's drawn on. It's not. A pinhead of bright red blood forms on my fingertip. I suck on the finger, a whisper of iron on my tongue. Why do I always have to learn things the hard way? From within the clear patch of mirror, brows drawn together, my mother scowls back at me.

I'm getting used to it. The auburn hair, angular features, pale skin and murky green-brown eyes are all hers, the likeness stronger than ever these days, but there are differences. For one thing, she was always exhausted, with big dark blue circles under her eyes. Hardly surprising with four kids and a full-time job. Nobody even suspected it might be a physical problem, until it was too late. I don't miss her anymore. Not really. She's been gone so long. It's just a fact of life, an old scar that rarely itches. Anyway, I reckon the longer a person spends staring into mirrors, the less likely they are to find anything useful there.

It takes me five minutes to dry myself and get dressed. I tuck the flare gun into the waistband of my jeans, at the back, Hollywood-style, and peer out of the room's one small window, checking as best I can for bears before opening the door and stepping outside.

> • <

Grant looks up. I didn't knock.

'Bears,' I say. 'Didn't want to hang around outside.'

'Really?' He jumps up and rushes to the window.

'Well, no,' I admit. 'I didn't actually see any. But there could be. You heard the guy.'

'Yeah, right.' He gives me a look and returns to his seat. He has his laptop set up and is running the survey plan.

A glowing grid of lines and coordinates scroll across the screen. Grant zooms the display back out, showing the perimeter of the patch of sea we're heading for, an elongated green parallelogram laid over the 87th parallel, pointing north. The shape is criss-crossed with red survey lines showing the course the *Polar Horizon* will sail, back and forth like a shuttle on a loom, threading together its pattern of data.

Ours is the first commercial survey this far north since the Arctic Protection Agreement of 2020 banned all exploration and drilling within the Arctic Circle. The area was mapped by the Russians years ago, but ownership disputes between the five arctic nations were still dragging on when the Chukchi disaster closed everything down. End of argument. Finally, however, despite the ongoing mess in Alaska, big money has found a way. As it always has. Always will.

'Can't do much more with this until we're underway,' says Grant, the light from his laptop reflecting in his eyes, making them glow. 'Nothing's set in stone until then.' He talks on about local conditions, tidal readings and the rate of drift of the ice sheet. None of it is news to me. I helped design the program that runs the calculations to keep us on course, but Grant likes to explain things and every now and then I let him. Keeps him happy.

His cabin is a mirror image of my own but has something extra that mine doesn't. Tacked onto the wall behind the bed is a polar bear skin, complete with head and claws. Surely that can't be real? I touch it. The surface hairs are course but underneath them is densely packed fur, disarmingly soft. If it's a fake then it's a good one. Jesus. The environmental protection lot would shit kittens if they saw this. The head of the bear is flat on the wall, looking down on the bed, black lips curled back exposing pink gums and killer teeth. The eyes are dark glass.

Grant is still talking. 'We've got a couple of days from port before we'll be in position. Should be enough time to get everything sorted, as long as we're not bothered about sleep.'

A bubble of silence follows. We both know we're thinking the same thing, remembering those times we willingly lost sleep together. A warm sensation grows in my chest, spreads to my stomach, moves further south.

'Stop looking at me like that,' he says, turning his attention back to the screen and squaring his shoulders. 'There'll be none of that on this trip.' He stabs determinedly at the keyboard.

I trace the familiar lines of his body, currently hidden beneath fleece top and jeans, with my eyes, notice a toe poking through a hole in his sock. What's up with him? Has he got himself into some kind of relationship? How annoying. There's never been any emotional involvement between us, just healthy, recreational sex when the opportunity arises. A friendly arrangement that works for both of us. Or at least it always has up until now.

The warm feeling persists. I perch on the table beside him but he pretends not to notice and keeps his eyes on the screen. I push the lid of the laptop closed, nearly trapping his fingers. 'You're not serious,' I say.

'I am.' He keeps his gaze fixed on his hands. 'Completely.'

'You don't mean that,' I say. 'Come on. We're out there for five weeks. Five. Whole. Weeks.'

Grant makes a half-hearted attempt to raise the lid of the laptop but I hold it down. 'We'll hardly see each other anyway,' he says. 'We'll be on rotation.'

'That's inhumane.'

'I know. But this job is important.' He's putting a lot of effort into maintaining his stern expression. 'We can't afford to get sloppy because we're at it every time people turn their backs.'

'I guess.' The company does have a lot riding on this job. Money, reputation, potentially a claim on the biggest untapped oil reserve left on Earth. Okay, it's a big deal. But five weeks without any distractions?

'I mean, for Christ's sake Izzy, the whole industry, the government, the media, fucking everyone is going to be all over our data when we get back.'

'Yeah yeah, okay, calm down. I get it.'

'I'm just saying. It's got to be clean. Unambiguous.'

'I completely agree,' I say. 'We'll keep it professional on board,' I slide a hand around the back of his neck and twist my fingers into his thick black curls, 'but we have time now.'

'I don't think that's the best...' He tails off and a smile slowly spreads across his face.

I pull his head back slightly and lean in close enough to lick his lips.

'Izzy,' he groans, his resolve dissolving, already a thing of the past. He reaches for me. I swing a leg over his lap, straddling him on the chair. He's already hard.

> • <

The bedspread has fallen to the floor and the sheet is a tangled series of damp knots under our bodies. Grant is on his back, breathing hard as he holds onto my hips. The beginnings of that helpless, slightly panicked look he gets when he's almost there steals across his face. 'Not yet.' I put a hand on his chest and slow my movements. If this is going to be the last sex for weeks, I want to make the most of it. The bear skin on the wall grins down at me, the lamplight reflecting from teeth and eyes. When I finally come, Grant thrashing underneath me, I hold on, bury my face in his neck, grip tight to his shoulders.

'Ah, fuck! Izzy!' He pushes me off and I tumble to the floor, land with a thump. I blink up at Grant as he kneels on the bed, his dick like a lowering drawbridge. A small laugh escapes before I can stop it. Grant glares at me. 'Jesus fucking Christ, woman!' He puts a hand to his neck and brings it away red. He stares in disbelief. 'What the fuck?'

ꓑ INSTALLATION 1

NY ÅLESUND
78.9250° N, 11.9222° E

2ND JUNE 2025

'Call me Isobel,' I say and extend my hand.

The captain ignores it and pins me under a hard stare.

Peder Bjornsen inhabits the role of captain so completely there's no need for him to introduce himself in return. Over six feet tall with doggish sandy hair, he's as broad as a door and wears a fisherman's coat buttoned over an Arran-knit sweater. His face looks like a weathered barnacle prised off a rock on some godforsaken shore. A vertical scar starts at his hairline, bisects his eyebrow, then picks up again below his eye and continues to the edge of his jawbone, cutting a shiny channel through blond-grey stubble. It's hard to place his age, but I'd guess at around fifty. His pale blue, end-of-the-world eyes look much, much older.

He exhales through his nose with a snort that could be

amusement or dismissal, I can't tell which. Maybe it's both. He turns away, waving an arm to the aft of the bridge room. 'You set up there. We sail in four hours.'

As he moves off I imagine I can hear the distant creak and groan of masts and timbers, the snap of wind in oiled canvas. Captain Bjornsen hauls centuries of salt-encrusted seafaring history in his wake.

Grant crashes his armful of hardware down on one of the two desks in the corner, kicks a chair aside and crawls under the desk looking for power points. He's still upset with me about last night, but also hacked off about the vessel setup. Usually the instrument room is a deck or two below the bridge in its own dedicated space, but the *Polar Horizon*'s incomplete refit means we're all lumped in together and have to improvise. The arrangement is less than ideal.

I can see two parallel scratches on the side of Grant's neck as he wrestles with cables on his hands and knees. Can't imagine how I could have made those marks with my teeth. I've no aversion to garlic or sunlight. I bite down on the pad of my thumb, testing a canine for sharpness.

Oh well. I have bigger things than Grant to worry about.

I'm not sure how I feel about being here, on this survey. Never saw seismic as a permanent career, only a way to make some money – two or three years maximum. But I passed that self-imposed limit a couple of years back. There's always a reason not to quit. The pay is good and I've not seen many other uses for a Maths degree that don't involve a desk-bound, nine-to-five existence. I rationalise my choices, of course. We all need to make a living, to survive in the environment we're born into. If I didn't do this job, someone else would. I'll get out before I hit thirty. Gives me a couple of years to figure out how.

The survey vessels we work on are looking for oil and we're helping them find it, so the obvious conclusion is that we're part of the problem: aiding and abetting, or at least enabling, the plunder of the world's natural resources. That's not the way I choose to look at it. We are simply explorers, charting the terrain at the bottom of the sea, pulling information from deep within the bedrock. We are in no way advocating what people do with that information. We only provide it.

This lie is easier to stomach in hot places: off the coast of Mexico or Mozambique, where nature seems abundant, inexhaustible. There, it's easier to believe we're insignificant.

But here I can sense the world working. The raw machinery of it. I can't avoid the feeling that this whole frozen region is a vital piece of the engine that drives the world along. Earth's crankshaft. If we mess this up, we're all fucked.

Not all that long ago, everything around here was untouched by all but a very few people. Now, icebreaker-class cruise ships sail to the pole in summer and tourists crawl over it, taking selfies. I've even heard that the operators break up swimming-pool-sized areas of ice to let holidaymakers bathe in the sea right at the point where all latitudes and time zones converge and the only direction is south. Extra snow has to be flown in to keep the area from looking like the damp patch of trampled slush it's rapidly turning into.

Not much anyone can do about that. I need to concentrate on the job at hand.

That bear skin though. Its claws have snagged a memory and pulled it forwards, looking for a match.

It was back at the start of the year. I'd been clock-watching as another claustrophobic day in the office dragged by, when I saw white fur moving along the corridor. Shockingly white. It had a synthetic look and I could almost feel the static electricity fizzing around it. Then I noticed what looked like ears, smallish and set wide upon what was now unquestionably a head – a broad face punctuated by round black eyes, and a snout with black lips and nose.

The bear stopped and looked at me over the partition.

'Alright?' he said.

No one else had noticed him. Heads remained bowed over keyboards, voices murmured unperturbed into headsets. The air conditioning exhaled one of its sporadic death rattles and a muted ping from my PC told me another email had landed in my inbox. A bear presented a far more interesting prospect.

'Yeah.' I smiled. 'Thanks. I'm grand.'

The bear nodded and although his facial expression was static, I felt sure he smiled back.

'You looking for anyone in particular?' I asked.

'Your boss around?'

I liked his voice: deep and resonant but disarmingly casual, in charge without having to try. The hint of an accent, not enough to place the country of origin but enough to convey that English wasn't his first language, but he had complete mastery of it. A voice that implied much about the intellect behind it. A good voice for a bear. I wondered if he was putting it on as part of his disguise or if he sounded like that all the time.

'I think he's in the admin office downstairs. I can go and get him if you like?'

The bear raised his paws, black pads towards me, claws curling inwards. 'It's okay. That his office there?' He nodded towards the large glass-fronted room on the other side of the corridor.

'That's the one. If you wait here, I'll—'

'No. Thanks,' he cut me off, turning away as I got up. 'We'll go and wait for him there.'

'We?'

He motioned towards the stairwell. Half a dozen bears walked calmly into the office and sat down around the conference table.

I followed the last one in.

'We're going to have to close that door,' said the bear. It was difficult to tell them apart, they all appeared to have sourced their bear suits from the same place and wore almost identically inscrutable expressions. But I recognised his voice. 'You can wait in here with us if you like.' He pulled a chair out and offered it to me.

I hesitated. The company of bears, even fake bears, appealed more than spending another long afternoon pounding out bug fixes and answering support calls.

'I think I better wait outside. But thanks for the offer.' Consorting with strange bears in my boss's office wouldn't help my prospects of a pay rise. 'Before I go, can I ask what you're doing here?'

'We're protesting your company's role in the destruction of the arctic environment.'

'Really?'

'Yes, really.'

'I think you might have the wrong office.'

Surely there were better candidates for staging an environmental protest? Our involvement in the Arctic, at that point, was peripheral at most. Admittedly, we were working on a new add-on for Proteus to increase the accuracy of surveys conducted in pack-ice. And fair enough, we all knew that probably meant it would be used in the Arctic, but we were focused on drift mapping and sensor depth, details of how the physical conditions would affect data acquisition, the implications for navigation and processing. Our concerns could be shepherded, with logic, into discreet mathematical challenges. Bears didn't come into it.

The bears sitting around the table exchanged anxious glances. 'This is Seismic Systems, right?'

'That's right.'

'And you do manufacture navigation software and hardware for vessels that, even as we speak, are getting ready to plough up the Arctic as if it was a farmer's field, facilitating the inevitable drilling, putting polar bears and other arctic species out of a home and driving them to the brink of extinction?'

'Well,' I expelled a sceptical breath, 'I'd say that's a bit of a stretch.'

The bear tipped his head to one side. 'How so?'

'It's true we make navigation tools, but we could hardly be held entirely responsible for the destruction of the Arctic.' I wished my voice hadn't sounded so defensive.

The bear took a couple of steps towards where I was hovering in the doorway. 'If you guys weren't so busy profiting from working out ways for the ships to get up there and find the oil for the rigs to pump, then perhaps none of it would be happening.'

'Well…'

'Don't tell me, you're just following orders?' He paused and let the implication settle. 'Everyone in the chain is responsible. Some more responsible than others. We are here to hold your company accountable for its significant link in that chain.'

'By dressing up as polar bears?' This was starting to feel personal. Him standing there in his ridiculous costume, having a go at me, implying I was some kind of environmental fucking Nazi.

'Whatever it takes.' He folded his arms and sat back down.

'Right.' He was getting on my nerves now. I'd heard all this before, mostly from a small voice at the back of my own head, and labelled it Not My Problem. 'Tell you what. You make yourselves comfortable and I'll see if I can find someone to help you.'

I backed out of the office and one of the bears wedged a chair under the door handle. I should probably have taken the whole thing more seriously but it was hard not to find it funny. The ridiculous show of it.

〉•〈

Niall Cameron, our not-so-illustrious leader, came blustering up the stairs. I hoped no one had told him I'd shown the bears into his office, and had been casually chatting with them.

'What the holy fucking fuck is going on here?' Niall shouted, rattling the handle to his office. The bears turned in unison and waved jovially. A large hamper had been placed in the middle of the table and the bears were handing out paper plates, triangular-cut sandwiches and small cakes. One poured what looked like Ribena from a polka-dot teapot. It was all very amicable.

Niall's face turned an alarming shade of purple and he was raising his arms and dropping them as if someone had commanded him to fly. His frustration at this being plainly impossible didn't free him from the obligation to try. He puffed air in and out and spluttered half-formed sentences. 'Work to do— My fucking office— Shit for brains furry bastards.'

He put his shoulder to the door and heaved but it had no effect. 'Well don't all stand around gawping. Someone phone the fucking police!' I thought about suggesting an ambulance because Niall looked look like a heart attack waiting to happen.

The police took their time and the press arrived before them. The bears must have tipped them off in advance. What would be the point of a stunt like this if there wasn't any publicity? There had to be photos or, even better, a live news crew. As it was, they got a single local news drone. But that was enough. It buzzed around the car park before it spotted the waving bears at Niall's office window, moved close and hovered there, remote-control camera taking it all in as the polar bears drew various slogans, first on Niall's whiteboard with the red and green markers, then on placards which they happily held up and posed around.

Stop polar destruction
Save the bears
Homeless, please help

> • <

It was in a monthly planning meeting a few weeks after the occupation that Grant and I first found out we were to be more directly involved with the project than number-crunching in the office.

There were ten of us in the boardroom: Niall, a couple of guys from support, the obligatory what-the-fuck-does-he-do-anyway middle manager and half a dozen field engineers. Jobs for the next six months were being given out. Stewart and Angus got the Gulf of Mexico. Erik and Alan got the Indian Ocean, off the east coast of Africa.

'Grant, Izzy? You'll be taking the arctic survey.'

'I didn't know there was one,' said Grant, sitting up straighter in his seat.

'You're both on the icebreaker development team aren't you?' Niall made a show of consulting his notes. 'What did you think it was for?' He glared at Grant, who reddened now the whole room was looking at him, wondering how long Niall was going to roast his arse for and at how high a temperature.

'I mean, I didn't know we had a contract.'

'I'm sorry Grant,' the sarcasm dripped from Niall's words, 'as a field engineer, of course you should be privy to all the decisions made at board level. My apologies. I'll be sure to include you in future.'

'The software's not out of testing yet,' I put forward. It was true. The add-on module was still in development and had a long way to go before it was ready to integrate with the rest of the Proteus system. Grant shot me a grateful look as Niall turned his attention to me.

'Make sure testing is completed by May. It's a five-week job, minimum, starting in early summer. You'll get the usual offshore rate, of course, and there'll be a little extra bonus if you can bring it off to the satisfaction of the client.'

The other engineers eyed us sharply, their sunny destinations suddenly looking less sunny.

'It's a tricky job though. Difficult conditions, and they want the data quality within very tight parameters. Plus there are some special conditions attached.'

'Like what?'

'We'll discuss everything nearer the time. For now, just make sure that software is ready.'

> • <

Some days later Niall took the two of us aside and outlined what those special conditions were. He looked terrible, like he'd aged years since the meeting. His skin was grey, his shirt crumpled. I detected the faintly sour smell of badly slept-on whisky.

The deal was we were to talk to no one outside of the company about the exact timing or location of the job. That included friends and family. We were not permitted to take any internet-enabled mobile devices on board. The oil company rep would maintain a communications link with their head office, and Proteus' network capabilities were to be limited exclusively to satellite positioning and tidal data.

Grant and I traded eye-rolls. There was no way they could enforce something like that. Someone would get around it. What were they going to do? Frisk us? Cavity searches?

'Any breaking of these conditions will not only mean loss of bonus, but will result in dismissal from Seismic Systems.' Niall sounded like he was reading from a prepared script.

'That's a bit extreme, isn't it?' I said, though I'd already decided it wouldn't be worth my while flouting the ban.

'Those are the terms. If you don't want the job, I'm sure I can find someone else who does.'

'Why all the cloak and dagger stuff?'

Niall sighed. 'Bloody tree huggers. Blah blah, chuck another mung bean in the pot, whatever. Not usually a problem. Nothing we haven't ignored many times. But this time the client is concerned that a bunch of extremists might be planning something.'

'What sort of something?'

'Christ knows. Chain themselves to a penguin. Who the fuck cares?'

'That's the Antarctic,' Grant murmured.

'What?' Niall glared at him.

'Penguins. They only live at the South—'

'Fucking whatever, Grant! The point is, we don't need the bad publicity or the disruption. But,' Niall massaged his temples, 'we do need this contract, so whatever the client wants, the client gets. Got it?'

❯ • ❮

Aboard the *Polar Horizon*, I'm minding my own business,

plugging in cables, testing connections. I'm getting some sideways looks from the other crew members. Men at sea are still unsettled to see a female engineer or navigator. Seamen of all varieties are still haunted by the old superstitions. It's not just women, there's a ridiculous variety of ways for bad luck to board a vessel. Flat-footed people, red hair, sailing on a Friday, albatrosses, saying 'drowned', bananas. I pull my woollen hat further down over my ears. Partly because it is bloody freezing but mostly because I think the revelation of my red hair is best saved for later.

We get everything hooked up, install the software and start running system tests. Bjornsen comes and watches us for a while.

After an hour or so the room warms up with all the bodies moving about and machines running. My hat is making my head itch. I pull it off and push my fingers through the liberated curls to give my scalp a good scratch. There's a sharp intake of breath from one of the younger crewmen and I see him glance apprehensively over to his captain.

Bjornsen stares at me with his eyes from the end of the world, shakes his head and turns away. The younger crewman averts his gaze and I wonder if he's resisting the urge to cross himself for protection. Short of shaving my head or wearing a wig, there's not much I can do about my crowning glory. We're all stuck with it. It's not like I deliberately brought a crate of bananas and a pet albatross on board. I'm not keen to get thrown overboard.

In the Middle Ages, if a ship got caught in a storm they'd throw any female passengers overboard to appease the sea. Things might be different now, but then again they might not. I'm not letting my guard down.

I try to stay as sexless as possible at work, especially offshore. Definitely easier in this climate, as we're all wrapped in jerseys and coats most of the time. The unwritten rules of working in a male-dominated industry are: your gender is an unfortunate disability that you're doing your best to overcome. If baited on the subject, out-swear your opponent without compunction.

So, no, I have no motherfucking bananas.

2 CONFIGURATION

78.9250° N, 11.9222° E

3RD JUNE 2025

The second officer is a peach. Jules Guerin is tanned and lithe with eyes the colour of melting milk chocolate. It's hard to resist the urge to stroke his honey-soft hair. He is delicious and, like a pampered house pet, he moves as though he knows it.

He's conferring with Captain Bjornsen in Norwegian, the pair of them glancing over to where we're working. Fuck's sake. How distracting. He makes everyone else look like the house lights have just gone up after last orders. Well, if the nights get lonely and Grant sticks to his ban on extracurricular activities, then maybe... But what am I thinking? There are no nights here at this time of year, not at this latitude. Svalbard is 78° N and the survey area lies somewhere just beyond the 87th parallel. Top of the world. Soon there'll be hundreds of miles of sea between us and night.

A small contingent of onlookers has gathered at the dock and watches as we lug the navigation units and trigger systems on board. Ny Ålesund, the most northerly inhabited place on Earth, hosts several environmental research stations from different countries. I suppose there could be a few of Niall's tree huggers in their number. Not that there are any trees here to hug. They'll have to content themselves with finding some lichen to stroke.

I wonder if they're all sworn to secrecy about our presence here. Or bought off. It's pretty obvious what we're about. The *Polar Horizon* started life as a seismic survey vessel but was sold to an environmental agency and refitted for scientific research over a decade ago. It's spent most of its time since then noodling around full of scientists and academics with theories about the colour of algae, or the musical preferences of arctic cod, or whatever. Perhaps some of the glowering scientists on the dock even sailed on it. Its resale to a contractor and retro-fit back to its original purpose was supposed to be completed by now but clearly hasn't been. Whole sections of the ship's interior are gutted, wall-panels yawning open and wires trailing where equipment has been removed. But we're here now, the survey is going ahead regardless and we've no choice but to get on with it.

> • <

There are eight levels, numbered from the bottom of the boat upwards: one is a place no one goes, a space with only metal entrails and an inner hull; two holds the engines; three for gym, laundry room, steward's and engineering quarters;

four to eight comprise the above-deck superstructure, equipment room, galley, day room and crew quarters, officers' quarters, bridge. The bridge is deck eight, right at the top of the food chain.

We have the usual mix of nationalities on board, with a few wild cards like Jules thrown in. Apart from Ralf, the Aussie third mate, and Hannes, a towering Swede in charge of the seismic hardware equipment, the officers are mostly Norwegian or Danish, the self-appointed aristocracy of the sea. All gruff bulk and swagger, with a faint edge of mournfulness for the passing of the glory days of the Vikings. The crew is mostly Russian, good workers, excellent mechanics. They keep themselves to themselves, don't trust the Norsemen, and certainly don't trust us.

Our nationality isn't of any interest to anyone – being Scottish generally raises no more comment than a few jokes about haggis and whisky. It's our role as navigators that isolates us from both the officers and crew. They need us. But they don't like us. We call the shots, and everyone on board is forced to defer to our judgement in the interests of the survey. We dictate headings and bearings and decide when to stop and start the acoustic guns and recording systems. The priority is to work the survey area tightly, silencing the guns only on turns so the whole undertaking has to be planned and executed with hard-nosed efficiency. We sail twenty-four hours a day for as long as it takes to gather the necessary data. Two navigators working in shifts to ensure there's no downtime. At a cost to the company of several thousand per minute, downtime is something everyone is keen to avoid, with its attendant buck-passing, arse-kicking and rolling of heads.

The only person more isolated than us on board is the oil company representative, the money man. His job is to keep track of how much everything is costing. In the event of disagreement, his decisions can overrule ours. I've never experienced that situation on board a vessel and don't want to. The oil reps are usually quiet guys who keep themselves to their spreadsheets. We've not clamped eyes on the rep for this survey yet, he's not emerged from his cabin, but he's rumoured to be a Kiwi.

This is our sailing dis-united nations. Strata of nationality squashed together into an unappetising, floating layer cake.

› • ‹

Bjornsen creaks over to where Grant and I sit at the control station and his huge shadow falls over both of us. 'Underway in three hours,' he growls. 'We reach the survey area sixty hours after that. Everything will be ready?' The very slight upward inflection at the end of his voice is only there for verbal punctuation, he doesn't intend it as a question.

'Sure,' says Grant. 'Once we've deployed the streamers and run some tests, provided everything is as it should be, we'll be ready to fire the whale shots.'

Bjornsen's face creases up like an old leather football slowly crumpling. He plants a heavy fist on the desk, making it groan under his weight as he leans in, and squints suspiciously at the numbers and charts flickering over the display screen. 'What is this, whale shots?'

'A new addition to the software.' Grant's voice has climbed half an octave. We both knew this feature wasn't going to go down well with the likes of Bjornsen. 'There's been some bad press back home. Environmentalists lobbying parliament, online petitions. Apparently, the noise coming from our acoustics interferes with the sonar of whales, even from long distances. It affects their ability to navigate and communicate, which screws up their mating.' Grant gives a high-pitched giggle. 'No pun intended.'

Bjornsen stares at Grant, silencing him. We wait as he digests the information, his expression unreadable.

'So,' Grant continues, talking fast now, wanting it over with. 'The idea is that we fire a series of shots as we approach the survey, as a warning to any whales in the surrounding area. Hopefully they'll get the idea and clear off to a safe distance.'

Grant has described the idea perfectly. The fact that it's a staggeringly stupid idea isn't really his fault. We all know it's bullshit. If the acoustic disturbance from the survey messes up the sex lives of whales, it's not going to mess them up any less by starting earlier. And that's ignoring the fact that whales mate in warmer waters, coming to this area only to feed. It's a sop to the environmentalists, an attempt to portray the company as sensitive to the local marine wildlife. You don't have to be David fucking Attenborough to see it's an exercise in futility that could only pacify the wilfully ignorant.

Bjornsen is staring incredulously at Grant, who is pretending not to notice and cycling through the on-screen displays in a way I know is of no technical value. It's Grant's attempt to appear absorbed in his work and not at all intimidated by the two hundred pounds of angry Norwegian towering over him. Poor guy. He always gets landed with talking to the officers, because so few of them consider approaching me first. Grant has gone slightly pink. When he turns his head in a pretence of consulting his notes I see the scratches on his neck, less angry looking now but darker, starting to heal. I wonder how long he's going to stay pissed off with me.

'See this,' says Grant nodding to one of the displays and glancing up at Bjornsen. 'The blue markers here,' he points with the tip of a well-chewed biro. 'These show where we'll be firing the whale shots before the lead-in line to the survey.'

Bjornsen narrows his eyes to laser sights and scrutinises the display.

I think about the poor, sex-starved whales. Can't be easy for them, the whole mating game. Even without us coming along and making a racket, the logistics are a nightmare. It's not just a question of grabbing the nearest warm and willing body. Oh no. First there's all that swimming and hooting in miles and miles of ocean looking for another whale they like the look of, and even when they achieve this unlikely meeting the act itself is comically difficult. I remember seeing a programme about it on the Nature channel. Might have even been narrated by David fucking Attenborough. These two whales had to swim miles apart then straight towards each other at a ridiculous speed, like a massive underwater game of chicken, then, at the last moment, they reared up out of the water and slammed together achieving penetration and ejaculation all in one crushing crescendo of smashing flesh and exploding water, before falling apart and back into the ocean. Done. Mind blowing. They must have some powerful sex drive to bother going through with all that.

Bjornsen straightens up and shakes his head. 'Stupid,' he says, and lets the word sit there, heavy and final.

'That's probably true,' sighs Grant. 'But it's company policy now. Something we have to do, on every trip. It doesn't make any difference to the main survey.'

'Makes no difference if you play them a polska. Stupid. How far from the survey you need to do this?'

'Just a couple of kilometres. I'll let you know.'

'Ja, you do that,' Bjornsen huffs and mutters something in Norwegian before heaving off.

Grant's shoulders relax a little and he looks over. It's the first time he's acknowledged my existence since that night in Longyearbyen. He must realise this too because he quickly looks away. Not forgiven yet then.

Bjornsen is telling the second mate about the whale shots. The Frenchman glances over at us and smiles. We've been told he's doubling as our MMO, which is unorthodox, but may mean he'll be more sympathetic. Every marine survey has to have a Marine Mammal Observer. Usually that's their only job but, as we're beginning to realise, the *Polar Horizon*, in addition to being poorly refitted, is only partially crewed. But it's easy to lose track of my concerns when looking at Jules. Oh, but he's lovely to look at. I wonder if female whales have orgasms. And whether they consider them worth all the effort.

> • <

As we're still in dock, I'm unprepared when the deck takes a violent lurch to starboard, knocking me off balance. I'm thrown one way, then the other as the vessel rights itself and I trip over Grant, who has already gone sprawling. By the time we pick ourselves up, everyone else's attention is fixed to port. We join them at the window, our footsteps wavering slightly as the tilting deck settles back to the horizontal, both of us resisting the impulse to grab on to each other for balance.

'Fuck me, that's an ugly bastard.' Grant lets out a low whistle. 'Must be a hundred, hundred and twenty metres, would you say?' He directs this question towards Jules who is standing between us.

Jules shrugs in a cartoonish Gallic style. 'Yes, at least that. Maybe more.' The slight tremor in his voice, combined with the studied indifference, tells me he's as gobsmacked as the rest of us. And that it matters to him that we don't know this.

The icebreaker is a hulking beast of a thing. An old vessel, not one of the modern sleek, clinical affairs, this one has seen plenty of service. Its massive snub-nosed hull is matt black, the superstructure a blood-red block stuck onto the deck. Streaks of rust give the impression that the vessel is gradually dissolving, or defrosting like an enormous chunk of meat. We watch it turn and surge past us again, close enough to make the *Polar Horizon* sway in the water, forcing us to grab onto whatever we can to stay on our feet again. It towers over us and throws us into deep shadow. There are jaws painted across its bow, serrated white and ready to bite. Some of the teeth are chipped and corroded which only adds to the impression of extreme menace. The words АРКТИКА КОЧ are painted in metre-high white capitals on the hull, followed by the hammer and sickle, with ARKTIKA KOCH in smaller lettering underneath.

'Tell those bastards to stop fucking about. I want them at least five hundred metres away,' Bjornsen shouts at one of his officers, a dough-faced lad with unfortunate ears, who in turn shouts into a radio handset in an attempt to raise someone on the icebreaker. Either there's a fault with the radio or they're deliberately ignoring us. I suspect the latter.

Bjornsen, although definitely pissed off with the *Koch*'s behaviour, shakes his head in grudging admiration. 'Double hull, nuclear-powered. Not seen one of them in a long time. Thought they were all made into museum pieces.'

'Well, not this one. Apparently,' I say.

He lets out a short grunt. I'm pretty sure it's a laugh, and almost certain that's a small smile to go with it. 'Ja.' He nods. 'Apparently.'

As if in reply, the *Koch* lets out a deep klaxon blast. The sound reverberates through my skeleton before landing like a heavy sonic harpoon in my chest. I press a hand to my breastbone and bend forward, like an idiot. Of course there's nothing physical there. I force my hand down and glance around to make sure no one saw my reaction.

Jules catches my eye and smiles. 'I know,' he says, 'I felt it too.' He taps the centre of his own chest with slim, tanned fingers. 'Here.'

I feel my face begin to colour and turn away from him.

The *Koch* curves away and powers out to a safe distance sending back a bow wave that slaps lazily into our side.

'Did you say nuclear?' Grant pipes up.

'Ja. All those big icebreakers are nuclear. They carry two reactors on board. One for power, another for backup.'

Grant's mouth falls open and he shuts it again just as quickly, his teeth clacking together. He scrunches his eyes closed and presses at his temples with both hands, as if trying to massage the unpleasant reality into his head. 'You say that like it's a sensible thing, to be sailing around the Arctic with a dirty great nuclear reactor, sorry, two dirty great nuclear reactors on board.'

Bjornsen gives him a scornful look. 'At that size, they're better than the diesel alternatives. Faster, cleaner. Been operating up here since before your mamma squeezed you out, so don't get your little whale-loving panties in a twist.'

This shuts Grant up but he looks dismayed. I'm not sure whether he's more bothered about the *Koch* or the fact that Bjornsen has pegged him as some kind of eco-fairy.

> • <

One by one, everyone disperses to whatever they were doing before the icebreaker arrived, leaving only the two of us by the window. Grant is still fizzing, his agitation polluting the air around him. 'Why weren't we told? I wouldn't have agreed to work this survey if I'd known we'd be sailing behind that floating fucking nightmare.'

'Can't say I'm ecstatic about it either.'

That's as far as I'm prepared to go. I won't admit it to Grant, but the thought of trailing in the wake of those twin engines has started a creeping dread in the pit of my stomach. I push it down; I'm well-practised in the art of self-deception. It's a matter of survival in a conflicted world. We clip and trim what we choose to think to fit in with what we need, and how we need to be in order to get it. We all do it. I try to stay honest with myself about that.

Grant can be such a child sometimes. I try, unsuccessfully, to keep the impatience out of my voice. 'We're here now. There's nothing we can do about it. And we do need something big for this job.' We watch the shrinking vessel. 'Certainly looks like we got it.'

'Aye, careful what you wish for, eh?' Grant mutters. He retreats to his workstation and crawls back into his nest of cables.

The *Koch* dwindles into the distance. Its receding shape growing blacker the smaller it gets, a black hole drawing in every fugitive scrap of darkness from the surrounding area, sucking up all the shadows and crushing them.

3 DEPLOYMENT

87.2234° N, 29.5693° E

6TH JUNE 2025

Everything is connected. The real-time navigation unit, the triggers, the processors, six display monitors. We test Proteus with old data from a previous survey and everything appears functional. We are ready to go.

The *Polar Horizon*'s engines start up and as the entire fabric of the ship begins to hum with the vibrations from below, the crew shifts into gear. Everyone moves quickly and deliberately, turning and pivoting around each other as they go about their appointed functions. Everything is checked and double checked. But underneath all this adult efficiency I can detect a bright strand of heady childish excitement. It's always there at the start of a survey. Nobody acknowledges it, and I've certainly never spoken about it to anyone else, but I like to believe we all feel it.

We're going on an adventure, running away to sea. We'll

sail off through night and day and in and out of weeks and almost over a year.

Only this time there will be no nights.

> • <

Bjornsen gives the order and the icebreaker moves off. The sea is free of ice around Svalbard but we'll need its reinforced hull soon enough. When we reach the pack-ice, it will go crashing through, opening a safe channel for us to follow.

I wait until we motor out, following the icebreaker, heading north. It's still at least forty-eight hours before we need to deploy the streamers.

'You okay here for a bit?' I ask Grant.

He doesn't turn his head. 'Yeah, sure, on you go.'

I like to watch the land recede and disappear. There's an addictive buzz, imagining I'll never see it again, that I'm leaving behind everything I've ever known. Perhaps it's the idea of starting again, nothing but clean slates and blank pages. The vertigo of sudden and dramatic change. It's a dance on a cliff edge. I don't know why I need to feel this.

I'll come back, I always do.

The light on deck has a pearly quality, the sun high and veiled by long skeins of cloud. The sea placid, churned to a milky froth at the bow. Occasional jagged pieces of ice bob past at a distance, looking like little ice castles adrift from the shores of some distant Lilliputian civilisation. I watch the dark mountains of Svalbard diminish until they're no more than a raised eyebrow on the horizon. Then gone.

I turn and lift my chin to the oncoming wind.

> • <

The accommodation is basic. My cabin is furnished in a spectrum of greys: stormy slate lino on the floor, walls of ash rising to a ceiling of thinned-out smoke. There's one small window, square with blunted plastic-trimmed corners. It's like being inside a cinder block. There are bunk beds, the frame painted a military-looking gunmetal, a scratchy cement-coloured blanket tucked tightly around the mattress.

At least I have a cabin to myself this trip. I've been on jobs where everyone except the officers shares bunks and sleeps in rotation, meaning when you eventually get to bed, it's still warm from the previous occupant, redolent with their latent farts lurking in the crumpled sheets, their sour breath smeared across the pillow.

My rucksack is where I left it in the corner, not yet unpacked, not that there's much to that task. We travel light on surveys. The heavy equipment takes priority, and since it's all lumped together and charged for at airports, there are tight restrictions on what we can carry for personal use. Maximum two changes of clothes. Toothbrush. Not much else. Basic toiletries are usually provided on board. I take my few possessions out of my bag and stow them in the tiny overhead locker.

I'm still pissed off I forgot to pack a fresh notebook. It's a bit old school but after long hours of staring at screens I like the slow, deliberate feel of it. The resistance of the pen pushing across the grain of the paper, leaving its looping trail of ink. For all it can't be easily backed up to the cloud, it feels more permanent, more real somehow, but private, mine. I'm having to make do with writing on the blank sides of the Operator's Manual printout. Most of the documentation is electronic but we still bring a hard copy of the basic core manual in case the electronic version can't be accessed for any reason.

As I write, chapter heads in heavy block capitals periodically ghost backwards across the top of the page. Below them, I write on the shadowy turned backs of paragraphs, recording my reality on the flipside of the official version.

No one ever reads the manuals. Hence the acronym. RTFM: Read The Fucking Manual. It's not meant as a serious suggestion, more a coded way of calling someone else an idiot. Actually reading the fucking manual would be seen as an admission of weakness, the same way as asking for directions reveals you're lost.

Nobody will read this side of the paper either. I'm not writing to or for anyone else. I have no audience in mind. I'll likely chuck the filled-up pages into the recycling bin at the end of the trip, like I usually do. Or who knows? Maybe this time I'll keep them, re-read these words one day in the future, when I'm old and bored enough. In which case, hey old me – perhaps you should be getting out more? The idea of offending my future self makes me laugh. But the more I think about this touchy future ghost self, the less funny and more disturbing she gets. Like she's looking back at me and making her own judgements. The smile fades from my lips and I let her go.

My bunk is narrow and the mattress is thin but I've had worse. I think about putting in a request for extra pillows but quickly decide against it. It'd be interpreted as soft, as wanting special treatment. I remind myself, nevertheless, to ask for something to cover the window, something that'll do a more thorough job of blocking out the light than that flimsy blind. Even when drawn right down, light floods the cabin. My few attempts at sleep since coming aboard have been woeful, and left me feeling stiff and irritable rather than rested.

> • <

'There you are.' Grant swivels in his chair. 'It's all yours. I'm going to get something to eat.'

I can tell by the way he swerves past without even glancing in my direction that we're not mates again yet. How tedious. I stifle a yawn. It's going to be a long five weeks if he keeps this up.

As he leaves the bridge, Jules arrives. 'Ma belle Isobel,' his sing-song voice is teasing with a layer of self-mockery which stops it being annoying, 'have we tired you out already?'

'No, no. It's just… I don't suppose you know where I could get something to block the light from my cabin window, so I can sleep?'

'Ah. The light. Of course. One moment.'

I watch him go, take in his lean build, allow my eyes to slip down for a moment to his, it has to be said, absolutely perfect derriere. Enough padding on the muscle for a rounded shape, that beautiful dip and curve out from the lower back. Nice. Very nice.

On the display, the *Polar Horizon* is a blinking green rectangle, pointed at the bow end. The icebreaker, despite its far greater size, is an identical shape. Both shapes are tracking steadily north towards the ice sheet, the icebreaker now pushing into its ragged edge. I click through screens of data. This part is watching and waiting for the real work to begin.

My gaze wanders around the bridge and stops on a sign tacked to the door to the outside deck. It says WARNING and underneath there's a silhouette of a polar bear, which appears to be ambling along minding its own business. Perhaps the sign would work better if they showed it roaring, all teeth and claws and charging towards you. Below the bear, the sign says:

> POLAR BEAR ALERT
> DO NOT ASSUME
> THE COAST IS CLEAR
> A POLAR BEAR MAY
> BE OUTSIDE THIS DOOR

I feel suddenly cold and tug the cuffs of my fleece down over my knuckles. Why am I thinking of a paw print in thick frost? I have a clear image of it in my head, a large central pad surrounded by five toes, each of them with a calligraphic claw mark gouged before it. I'm puzzling over this image, pulling at the edge of what can only be a dream but feels more tangible, more like a memory, when I become aware of Bjornsen standing next to me. I jolt in my seat and try to cover my reaction by reaching for something under the desk. I don't think he's fooled for a second.

'Bears can't really get onto the vessel, can they?' I realise before I've finished asking that of course they can, and in fact must have done so in the past, or the notice wouldn't be there. They're not given to frivolous signage at sea.

'They're curious as cats, and smart too. They're attracted by smells. Our food, our garbage.'

I think of the containers on deck. Environmental protection laws prohibit the dumping of waste in the Arctic Circle so it's all stored in inadequate-looking vats. Even with only a few days' worth of waste in them, the rancid smell is hard to miss if you stand down-wind.

'Have you ever seen one?'

Bjornsen gazes at me for a long moment, his expression glacial. He looks about to answer when Jules returns and hands me a folded bundle of waxed canvas and a roll of duct tape.

'Blackout material,' he says. 'Cut it to size, double it up for good measure, and tape it down around the frame.'

'Thank you.' I take the material and tape. 'Maybe you guys are used to it, but I can't sleep with all this light.'

'Well, some of us don't need sleep,' Jules looks at Bjornsen, 'but us mere mortals rely on this stuff.'

'We'll be moving into the ice soon,' says Bjornsen. 'Better make sure you're ready.'

'Let me know if you need any help with that,' Jules says, and squeezes my shoulder before following Bjornsen. A little over-familiar, I think, watching him walk away, but not exactly unpleasant.

Left alone with Proteus, I wonder if I said something to offend Bjornsen, or if he was just bored by the polar bear question. His demeanour makes me curious. What is he hiding?

My thoughts are interrupted by the arrival of Max, the

representative from Pilgrim, the oil company. No one else is employed directly by them. Seismic Systems, the Norsemen and the Russians, we all prefer to distance ourselves from the balance sheets and outcomes, even though we know we're at their mercy. We're all, to various degrees of directness, working for Pilgrim, and they in turn work for the great god of consumption. The beast must be fed. That's what we're all doing here, ultimately – searching for the system's next meal.

Max is not popular with the crew. There are no overt insults, no open aggression, just a coldness, a way of excluding him from the casual banter that sustains the rest of us. That goes some way to softening my own attitude towards him, I can't abide bullying. But to be fair, he is hard to like.

His shoulder blades jut from his stooped back and he picks his long legs up as he walks, moving his head from side to side, peering at anything that catches his eye. The impression is of some kind of wading bird. I wouldn't be surprised to see him dart his face down and come back up with a worm between his lips.

He's standing too close. Because he can. I can't leave my workstation and asking him to step back would imply I had a problem, which would inevitably tip over into me being the problem. Not going to give him the satisfaction. But if he gets any closer he's definitely in danger of me accidentally elbowing him in the nads.

'You people will be working shifts in rotation when the survey starts, ah geese.'

He's a Kiwi and has a habit of ending his sentences with 'I guess', which in his accent sounds more like 'ah geese'. You can't blame a person for their accent, but the way he slides the geese in at the end of everything he says feels malicious, like he's insinuating something. It'd sound just as fucking irritating in any accent or language, coming from him. I'm just waiting for him to say it again.

> • <

A flock of gulls has followed us from Ny Ålesund, no doubt mistaking us for a fishing vessel, or hoping we'll be helpfully messy with our rubbish. These aren't the pretty ivory gulls or the subtly hued grey and white ones I saw back on Svalbard. The ones following us now are huge brutes, with lizard eyes and vicious beaks.

'Black backed gulls,' Jules tells me. 'The biggest gull species. Just as mean as they look. They'll eat anything. Rubbish, carrion, other birds.'

We watch as they scream in a thick cloud behind us and take turns landing on the deck in raucous gangs of a dozen or more at a time. 'I don't suppose they're helping with the sleeping, are they?' Jules asks.

I shake my head. 'They never shut up.'

Just then, Ralf, the Aussie third mate, bursts onto the bridge, his hair sticking out even further than his ears. He's been woken by a gull squabble breaking out right next to his cabin window.

'Right! That is fucking it. Time to let fly the dogs of war.'

Jules grins at me. 'Oh, you'll like this.'

'Give me a second,' says Ralf, busy at one of the control stations. I lean over his shoulder. He's loading a file into the klaxon system, setting the volume to maximum. 'You asked for it, you evil fucking dino chickens!'

He hits activate. A pack of wild dogs, barking, growling and snapping, a rabid, furious barrage of canine menace erupts from the speakers.

The gulls explode into the sky in a clatter of wings. Ralf kills the klaxon and in the silence that follows a drift of white feathers fall softly to the deck and cover it, like snow.

Real snow greets us as we move into the ice, or rather into the channel of open water cleared for us by the icebreaker. The temperature drops and a stiff wind carries a ragged smattering of flakes. The edges of the passage become more clearly defined as the quantity of ice displaced in order to clear it increases. At first it seems we are being led into a maze with equally wide openings off on either side, but gradually these openings narrow and become fewer and further between, until the only path we can follow is the one cleared for us. It stretches ahead over the moving ice field, broad as a six-lane silver motorway. In every other direction, irregular slabs of ice lie scattered across the sea like an impossible, abandoned jigsaw.

It's time to deploy the streamers.

Seismic streamers are not the graceful, decorative ribbons the name suggests. Not the sort of thing flicked through the air by tiny gymnasts or tied in a bow around a bunch of party balloons. They're cables as thick as a docker's bicep, wound onto reels as high as your head and mounted on sturdy metal frames on the back deck, the whole apparatus bristling with bolts and restraints. The cables are a kilometre long and made of clearish carbon fibre tubing, strong but flexible in water. Onto these tentacles are strapped and secured by various means all our ways of seeing and hearing, which put together, we like to believe, amount to knowing.

There are depth sensors, velocimeters, acoustic receivers, DGPS and RGPS positioning devices, compasses, laser positioning systems, salinity gauges. There are fin-like devices to help drive the streamers side to side, or up and down, to adjust their position in relation to the survey lines and each other. They are our eyes and ears in the water, our antennae. Without them we are blind, deaf, senseless.

Grant goes to the back deck to supervise the unwinding while I stay with Proteus and watch the multitude of compasses and sensors come online and start sending their data. At first the signals are chaotic as the streamers whip side to side like the tail of an angry cat, but as more and more length is fed out the weight pulls them straight. I employ the fins to help them along and finally, after an hour or two's work, the twin streamers are trailing straight and parallel behind us, everything online, Proteus happily munching on a steady stream of data.

> • <

Now our long day begins. I'm already starting to lose track of the number of days I've been aboard. Is it three or four? We persist in grouping the hours into units we can understand, calling them day and night. This practice feels more deluded with every lighted hour that passes, but what else do we have? If we don't measure, divide and account for time then what is it to us? What are we to it?

4 START-UP

87.5331° N, 26.4434° E

10TH JUNE 2025

We manage to complete the stipulated whale shots without any disruption, other than the back-and-forth of whale-related sexual innuendo the rest of the bridge crew contribute. I can't help feeling sorry for the whales having their date-night ruined: the confused guy whale veering off course, his massive hard-on waggling uselessly in the current; the female whale feeling let down, believing her mate's just being an arsehole and not bothered to turn up at the time and place they'd agreed. Hopefully they'll have a chance to clear up the misunderstanding another time, in some quieter corner of the ocean.

> • <

It's when we're approaching the lead-in to the first line and have enabled the live survey that all the screens go blank.

At first we think it's a power supply problem, but the base units are still running, fans whirring, lights flickering. Everything else on the bridge is still operational. Grant and I gape as the screens go from empty to displaying a swirl of static that circles then seems to press against the inside of the monitor screen, like it's trying to escape. It feels, and I know how crazy this sounds, like there's something alive in there, more than alive – sentient. It only lasts a couple of seconds, although it feels longer, before the screens flicker and, as suddenly as it went down, the whole system returns to normal.

'The fuck was that?' says Grant.

'No idea.' I'm already checking the configuration but not finding any obvious flaws. 'I'll run diagnostics and get a full debug report. But in the meantime,' I shrug, 'I suggest we just get on with it.'

No one else saw the glitch. Max, thankfully, is preoccupied with his own laptop on the other side of the room. We both know he won't want to delay the survey before it even gets started, and for no reason we can explain. Grant rubs his chin. 'Ah geese,' he says, in a bad imitation.

I smile, still uneasy, but at least this shared secret disperses the tension that's lingered between us since Svalbard.

> • <

Now we're underway, the work settles into a pattern. Grant and I barely see each other, apart from handing off at shift changeover, which is amiable enough. The rest of the crew has relaxed into each other's company, and even Bjornsen indulges in the odd joke.

All the same, there's something I can't put my finger on. It's as if I'm staring too hard at a 'Spot the Deliberate Mistake' picture and can't, no matter how carefully I look, see the damn mistake. This foreboding distracts me, an itch I can't scratch. Added to that is the persistent prickling sensation of being watched. It's as though there's someone standing right behind me, looking over my shoulder as I work. Sometimes this feeling is justified and I'll find that creepy fucker Max standing there peering at me like I'm a caged animal in a zoo. But most of the time it's just thin air.

I tell myself I'm imagining things. Probably the lack of sleep. The unrelenting daylight is so wearing. The sun moves around the sky, slowly circling us like a predator with all the time in the world.

> • <

I get up from the monitors, stretch my arms above my head and walk around to ease the stiffness from my legs. It's mid-afternoon on the eighth day, like that means anything out here. I stop by the window and try to exercise my eyes by focusing on objects in the distance. With a total lack of landmarks and precious little variation in the surrounding expanse of ice, sea and sky, this isn't so easy.

Without a point of reference, the eyes don't see distance and nearness in the normal way and the mind fumbles over the incomplete data. So when I do see something, I think at first my brain is simply trying to be helpful by providing something to meet demand. Not so much a hallucination as a visual anchor. I watch for a while, unbothered by whether it's real or not. But gradually, realising the hallucination, or whatever it is, isn't going away, I really look at what I'm seeing.

Grant joins me at the window. Soon he too stands stock still, his attention fixed in the same direction. A few more crew members come over, drawn by contagious curiosity. By now I'm relieved to know I'm not the only one seeing this. It isn't only in my head. It's real.

In the distance a patch of something off-white, a different shade from the ice and snow, is moving from floe to floe, sometimes disappearing and reappearing, getting closer all the time. Until it's close enough for us to get a good look.

'Fucking hell,' says Grant, 'is that really what I think it is?'

The bear stops and stares, his long neck extended, head low and level with his massive shoulders, his feet planted wide, claws hooking him into the ice. We gather in a hesitant knot at the window and watch him watching us. There's no doubt he's thinking, reasoning, cataloguing our size and speed, weighing up our intentions.

'Polar bear, ah geese,' says Max.

It's disconcerting to see one close like this, in the wild. There are so few left in the world at all. It should be a privilege, but that isn't how it feels. I flex my hands, realising I've been clenching them into fists by my sides. I'm breathing too fast and sweat prickles under my arms. I look at the bear's forepaws, big as dinner plates, the way his jaw hangs slightly open so I can see the black line of his lower lip, and behind that teeth. The bear is terrible in his whiteness.

He turns and walks alongside us. Surely we're going faster than polar bear walking speed? The way he proceeds across the ice field with singular purpose and utter certainty, the weighty roll of his shoulders and swagger of his back legs, seems to say that he is in charge of that sort of thing: speed, distance, time. They belong to him, not to us, and he will do with them what he wills. The way he plants each foot on the ice stakes his claim. Mine, mine, mine, his footsteps say. This place belongs to me, it is of me and you are trespassing.

I doubt he will forgive us our trespasses, this great white god of the north.

> • <

Bjornsen's face is set, his gaze fixed on the moving figure. I'm tuning into the vibrations he gives off. I wouldn't claim to know or understand him, I imagine there are few who could, but I can sense his bearing, the way he holds himself. Now, the emotion coming off him is an electric storm, his muscles taut and singing like high tension wires, carrying a message of… is it recognition?

'Is that a male or a female? Can you tell?' asks Grant, his voice little above a whisper, as if the bear can hear us.

In the unsparing light, the scar running down Bjornsen's face seems to writhe and pulse like an artery under his weathered skin. 'Male,' he says, delivering the single short word like the clang of a bell prematurely silenced.

I'd assumed the bear to be male because of its size. It's difficult to be precise about dimensions over the distance but he looks no less than five foot high on all fours and maybe twice that nose-to-tail.

We're all looking at Bjornsen now, sensing something under the tension, none of us brave enough to ask him about it directly. We all hang suspended in the dense silence and

I half expect him to turn away and leave us dangling there. But he seems to relax a little, nods to himself.

'I know this bear,' he says, fingertips tracing the line of his scar. 'Don't know how old he was when he gave me this but he was full grown, not a cub. He seemed then the biggest bear I'd ever seen. Watch him now though. That Nanuuk is no skinny old wreck.' Bjornsen shakes his head. 'This is not possible. Bears live only twenty, maybe twenty-five years.' Outside, the bear paces, his footfalls rhythmic, marking time. Bjornsen's voice catches. 'But there he is.'

We all gaze at the bear, who has stopped again and is looking towards us, not just at the ship but straight through the glass and into the bridge. Surely he can't actually see us? And how can Bjornsen possibly think it's the same bear? Still, there's something in the intensity of the bear's scrutiny that could make a person question every thought in their head. I'm happy to turn my attention away from it and back to Bjornsen's story.

'It was many years ago. I was with my brother. We'd come up here in the summer when the ice melted to net fish. Dangerous and illegal, yes, but also enough profit to be worth the risk. We had families to feed. We did what we had to. Like everyone.

'It was going well until this brute got his eyes on us. He scoped us out, same as he's doing right now. Not worried about us seeing him. There is a saying, "The bear you can see is not the bear that will kill you." Mostly that's true. He didn't come close and after a while he disappeared. Not a sign. This was not good, we were on edge. Now he was the bear we could not see. But we could feel him, his presence, hunting us. We wanted to finish and get back to shore, to once again have land under our feet and roofs over our heads. And we nearly made it. It was the last catch.

'Our little boat was full and sitting low in the water, sheltered on one side by a high berg and surrounded on the other three by broken-up sheet-ice, one piece long and thin behind. We were hauling the nets in when the sea exploded. That's the only way I can tell it. It was like a depth charge went off, and that bear,' Bjornsen looks again to where the bear keeps pace, occasionally turning his head and looking towards us, as if he's part of Bjornsen's audience. 'That now very visible bear was balanced like a fucking ballerina on a slice of ice so thin it should not have taken his weight. I swear he smiled, he would have said boo if he'd had a voice. We dropped our nets and fell back. My brother, Eyolf—' the name comes out like an expression of sudden pain and Bjornsen breaks off for a moment, his jaw clenching and relaxing several times before he continues. 'It was only a fraction of a second but I've gone over that moment so many times. Now it's hours long. Days. I never saw Eyolf so white. Like he was frozen, waiting for time to start again.

'When it did, it went too fast for me to understand. Eyolf took off like a rocket from the deck, straight up in the air, and blood came raining down from him, red landing all around on the snow, in the sea, on the boat, on me and on the bear too. I grabbed the gun and aimed. Eyolf's body landed on the ice. The bear charged me and I fired. I thought I got him, right in the head. But the shot must have gone wide. It didn't stop him. He opened up my face like a can of meat paste. I must have passed out. When I woke, I was alone. The bear was gone and so was my brother. Only a red drag mark on the ice where his body had been.

'I was half blind and my face was nothing but pain. I didn't know how long I'd been unconscious. Somehow I got the motor started again. The floor of the boat was covered with blood – my own, Eyolf's, and I thought the bear's too. Bears can smell blood, especially fresh, a kilometre away. I don't know how I got back to Svalbard alive.

'I wanted to believe he was dead. The bear. That I had killed him. But I never could completely believe it. Now I know why.'

It's Max who breaks the silence. 'How can you be sure it's the same bear? Don't they all look the same? White fur, big teeth, bad attitude?' He gives a quack of laughter, which squeaks to a sudden stop under Bjornsen's glare.

'It's him. I know it.'

We stand and watch as the bear, closer now, turns his face full in our direction.

'My god,' breathes Grant. 'He sees us.'

His eyes are two dark patches. I frown and squint, willing my vision to telescope out far enough to make out the detail. I feel like I've stepped into the icy water. The bear's eyes hold a deep, cold darkness that glints with light reflected a million times through miles of ice and underneath that a black emptiness, an absolute night, which is looking back at us.

> • <

When I get off shift, restless and hoping to tire myself out enough to sleep easily, I go to the gym. The ship's previous crew of scientists were either extremely fit or wanted to believe they could be. The gym is immaculate, located in a long, windowless room below decks, well-equipped with treadmills, rowing machines, cross-trainers, weights, the lot. I'm no gym bunny back home but it passes the time offshore, and it's one way of working up a decent sweat, getting a fix of endorphins. I make my way around the room, using all the equipment and interspersing cardio with resistance work, but spend longest on the treadmill.

They've got some seriously good kit. The treadmills have big screens offering a virtual running path, which will speed up and slow down to match your pace and incline. You can choose between athletics track, urban, beach and woodland. I go for the forest and am presented with a grass-lined trail through tall pines, the occasional deer flicking through the shadows and birds calling from the branches. Hypnotic. I go into a kind of trance, my trainers pounding away. I realise I've been running for almost an hour when I pass the ten kilometre mark, but I don't stop. I feel like I could keep going for another ten without getting tired. It's somewhere around fifteen when I smell burning and wonder if the machine is overheating, but the smell is wood smoke, not hot metal and plastic. I look down at the belt spinning under my feet and see no smoke but when I look back up at the screen, the woodland scene has darkened, the path narrowed. A reddish light flickers between the trees and the smell becomes overpowering. I stab at the red button and stagger to a stop holding onto the hand rails as the treadmill judders to a halt. As soon as it's still, the screen goes blank. Blameless. The smell dissipates too, as if it never was.

Blood's pounding in my head and I'm breathing heavy. Why would anyone program something like that? I start up the program again but keep the speed to walking pace. The forest track comes back, green and peaceful as before. I walk slowly until I get my breath back then climb off.

I drink cup after cup of water from the cooler and tug the front of my sweat-soaked T-shirt off my body. So now I'm having full-blown hallucinations? Must be another side effect of the sleep deprivation. It's burning bits of my brain out, knocking holes in the walls between imagination and reality. Yes, definitely something to do with that. I'm not simply losing my shit. It'd be too much of a coincidence. I don't buy it.

While I'm wiping water off my chin, a couple of muscle-bound Norwegians come into the gym. I squint at them. I've given myself brain freeze from gulping down too much cold water too quickly. They're all blond buzz cuts and bulging lycra. They take up their places in the weights area and spot each other while they strain and grunt.

I ignore them and do some quick stretches. My back is tight from too much time spent hunched over a keyboard. After stretching it out, I sit back on my heels and gaze at the sweaty transfer of my handprints on the blue exercise mat. The blocky shape of the palms diminishing and distorting, the fingers thinning to claws as the prints slowly shrink and melt away.

After my shower I stop by the galley, hoping for a sandwich before making another attempt at sleep, and see Bjornsen sitting on his own, nursing a mug of hot chocolate. Who'd have thought he'd have a sweet tooth? He grunts when I take the seat opposite him. His story about the bear is the most I've heard him speak since we've been aboard.

'Are you okay?' I ask. He looks drawn. 'That was some story.'

'It wasn't a story,' Bjornsen growls, leaning back in his chair and crossing his arms.

'No, sorry. Poor choice of words.' I kick myself. 'That's not what I think.' I take a scalding gulp of coffee. 'So, what happened after you got back to shore?'

Bjornsen regards me steadily. After a few moments he uncrosses his arms. 'They flew me to the hospital in Tromsø. Said at first I would lose the eye,' he touches the socket of his left eye, 'and that I might have blood poisoning. They told Gretel, my wife, not to hope. But she stayed at my bed, slept there with the children, they were only babies then, in a cot next to my bed. The doctors tried to make her leave but she wouldn't. She gave me my life back, her and the children. My life and my sight.'

'So why did you come to work offshore again?'

'Ha! You sound like Gretel now.'

'I wasn't having a go. I mean, I don't think I'd have had the nerve after something like that.'

Bjornsen gazes at the table where he's pinching grains of spilled sugar together into tiny pyramids. 'For a long time I stayed away from the sea. I got work fixing the machines in the canning factory and driving snow buggies for visiting scientists. But the work is patchy and doesn't pay well. I missed the sea. I missed Eyolf more, but he was gone. So…' He turns the palms of his huge hands up, lightly frosted at the tips with sugar. 'Staying away wasn't going to bring him back.' He nods fractionally then shakes his head, a private argument he's plainly had with himself countless times before. He sighs. 'I never got to say I was sorry.' He presses down hard on a miniature sugar pyramid and grinds the grains to dust.

'It wasn't your fault. The bear—'

'We fought. Before the bear. I was so angry with Eyolf and I can't even remember what it was about now. Probably money. Him not paying his way, not being responsible. We argued a lot about that. I'm not sure of the details. All I remember is the anger and then the bear, and sometimes looking back on it, it's like they were the same thing, you know?'

I don't have an answer for him. I wish I did but can't think of anything that doesn't sound glib or inadequate. In the over-long silence he brushes powdered sugar to the floor and dusts his hands together.

'That bear is nothing like the one I saw in the zoo when I was a kid,' I say.

Bjornsen blows on his hot chocolate.

'I must've been seven or eight. It was much smaller, a female, apparently rescued by the zoo from getting herself into trouble and most likely shot.' I keep talking, fast, keen to disperse the lingering awkwardness. 'She'd been hanging around some village in Greenland, going through the rubbish and generally pissing people off. The zoo called her Mercedes, which I remember thinking was really stupid. She didn't look anything like a car. My dad told me it was from the Spanish name for the Virgin Mary. Maria de las Mercedes – Mary of Mercies. From the Latin word *merces*, meaning wages or reward, which in vulgar Latin was used to mean favour or pity.'

'Your dad some kind of professor?'

'Dad was a lot of things,' I smile ruefully, 'but he was never anything like that.'

'Ah. I'm sorry.' Bjornsen has picked up on the was.

'No, no, he's still alive. He's just not… He's not working anymore.'

'Retired?'

'Kind of.' Why don't I just say he's dead? It'd be simpler. Truer too. 'He never had the sort of job you'd retire from but he was always studying something. Mostly self-taught. Knew all kinds of obscure stuff, not much of it any actual use to anyone. Practically.'

Bjornsen frowns and I look away. I know my tenses are fucked up. I can't help it. It just happens whenever I think about him. His empty eyes and sunken mouth. The way his body keeps on breathing. The man I knew now only exists in the past. He'd been selfish, infuriating, impractical, emotionally stunted, but also whip-smart and most of all vitally, strikingly alive. What's left in the present is… I don't know. Not him.

I put my mug down and coffee splashes onto my hand. I wipe it on my jeans. 'Maybe the zoo thought they were doing that bear a favour, taking her into captivity,' I say. 'But it didn't look like much of a favour to me. Her coat was this dirty yellow colour. She was virtually catatonic, just sprawled out on a pile of slimy rocks. Nobody stayed long to look at her. It was too sad.'

Bjornsen nods slowly and scratches his chin, making a dry rasping sound. 'You think they should've let her get shot?'

I shrug. 'I heard they finally moved her up north, to the Highland wildlife park. More room for her to move around.

The first time it snowed, she hid inside and refused to go out. Didn't know what to do. She'd forgotten what snow was. After a few days she finally launched herself into it, sliding down slopes, rolling and playing, white spray everywhere. There were pictures in all the papers – Mercedes happy at last. She died soon after. They said it was just her age. Time catching up.'

'Maybe it was her memory,' Bjornsen is looking at me, his end-of-the-world eyes a clear arctic blue.

'How do you mean?'

'Finally understanding everything she could never get back.'

5 OPERATION

88.1594° N, 27.1418° E

15TH JUNE 2025

Two weeks in and already tensions are surfacing, which does not bode well. It takes a certain temperament, like an astronaut, to be confined to a vessel for prolonged periods of time with only the company of your crew mates. We watch films in the day room. What's showing depends on who gets there first when a shift changes. Mostly it's old action flicks from the 1980s and '90s. We found a huge stash of ancient DVDs in one of the cupboards, presumably left behind by one of the *Polar Horizon*'s previous team of scientists, and now the current crew are competing to select the cheesiest examples of the genre. I've developed a fierce aversion to everything about Steven Segal, and Claude Van Damme's thighs bother me. All that high-kicking sinew makes me wince and cross my legs.

If Hannes, our Swedish seismic engineer, gets to the controls first, it'll be the even older films, British epics like

Dr Zhivago, Zulu, Lawrence of Arabia. These remind me of the days before I left home to go to uni. My dad liked to watch the exact same films, curtains drawn, sitting in the dark with a bottle and a glass for company. When those films were made, he'd have been in his twenties. Mum wouldn't even have been born. Perhaps going back to a time before she existed made it easier for him to tolerate a world without her in it. I don't know. We never talked about it.

'Look at all that sand. So warm. So dry,' sighs Hannes, stretching his legs towards the screen and flexing his feet as though warming them at an open fire.

Peter O'Toole, strapped into the saddle, gallops his horse across a baked landscape of dunes, getting smaller and smaller until he disappears into it, swallowed by golden sand. The camera rests on the empty rippling desert. Another kind of sea. So many ways to drown.

> • <

There are card games, backgammon, reading, writing this journal. There are long sweaty gym sessions. There is hardly any sleep. The horizon is often obscured by shifting fog and flurries of swirling sleet and snow that hiss and shiver at the windows. The days blur and run into each other.

Despite being over-supplied with time pieces – atomic clocks, satellite data, all kinds of ways of pinpointing time to fractions of tiny fractions of a second – without the roll of light and dark some primitive need in our bodies is unmet, and we're all starting to unravel just a little. I find myself doubting our instruments, running more tests than are strictly necessary. Grant is doing the same, and I don't question him about it. But I see it in his eyes, those same restless doubts that won't let me sleep. Something is very, very wrong. The sun never sets.

This uncertainty is mirrored in the others as well. Tempers start to fray. Only Bjornsen is changeless, steady as a rocky promontory, he watches us with his far-away eyes as if we amuse him in some tragic way, as if he's seen this all before and knows how it ends. That man will never die, he'll be eroded, over centuries.

> • <

The deliriously delicious Jules is a welcome distraction. He looks more edible every day. His stubble is strokeable, tawny. I let my thoughts stray while watching Proteus' data pile up, imagine the feel of his facial hair under my fingertips, soft yet resistant, pleasantly rough. The rub of it on my face, neck, chest, legs, his breath hot against my…

'The quality stats for the last line. Hello?' The nasal whine of Max's voice breaks into my daydreams.

'What? Yeah. Sure. I'll mail the files over to you.'

'Can't you just talk me through them here?' He swipes at his raw-looking nostrils with a cloth handkerchief.

I bring some graphs and comparisons up on screen for him. There are endless combinations of data, interminable things that can be compared with other things. The numbers can be made to do almost anything, depending on which sets of data you compare and the parameters of the comparison. I show Max something bland and reassuring and talk him through it in a monotone which

I hope will lull him into a sense of leaving well alone and fucking the fuck off.

'That's good enough eh? Ah geese...'

'Yes, ah geese,' I say, and he gives me a beady look. 'Absolutely within our quality parameters at this stage, everything functioning within specification.'

He tips his head and stalks back to his own console where he pecks away at his keyboard with long, thin fingers.

I try to hate him a little less. Remind myself that he probably got beaten up in school a lot. I need a break. I wrap myself up in my thick coat and pull my hat down over my ears. 'Just going to get some air,' I say.

> • <

We're almost as far north as it's possible to be so the sky comes curving straight out towards you from the horizon, low and edgeless. The sky and sea pressing together like two huge rollers and the ship heading for the join, pulled in towards that vanishing point. I wonder if we will be crushed or turned out on the other side, and what might be there beyond sea and sky.

The sun doesn't set, but the quality of the light changes. Now we're approaching the summer solstice, the sun only climbs and falls by a single degree in its entire cycle. Desperate for variation, some relief from the constant light, I devour the smallest deviations like a starving woman, gnawing and sucking greedily on every detail.

When there are no clouds the punitive white light glares like the radiation it truly is. It blanches the exposed skin on my hands and face. My outer edges fade to translucence, my bones glow silvery blue. I become an animated x-ray of myself. At other times, when the sun is shrouded and dips that crucial degree, the water turns from ultramarine to navy, the ice from white to azure, the fissures edged with jagged indigo shadows. All the colours of a painted ocean.

These changes feed me but leave me unsatisfied. I have begun to crave darkness, physically. There's a deep-down ache, a tightening in my chest, a clawing hunger pulling at the back of my throat. The forgiving, enveloping peace of night.

Back in the non-polar world, no matter what happens on any given day, night always comes with the free gift of a clean slate come morning. But here, now, with one long perpetual day stretching ahead of us, there are no real tomorrows and there can be no forgiveness. The bright light of day exposes all our mistakes to constant visibility. There is nowhere to hide.

We've left behind the open sea and are deep into the pack-ice now. The sea still moves and rolls, but covered in a patchwork quilt of ice it looks deceptively solid, giving the impression that we're gliding through frozen countryside, snow-covered fields slipping away to either side. A dream-like unreality lies over everything. It's the sea but different, it's the sky but changed, it's the world but there is nothing about it that feels like home.

Up ahead the icebreaker grinds onwards, always north, shouldering aside the smaller floes, pulverising the larger ones. The shearing, scraping noise of metal on ice drifts on the wind and sets my teeth on edge.

> • <

Fucking pickled fish again. The Norwegians can't get enough of it. Since they own the vessel and the chef they get to choose the food.

It's laid out like a continental-style buffet on a table to the left of the serving hatch that opens into the kitchen. I can hear Rune clattering around in there, shouting at his kitchen boy one second then humming contentedly under his breath the next. Perhaps he's shouting encouragement, but it doesn't sound like it. His boy, who is actually a tiny wizened old man, scuttles around the steaming pans fetching and carrying and dodging Rune's heavy hands.

I look at the fish. Roll mop herring, I believe. Little bundles of rolled up white fish with bits of pickled gherkin poking out from the middle. The white flesh has a pearly shine to it. I'm sure this stuff must be good for you, full of all kinds of vitamins and oils and the like, but it tastes revolting. Probably it's a taste you have to be brought up with, weaned on. Especially for breakfast. What kind of a person seriously wakes up and thinks the first thing they want to put in their mouth is a bit of cold, vinegary fish?

I wouldn't mind so much but the Russians have nicked all the pastries again. They can't get their heads around the idea that such luxuries have been provided for and will reappear regularly. They fill their pockets with all they can hold each day and stash them in their cabins, as if they're hoarding for a long winter. They have no shame about it, pushing each other and grabbing at the food, cramming croissants and Danish pastries into their pockets. I can't help wondering what these guys eat at home. Most of them are tall and muscular. What's been fuelling that growth? They smell of the ship's intestines: hot metal, oil and grease. They stick close together and mutter gloomily in Russian, rarely conversing with the others on board. Sometimes they use English, which they exchange with the Norwegians in short, abrupt sentences, no more than is needed to get the job done. English still functions as a lingua franca for most international crews, clinging on to its dominance as the language of the sea.

The sea has its own language and it's not one we understand. We're not even listening. We're sailing along on the crest of a massive communication failure. And the sun is always in the sky.

I pour myself a black coffee, claim a wedge of dark brown bread and sit at a table in the corner. A group of Russians are huddled around another table and they pay no attention to me. The coffee, at least, is good. I take small sips, inhaling the sharp earthy vapour and riding the wave of caffeine. The bread is dense and tough. I tear small pieces off and dip them in my coffee making soft, bitter dumplings. I haven't slept well, again. I've not slept properly so far on this trip and am beginning to doubt whether I will before it's over.

My onshore life, with its orderly progression of days and nights, seems unimaginable now. I concentrate, trying to bring to mind the full moon, bright in a black sky. Remember the stars? Laid out across the darkness? Even a city night, wet tarmac streaked with orange streetlight, car headlights sweeping shafts of light over the dark glass of sleeping offices. It all feels unreachable, like a story told by a stranger about a place I've never been. But I long for it with something like homesickness. It's an unfamiliar feeling. One of the main reasons I took this job in the first place was the travel, the freedom of being tied neither to a specific place nor its obligations and complications. Freedom is important. But maybe my avoidance of attachment to a specific where, is what makes me more dependant upon the when. Everyone needs an anchor.

〉•〈

'Lost in thought?'

I'm startled to find Jules standing next to me.

'Sorry, yes, I was…'

'Miles away?'

'Oh, I wish. A few hundred miles away. Somewhere warm, around sunset, drink in my hand.'

Jules gives a gentle laugh. 'Still not sleeping?'

'Is it that obvious?'

'It's to be expected. In fact, you should be worried if you weren't finding it difficult. We're not suited to these conditions.' He pauses and looks over his shoulder before continuing. 'This place isn't meant for us. Humans don't belong here. I feel that strongly. Don't you?'

Yes, I do feel that, exactly. A sense of trespass. Wrongness. But, it's not going to do any good talking about it. Much as I like looking at Jules, I don't fancy taking this particular conversation any further. I'm already tired and bad-tempered, I don't need extra helpings of environmental guilt thrown into the mix. I swallow the rest of my coffee and make to get up. 'Well, I better get back to it.'

He touches my arm. 'I'm sorry. That came out wrong. I'm just…' he takes a breath, 'not sleeping much either. It makes for poor conversational skills.' He picks up my empty mug. 'More coffee?'

I decide to give him another chance. If he starts in on the we-don't-belong-here stuff again I can always leave.

While he gets the coffee, I roll my shoulders to release some of the tension locked into the muscles. Grant's still hardly talking to me, the rest of the crew are increasingly tense and preoccupied. A little human contact, with someone prepared to at least make the effort, might be good. He returns with two steaming mugs. I smile my thanks.

'So, tell me,' he says settling into the seat opposite, 'what are you running from?'

'Excuse me?'

'It's a theory of mine. Everyone working offshore I've ever really talked to has something back home they're trying to escape. I've never been wrong. Everyone has something. So what is it with you? Unlucky in love? Bad debts? Family problems?'

'Are you always this nosy?'

'Always.' He holds my gaze, mock-serious.

'Okay. You've got me.' I hold my hands up. 'All of the above. I'm broken-hearted and bankrupt and I've run away to sea.' I adopt a far-away look, press a hand to my brow and sigh dramatically. 'To forget.'

He laughs appreciatively. 'You'll tell me eventually.'

'Don't get your hopes up. There's nothing much to tell, honestly. What about you? What's your thing?'

'With me it's simple. Boredom. I can't cope with it. I have

a restless spirit.'

'A tortured soul?'

'That too.'

'Brilliant. Doomed romantics are such good company.'

We spar gently this way for a while, both of us enjoying the dance around the ring. I deflect his jabs at my defences, he counters with easy intimacy. We talk about home. Or what passes for it for each of us. Like me he spends a lot of time offshore, so our lives on dry land are similarly sketchy, those untended attachments harder to revive each time.

'I love being at sea,' he says, 'but this way of living, it has its costs.'

There's a lull in the conversation while we both peer inward at our personal balance sheets, those unsteady columns of costs and benefits. The mood dips and a melancholy chill starts to creep around us.

'I feel more and more, especially on this trip, like it can't go on forever.' His voice is quieter, less sure of itself. 'I have this sense of time running out.'

'For you personally? Or generally?'

He puts his hands flat on the table, his expression shifts. The playfulness is back, but a different flavour. 'What if time is an add-on to the human brain? Like an operating system?'

'Um...'

'Say the body, the brain, all the nerves and neurons are the hardware.'

'Yeah, okay.' I have no idea where he's going with this but it's brought the light back to his eyes.

'And things like spatial awareness, language, creativity, sex drive, ambition, all of those things are software programs.'

'I could go with that.'

He smiles awkwardly. 'Bear with me. This is the sort of stuff I think about when I can't sleep.'

'No, no, carry on,' I say. I'm somewhere between impressed and sceptical. My own sleepless mind tends to wander in a daze between work issues, half-arsed plans for the future and vaguely erotic scenarios I'm too tired to get worked up about. But this guy amuses himself with theories about the nature of time. No shit?

'None of those programs,' he continues, 'take language development, could run without time. We literally could not string a sentence together.'

'Uh huh.'

'There has to be an order – a before and an after. They're fundamental to everything we are. So, linear time is the operating system.'

'Okay. And?'

'What if we could change the system?'

'You can't just get rid of time.'

'No, but—'

'Not and still have life. Birth, growth, decay, death. Without time, none of it makes sense.'

'Only because we're looking at them all lined up. Through our idea of what time is.'

I mull this over for a while. My brain, although drawn, magpie-like, to the shiny ideas, can't get a good purchase on them. Jules is still talking but I'm just watching his lips move. I've lost the thread and it feels like a lot of effort to latch back on. So much easier to just watch. The sensual way he uses his hands, the fine creases around his eyes. That mouth.

He laughs. 'Sorry. I'm boring you.'

'No. I—'

'It's alright. You're tired. Perhaps another time?' He stands up.

'Sure,' I say, holding the eye contact just long enough. 'I'd like that.'

¿ ALARMS & WARNINGS ¿

88.3562° N, 35.5748° E

18TH JUNE 2025

It's the silence that wakes me. I sit up in my bunk and bang my head on the cabin roof. The darkness is total. I've covered the window with blackout material and taped it all the way round to block out the midnight sun. Perhaps I've gone too far. I put my fingers to my eyes to check they're open; there's no difference between open and shut. How can anyone be expected to sleep properly out here? My body clock feels smashed, cogs and springs spewing out in all directions. So many tiny pieces and no idea how, or if, I can ever fit them back together.

The sun never sets, but in the small hours where the night should be it lowers almost imperceptibly in the sky and hangs there, watching us, red and unblinking.

I listen to the silence as I pull a thick jumper over the clothes I slept in. Something is wrong. Within a few days of any survey, the regular thump of the acoustic guns fades into the background, becomes part of the fabric of reality, like a heartbeat. You don't hear it anymore. Once that happens, silence acquires meaning, becomes loud – a warning. The guns have stopped.

> • <

Proteus is playing up. We spend every shift chasing alarms and warnings, and the monitor screens are an angry rash of flashing amber and red. No sooner do I resolve one, returning the status to green, than another demands my attention. Neither Grant nor I can keep up with the rate of errors and glitches. Even with both of us working longer hours so our shifts overlap, the workload is overwhelming. We're both tiring.

I drag open the cabin door, blunder into the narrow corridor and head towards the galley. No way I'm getting roped into sorting out system problems before I get some breakfast, or at least caffeine. Anyway, we can't be on a turn. It feels like too soon since the last one, but I no longer trust my perception of time.

At times my surroundings seem no more real than a dream and my dreams, when I have them, no less real than reality. It's becoming hard to tell the difference. If I could even dream of night, blessed night, that might be some relief but when I do dream, it is mostly of ice and teeth. When I wake there's a moment when even my own body feels strange to me, like my bones don't fit properly inside my skin anymore and I have to remind myself how to stand and walk. My jaw aches.

> • <

I rub my eyes and stumble slightly, swaying sideways into a cabin door. Just as my shoulder makes contact, and I tense to push off again, the door opens and I tumble through.

From my position on the floor of the cabin, I take in the sturdy work boots and the soft frayed edges of denim jeans. A trace of cedar wood aftershave reaches my nostrils. Jules looks down at me, a surprised smile on his face. He reaches down, grasps both my hands and helps me to my feet.

'Is-o-bel.' He pronounces my name meticulously, all tongue, lips and teeth, making the most of each syllable. I've never heard it sound that way before and hardly recognise it as my own. But I'll take it. 'You only had to knock.'

His smile is distinctly carnal. I realise I'm staring at his mouth and try to pull my hands out of his grip, but he doesn't let go. Instead he pulls me closer to him. A millisecond's consideration confirms that closer to Jules is not somewhere I object to being, so I don't. All tiredness has evaporated from my body and I feel more awake than I have for some time. His smile has faded, his eyes lowered, his face is close to mine, and before I've registered the transition from not-kissing to kissing, we are. This kiss goes from nought to sixty, gentle to urgent, in no time at all. He releases my hands and we are wrapped around each other, pressing the lengths of our bodies together as best we can through the layers of warm clothes we're both wearing – clothes which are beginning to feel conspicuously unhelpful.

Locked together, we shuffle further into his cabin. I extend a leg and kick the door shut behind us. We separate and stare at each other for a moment, breathing hard. I take hold of the rough wool of his sweater and tug it up over his head. He does the same for me and we continue trading items of clothing until there are none left, only two mounds of meekly uninhabited fabric on the floor. I don't feel cold, despite the chill of the air on my uncovered skin.

I'm burning.

I reach for him. He says something under his breath in French that I don't understand, and don't need to.

> • <

Some uncounted time later we are a single animal, damp cooling limbs, breath slowing, pulse subsiding and separating into two distinct rhythms. Jules, wearing a dazed expression, runs a hand over his forehead, dislodging wet strings of hair, making them stand out at startled angles.

We start to disentangle ourselves. Jules flinches. There's a deep scratch running from his shoulder across his chest, another on his hip. Blood on my hands. What have I done? He looks at me, runs the pad of his thumb over my lower lip. It comes away red.

I put a hand to my mouth. 'Oh shit. Fuck. I'm sorry. Did I hurt you? I didn't mean…'

Jules winces slightly but smiles and reaches for me, holds my shoulder. 'Don't apologise,' he says. 'I'll live.'

I can't explain it. The last thing I want to do is damage Jules's body. It's too perfect to spoil. I like him, why would I want to hurt him? I shake my head in disbelief. 'But I don't usually… I've never… This isn't something I…' A vision of the scratches on Grant's neck surfaces and I push it back down again.

He kisses me. Salt and iron. I wonder if he thinks I'm ashamed of the simple fact we've had sex, and so impulsively. I'm not. It's the damage, the blood... That's something new, something worrying. My memory of what happened after the clothes came off is already losing focus and receding into a reddish haze. I can't make out the details. Can't imagine what was going through my mind.

'Don't worry about it,' he says, maybe reading my mind, maybe reading the wrong page, but so what? I let it go. The deep satisfied ache between my legs is one thing I'm not confused or remotely worried about.

'Okay,' I say, getting up and dragging my fingers through my tangled hair. 'But right now I think I really should get to the bridge.'

'Ah yes, I should too.' He gets out of bed and stretches, starts gathering up his clothes.

I'm already pulling my combats on. 'No. You stay here for, say, half an hour or so at least? I don't want this all the way round the ship before lunchtime. Okay? If we show up together, looking all...' I gesture between us and pull an exaggerated swoony expression. 'You know? It's going to be pretty obvious.'

He looks like he might be about to argue, to insist that he goes first and it should be me who hangs back in the cabin, but he gives way. 'Sure, no problem. But we were making so much noise someone probably heard anyway.'

I don't recall being noisy, although when I probe my retreating memory, something growls. I can't tell if it was me, him, or... Or what?

'Shut up, Jules.'

He laughs, then shuts up and looks contrite.

'Right, I'm away.'

'Another time, yes?'

I grin. Despite the weirdness, and what just happened was a lot of weirdness, I know I won't turn him down. 'Hmm,' I say, pretending to weight it up. 'I guess, if I get bored.'

We part without lies or promises. A clean getaway.

> • <

Out in the corridor I lean against the door for a moment, close my eyes and focus on pulling myself together, mentally at least. When I open them again, Grant is standing there looking at me.

'You look very pleased with yourself,' he says, his eyes narrowing.

'What? No, not particularly, just tired, y'know?' I lick my lips. 'This constant daylight…' The taste of Jules's blood on my tongue. I turn sharply away from Grant and start walking.

'Uh huh?' Grant doesn't sound like he believes me at all, but follows close behind. 'I was looking for you. You weren't in your cabin.'

'I got a bit lost.'

'Really?'

'I was kind of disoriented. Must've gone the wrong way.'

Grant opens his mouth to speak again. He looks really pissed off. I can't be doing with jealousy. It's not as if he has any grounds for it. We've never made any promises to each other. I get in before he can start interrogating me.

'So, how're things going on the bridge? I noticed the guns aren't firing. Please tell me we're on a turn or something.'

Grant swallows and, with effort, refocuses his attention on the job. 'We're not on a turn,' he say, and looks at his feet, at a loss.

'Alright then.' I pick up the pace and swing onto the ladder to the next level. 'Sooner we get there, sooner we can get them firing again.' Max will be having a hissy fit.

> • <

Bjornsen watches us arrive.

'What have you two been doing? Fucking in the cupboard while everything goes to buggery? Ja?'

Grant chokes then coughs to cover it.

'Jealousy is such an ugly emotion, Captain,' I say. 'And you're so beautiful, it's a shame to spoil your pretty face.'

'Fuck you, Ginger,' he grumbles, smiling to himself.

'In your dreams, pretty boy.'

Bjornsen laughs and shakes his head. 'You're needed over there,' he says, and throws Grant a withering look.

'Come on, Grant,' I say, 'let's have a look.'

We sit down at the control station and he brings up the real-time display. The survey area is blinking green with the plotted lines and streamer positions overlaid in blue and red respectively. Small purple triangles represent dynamic obstacles, otherwise known as bloody great icebergs, otherwise known as a quick cold death if you run into them.

Grant flips to an alternate display as Max hovers up behind us. He keeps the data moving, showing Max some innocuous crap, talking about how we've already got good data and it won't be long before we're back firing the guns again.

'Do you realise how much money the company is losing every second this survey is not fully operational?'

'No,' I say, 'not exactly. But I bet you do.'

'Well, yes, let's just say it's a lot. So, let's just get this working, people.'

'Sure thing, boss,' says Grant and Max stalks off again.

I hate it when he calls us 'people'.

> • <

I wait until Max is engrossed in some readouts we've fobbed him off with then switch the display back and bring up the analysis of the data from the acoustics. There are the usual regular peaks and troughs of the guns but then, after the signal disappears from when the guns were disabled, there remains an oddly high level of background noise. Cross-referencing this and laying it over the depth sensor data gives me results that make no sense. I try again, mapping the positioning data and triple checking the projections are applied correctly, the magnetic variation, the tidal profiles, and on and on, but I keep coming up with the same thing. The mysterious noise interference appears to be coming from the ice itself.

I change the time parameters and see that the interference has been there all along, since we started shooting, and what's more, it's building in volume. It's outwith the limits of human perception, but not for long if it continues to grow at the same rate.

'What do you make of this?' I ask Grant in a low voice.

He chews his lip. 'Problem with the acoustic units?'

'All of them?' We both know this is unlikely. Verging on impossible.

'Do we have RGPS from the tail buoys?'

I check both of them. One is fine but the other is suspect. The data is ragged, with gaps. 'Kind of. Not what it should be. Damaged unit?'

'Only one way to be sure.'

He can't be serious.

'Someone is going to have to take the workboat out and have a look.'

Even in perfect weather, taking a workboat out is a hard manual task we try to avoid wherever possible. In these conditions, it'll be an absolute bastard of a job. At the same time I know he's right. This level of error in the readings could, conceivably, be caused by the equipment icing over, which would distort the signals. We could spend days digging around in the diagnostics, running tests and getting nowhere. We have to rule out physical problems before we can be sure it's a software issue.

I tell Max. He doesn't like the prospect of more downtime but I explain that if we don't physically check the antenna, the whole survey could be rendered meaningless.

Either myself or Grant need to be aboard the workboat and I volunteer. Not that I want to do it, but I want even less to deal with Grant pissing and moaning if I make him go.

'Your turn next,' I say to him with a pointed stare.

> • <

When Jules appears on the bridge I busy myself with loading the data I'll need onto a hand-held unit. He looks cool and casual as always, like nothing has happened between us. Good.

'If that's what we need to do then you better get to it,' says Max.

Bjornsen chips in. 'One of Viktor's boys will skipper for you. And take Jules, he could do with the fresh air and exercise.'

I look over, startled, and Jules grins at me.

'It would be my pleasure,' he says and performs a mock-chivalrous bow, sweeping an invisible feathered hat low in an arc past his knees.

I notice Grant scowl at him before turning his attention back to the displays and their accumulations of impossible data.

'Okay,' I say. 'Let's get going.'

Despite the difficulty of a workboat trip, the physical demands, the increased chance of falling into the sea and freezing to death in seconds, despite all of that, maybe it'll be good to be off the *Polar Horizon* for a while.

> • <

The survival suits are stored in a cargo locker on the main deck. Legally, there's supposed to be one for every crew member and a range of sizes available. This is hardly ever the case and this time is no exception. The bright orange suits are all one size – giant Scandinavian man-sized. Great. My five feet and nine inches make me taller than your average Scottish woman, but still several inches shorter and about a foot narrower than the template for these survival suits. I pull one on, push my boots into the integrated feet and try to hoist the excess material up to my waist and secure it with a thick belt. This is only partially successful. I look like a burst football. The two men fare better. They look at me, sympathy mixed with amusement. I ignore them and strap the ruggedised hand-held to my belt. We're ready.

'Make sure the gun is loaded,' says Bjornsen and I stop in my tracks. Gun? It's only then, exploding into my mind in a mass of roaring white, that I remember the bear. Bjornsen meets my eyes and nods. Shit, how could I forget about the bear? I've been so busy thinking about the equipment and the freezing water, the fact that there's a massive carnivore, at least one we know of, running around out there slipped my mind.

'Don't worry,' says Jules. 'The way we look, he'd be embarrassed to be seen in our company.'

'True.' I force a smile, but I doubt the bear is fashion sensitive.

Our workboat skipper watches Jules shoulder the rifle then reaches a hand inside his own coat and pulls out what looks like an old military issue revolver. A brutal, ugly thing. He expects us to admire it and, although my initial reaction is to recoil, as I glance over the ice-strewn water stretching forever in all directions, I quickly reverse my position. I'm glad we're well-armed. Bjornsen said it's the bear you can't see that will kill you, and I can't see any fucking bears.

He puts the weapon away and I offer him my hand. 'I'm Isobel.'

'I know,' he says, ignoring the question on my face and gripping my hand briefly in his. 'Ilia.' He turns away and says something in Russian to Jules, who to my surprise replies in equally fast and fluent-sounding Russian. They share a laugh and set about stowing the gear, winching the workboat free of the main deck and lowering it into the water. With the ropes still attached, we climb down one after another and into the much smaller vessel.

The way the workboat is gripped by the water is a firm reminder of who, or what, is in charge out here. The sea tenses and flexes around the sides like a muscle, or a fist, more than able to crush us at will.

Jules, perhaps sensing my apprehension, perhaps feeling it himself, says, 'Come on, let's do this, and later on you can show me your cabin, maybe?'

The thought provides some welcome warmth. I take a deep breath as we settle into the bench-like seats. Ilia disengages the ropes, starts the engine. With a strangled bark dropping to a growl, we motor away from the *Polar Horizon*, curving back towards the end of the streamers.

7 TROUBLESHOOTING

88.4852° N, 30.2410° E

20TH JUNE 2025

The *Polar Horizon* shrinks, inch by inch. We steal glances back towards it, over the open water expanding behind us. I wonder how long we could survive in this environment if we lost our way. We've no food as far as I know, a thought that makes me abruptly hungry.

The ice looks different up close. Perhaps it's the lower elevation: instead of looking down on the frozen world, we're part of it. This new perspective reveals strange formations floating beyond the edges of our clear channel like a drifting museum of malformed statues.

Ilia keeps the workboat scudding over the small waves at a steady speed, his eyes continually scanning the horizon, watchful and brooding. Sometimes his hand strays to the pocket where he stashed his gun and pats it, as if reassuring himself it's still there. Jules, in comparison, is almost jovial, as if we're tourists being shown the sights, with him taking on the role of guide.

'See right out there, just below the horizon?' He points with boy scout enthusiasm.

It's a jumble of whites, hard to make out the edges of anything properly. There's an impression of movement but it feels more theoretical than real, like trying to perceive the hour hand's progress around a clock face. But there's one area that looks to be moving slower than the other shapes around it.

'Iceberg. Probably calved from a glacier and now having little babies of its own as it melts and pieces break off. Could be from a glacier in Russia, carried round by the currents. The smaller ones will melt before they reach land. The bigger berg might end up bumping into Greenland, might not.'

Away from the ship, I'm also more aware of the sounds. The sea is by no means silent. There are muted crumplings and splashings as the statues, the pinnacles and minarets, fragile arches and buttresses collapse and loose bits of themselves into the sea, sometimes gently, sometimes with a crash. There is also a low, almost sub-audible groan coming from the pack-ice as it shifts, large slabs pushing against each other, setting off a chain of compression over miles until something shifts and gives way, creating new tensions elsewhere. Is this the background noise the acoustics have been picking up?

The cloud of gulls following the *Polar Horizon* from port has thinned dramatically, most of them gave up the chase, either scared off by Ralf's pack of disembodied dogs, or perhaps realising there will be no haul of fish here. A few of the persistently hopeful ones coast over us in the workboat. Their plaintive cries sound almost human.

>•<

Finally we reach the malfunctioning tail buoy. It's about the size and shape of a small dingy, plastic and belligerently yellow with a raised column at the back upon which is mounted the RGPS module and antenna. The signal light is still bravely flashing orange but it's easy to see the problem. The head of the antenna is coated with a great gob of ice, as if it has trawled through a giant-sized tub of ice cream and been left to harden.

While Ilia turns us in the water, Jules checks in with the hand-held radio to confirm our position. Bjornsen's voice coming faint and broken-up over the water is so much less reassuring than I hoped it might be. He sounds twenty years older, less sure of himself, less solid. Less everything.

We unlock the grab hooks and pull the tail buoy in towards the side of the workboat.

'I'll have to get on and de-ice it manually,' says Jules.

It's clear from the forced determination in his voice that he doesn't relish the job, but I'm glad he volunteered. 'Wait a minute.' I rummage around the equipment stowed in the workboat lockers. 'There should be a safety line here.' I keep searching, not looking up or meeting his eyes, mostly to spare him from my concern. Pointless emotion won't help either of us right now, whereas a simple fucking safety line...

'It's alright. It would only get in the way,' he says, gently enough to let me know he gets it and is grateful. 'Okay. Here we go.' He clambers up onto the side of the workboat, heaves himself over and onto the buoy. After an alarming wobble, he steadies and turns to face the antenna, feet straddling the buoy like it's a jet ski. He takes a large spanner from his pocket and starts bashing at the lump of ice.

'Very high tech,' I shout over.

'Sometimes brute force is the only way,' he calls back.

After a few hefty clunks, the ball of ice shatters. Jules laughs and leans back, holding on with one hand, using the back of the other to wipe powdered ice off his face.

'Very good, now get back over here.'

'Hey, look,' he shouts, pointing with the spanner.

'Will you stow the tour guide shtick for now?'

'No, really, shhhh. Just look.'

He's pointing past the bow of the workboat, to what looks to me like an empty bit of sea until a small grey-brown mottled island rises up and slides away again.

'What was that?'

'Seal. Watch. This one's curious.'

The seal pops its head out of the water then disappears back under, its side rolling like a wet stone, and surfaces again a little closer. It continues this way, pausing every ten feet or so to stick its head up and look at us. Not much more than twenty feet away from the workboat it stops and rises out of the water to a surprising height, its small head perched on the widening body, giving the impression of shoulders, like a human sentry standing in shallow water, arms by their sides. Although its tail and flippers must surely be moving under the surface, the seal is absolutely still. I can see its face, nostrils flexing as it snuffles the air, droplets of water spraying and collecting on its whiskers. The eyes are solemn black pools.

'I thought seals stayed closer to land in the summer?' I say, just loud enough for Jules to hear, hoping I won't startle the seal. Probably not likely, I decide, given it doesn't seem to have much in the way of ears.

'That was the old pattern but the sea-ice has become so unpredictable. Currents change, temperatures spike one year, crash the next. None of the animals know what to expect. All the usual habitats are unstable. They're forced to gamble between the coastline and the edge of the pack-ice. Sometimes it pays off, sometimes not.'

The seal stares at us as if it's going to ask for directions, or enquire politely as to whether we know where the best fish might be found. I'm wondering about its ears. Are they just holes in the side of its head or what? I feel vaguely embarrassed at my ignorance as it gazes back at me.

'And the bear too is forced to follow wherever the food decides to go.' This from Ilia.

Christ. The bear. How do I keep forgetting about the bear? He slips with ease behind any available distraction, finds blind spots in my consciousness and waits there, still and silent, until I remember. My stomach clenches into a small knot and I beckon to Jules. 'Come on. Enough with the nature watch. Let's get back now.'

Ilia steadies the buoy as best he can from the workboat and Jules makes to climb back on board. I glance at the seal. At that moment, its eyes suddenly widen and it disappears under the water. Not in a graceful roll but with a sudden jerk, straight down.

I look back at Jules and Ilia, who have frozen in their movements; they saw it too. We don't have time to speak before the bear breaks the surface of the water and claws sideways up onto a largish floe, his jaws clamped around the tail of the seal. The seal twists and its flippers waggle ineffectually as the bear drags it onto the ice, flips it round, anchors its body under one paw, then leans over and sinks his teeth into the seal's face.

I hear a hoarsely whispered curse from Ilia. We've both instinctively crouched down low to the deck, as if that's going to make us invisible, with our garish colours and chuntering motor. Jules is clamped to the mast of the tail buoy, not moving a muscle. Ilia begins to crab slowly towards the helm.

'Fuck are you doing?' I hiss.

He glares back at me. 'We need to leave. Now.'

'Not without Jules.' We both look over to the tail buoy where Jules faces us, eyes wide.

Ilia's gaze flicks between Jules, the bear, and me, weighing his options.

The bear has his own concerns. Wet ripping and crunching noises carry over the water. The bear's entire head is darkened with gore, obscuring its features. It appears faceless, just a thick neck fringed with teeth, tearing into the blubbery flesh where the seal's head used to be. For a moment it becomes a single creature, half-bear half-seal, joined at the neck, devouring itself.

Ilia's hand once again strays to his pocket but this time he brings out the gun and weighs it contemplatively. He looks at me. The thought fires across my brain – he could dispose of me easily enough, make up some story about Jules and I both falling victim to the bear, himself only narrowly escaping. But surely not. He might be a self-serving coward, but a murderer is a whole other level. He grins at me, and I wonder if I've misjudged him as he raises the gun in my direction, but he turns it away to aim at the bear. On the buoy, Jules is shaking his head furiously. I reach for Ilia's arm but he shakes me off and takes aim again.

Around the dead seal, crimson blooms outwards into a delicate rose pink that fades to nothing as the seal's life disperses into snow and ice. My senses are painfully heightened. Everything is sharp. The metallic tang of blood in the air, the cold clasping my face, the sea slapping rhythmically against the side of the workboat, and overseeing it all the sun, a boiling sphere of suspended time. Thick bile coats my tongue, the bitter taste mixing with the heavy smell of raw meat. I swallow, heave, swallow again, heave again then force myself to stop, appalled by the terrible, hot, slithering sensation in my throat.

The bear, having finished with the seal's head, rises up partially on his hind legs and sets about the body with his forepaws. With almost playful, cat-like movements, he seems to be toying with the corpse. Ilia still has the gun raised but doesn't look ready to fire. We watch, strangely hypnotised by the bear's skill as he, quite methodically, tears strip after sinewy strip away. He's skinning it.

In the impossible brightness I feel myself losing layers along with the seal, the relentless sun burning through my defences, flaying me alive.

The bear is preoccupied for the moment but how long will that last? It's not that he hasn't seen us – he has chosen to leave us be. For now. I make myself look away and hurriedly motion to Jules. He takes two steps around the buoy mast, lunges and grabs onto the workboat guardrail with one hand and my own outstretched hand with the other.

The air cracks. The workboat shifts in the water as Ilia staggers backwards with the force of the gun's recoil. Jules loses his footing and his grip on the guard rail. As he slips his arm twists and I try to hold on but his hand wrenches out of my grasp then he's in the water and it has closed over his head.

'No. No no no.'

A white streak in my peripheral vision. The bear has entered the water at the same time. Jules breaks the surface again several feet away and claws back towards the boat. I lean out and grab the arm of his survival suit and haul as hard as I can. 'Give me a hand here!' What is that maniac Ilia doing now? I whip my head round. He's at the helm, fumbling with the controls.

'Wait a—'

The boat lurches and the engine stalls. Jules, only halfway back on board, is nearly tipped back into the sea. I look around wildly as we drift sideways. The bear is nowhere to be seen. Shit. I grab onto Jules with both hands. It could be anywhere. Laying low behind that ridge of ice. Or submerged underwater, closing on us with teeth bared, feet away from Jules. I strain and tug, all the time expecting him to be yanked out of my hands and dragged under the water.

Finally he manages to clamber the rest of the way into the boat. His face is white with shock and he's coughing up water but the survival suit has done its job. He's alive and safe. For the time being.

I'm casting around for the rifle when the engine stutters back into life. Ilia throws the boat into gear, opens up the throttle and heads us back in the direction of the *Polar Horizon*.

> • <

Bjornsen is waiting on deck as the workboat is winched back into position on board the reassuringly sturdy larger vessel and the three of us clamber out. They'd been expecting more radio contact from us and want to know what happened. My body goes limp as the adrenalin overload washes away. The survival suit feels intolerably heavy and I sink down onto the deck, breathing heavily, my head down. Jules and Ilia are slapping each other's shoulders in boyish camaraderie I find hard to credit. Ilia has already apologised to Jules for the gun going off 'accidentally', and Jules has accepted this. The shot did go well wide of the bear. Whatever the truth of the matter, I don't have the energy to argue about it. I let them tell the story between them, watching Bjornsen's expression turn even grimmer than usual.

'Was it the same bear?'

The three of us exchange glances.

'A bear is a bear,' says Ilia.

I say nothing. I'm sure it was the same one but have only gut feeling to base that on. I sort through the images in my memory, already freeze-framed like a series of slides to be shown to armchair explorers in a safe, well-heated room far from danger, but in each one the bear is either a blur of movement or so covered in dark blood that it hardly looks like a bear at all. Comparing these images with my memory of the bear we saw stalking the ship doesn't provide anything conclusive. I shrug and look hopefully at Jules.

'Could have been,' he says, returning the gesture.

Bjornsen looks exasperated but shakes it off. 'Okay. You three, change out of those suits, then go to the galley and find something to eat.'

The galley sounds like an excellent idea. I'm starving.

> • <

This hunger is not going to be satisfied with bread and pickled fish.

'Hey, Rune. Don't you have anything else?'

'Of course. What does Madame desire? Name it. I live to serve.' He glowers and hefts a large carving knife from one hand to the other.

Jules leans over. 'Do you have any steak?'

Five minutes later the three of us are hunched over our meals, not talking, just eating. The steaks are thick and rare, red in the middle, oozing blood over the white plates with every cut. We eat quickly, concentrated on the task. As the edge is taken off my hunger about halfway through, it occurs to me how strange it is. Surely the scene we just witnessed should put us off the idea of bloody meat rather than sharpen our appetites for it? My knife slides satisfyingly through the tender flesh. Maybe not so strange. Are we not also predators, hunters?

I watch Ilia. Definitely more of a bear than a seal. He's mopping the last of the juices from his plate with a hunk of bread, leaving red-brown smears. He looks up at me and raises an eyebrow. I stare him down. I won't trust him again. He smirks as if to say he knows that and doesn't give a shit. He wipes his mouth with a paper napkin then sits back and belches, pushes his plate away and rises. 'I'm going to sleep now,' he says. We exchange curt nods and he's gone.

Jules and I finish our meals. 'Better?' he asks as we both lay down our cutlery at the same time.

I cover my mouth before I burp. 'Yeah. Much.'

'Do you think you could sleep now?'

'God. I don't know. Think I've lost the knack.'

'My bunk is quite comfortable. You're welcome to make an attempt there.'

I laugh. 'Somehow I have a feeling that might not be so restful. Anyway, I should go to the bridge, check everything's back up and running.' I make to stand but Jules reaches over and lays a hand on my arm.

'Grant can deal with things for a while longer. You need rest.'

There's that soft light playing in his eyes again, his head tilted to one side. I can't keep from staring at his lips as they part slightly and curve into a knowing parabola. 'I—'

> • <

His bunk really does seem more comfortable than mine. He was right about that. But surely everyone, apart from the captain, probably, sleeps on the same standard issue mattress? Maybe some mattresses are more equal than others.

'What's funny?'

'Nothing, nothing, just ignore me.' I twist my neck round and kiss his bare skin. We're wedged together on his bed, shoulder to shoulder, taking up the full width. The sex was tender in comparison with last time. There are no injuries, no disassociation, and although I feel a little high, my brain doesn't feel like it has been pulled apart and inexpertly put back together again. My body feels satisfied, comfortably heavy and, yes, definitely… sleepy.

〉•〈

'Why didn't you wake me? Fuck's sake! Ten hours? Grant will be going mental.'

'It's okay. Don't panic. I spoke to him and—'

'You did fucking what? What did you say?'

'I just told him you were exhausted from the workboat trip, and lack of sleep, all of which is true, and that you'd fallen asleep while we were comparing notes.'

'Ha! Oh, he'll have loved that.'

'And I suggested that perhaps he could, as a personal favour to you, work a double shift and let you catch up on some sleep, considering you'd been risking your life while he… wasn't.'

Grant definitely won't have liked that. Still, at least he'll probably bugger right off when I get to the bridge. He'll be knackered. I'm not sure if I feel rested or not. It's as though the last ten hours have simply been erased from my life without leaving so much as a shadow behind. I decide I don't have time to think about it, dress hastily and leg it out of Jules's cabin, his laughing 'You're welcome!' fading behind.

〉•〈

Grant's face looks like it's been used as a sleeping bag by a restless hippo, his eyes almost disappearing into dark pillows of skin. I'm braced for anger, sarcasm, resentment, or any combination of the three, so when I realise the look in his eyes is fear, I don't know how to react. He quickly looks away again.

Max flaps out of his seat towards me. 'Had your beauty sleep then?'

My fingers itch to make a fist and put it to use.

'Good,' he carries on, 'your colleague will no doubt bring you up to speed on the details but the edited highlights are that we've made a course change while you were having your little, ahem,' he doesn't even bother making the little coughing noise, just says ahem like it's a word, 'sleepy time.'

'Why?' I glance around the bridge and register the wider atmosphere. Bjornsen has his back turned to us but is somehow managing to exude displeasure like a gas through the cable knit of his sweater. Ralf is tiptoeing around him like he's an unexploded bomb. 'What's the problem?'

'No problem at all,' says Max, and I instantly don't believe him. 'I communicated with Head Office about the downtime suffered as a result of the positioning problems.'

Oh I bet you did. I bet you made absolutely crystal fucking clear who's carrying the can for that one, and that it's not you.

'They got back to me with a new set of pre-plots, some extra lines they want us to shoot, to make up the missing data.'

'What?' That doesn't make any sense. If that's what they want then they'd have us repeat the same area on our way back, not change course now. 'Let me see.' I squeeze in next to Grant who shoots me an anxious look, as if he's trying to tell me something without actually opening his mouth and just telling me. I stare at the display screens. We're heading away from the survey area altogether. This is crazy. I'm about to demand some kind of a sane explanation from Max, not that one is even possible, when I feel Grant kick me under the table. 'I… Right, okay. Give me a few minutes to get my head around this.' I stare at Max until he understands that what I clearly mean is piss off right now.

> • <

'Well?' I say to Grant when Max has cleared off to a safe distance.

He brings up the main display. Everything looks normal enough at first. My eyes flick over the symbols and numbers, mentally ticking off a checklist of potential issues. It all looks fine. The channel carved through the ice by the icebreaker is there and the line tracing our progress along it. Then I notice.

I look up at Grant and his expression tells me I'm not seeing things. Which is exactly the problem.

Not taking my eyes off the display, I take the mouse from Grant's hand and zoom out, scrolling around frantically. The icebreaker is nowhere to be seen. It has vanished from our displays. It has to be somewhere ahead or the channel wouldn't be there at all but the pointy-ended rectangular icon that represents the vessel on screen is conspicuously absent. 'But where…?'

'Fucked if I know. It's just…'

I glance towards the window. Although we often lose sight of the icebreaker in fog or snow, it's usually discernible as a black mark on the horizon when conditions are clear, as they are now. 'Have you looked for it? You know, with your actual eyes? Or a fucking telescope or something?'

''Course I have.'

'And?'

'Nothing.'

'Shit.'

'Yes. That's exactly what I was thinking.'

'Okay. Right. Let's keep calm. There has to be an explanation for this.'

'Isobel?'

I continue searching through Proteus' innards, hunting for an explanation, some clue as to when the fault started, anything. I'm digging deeper into stored data now, working my way back through Proteus' memory, minute by minute, hour by hour, and the further I go, the more baffling it gets. Apart from the irrefutable evidence of ice being broken and cleared ahead of us, it's as if all evidence of the icebreaker itself has been edited out of the system.

'Izzy!' Grant says, more insistent.

I still don't look up. 'What? What is it?'

'I need to tell you something.' Grant takes a breath. 'About Jules—'

Oh for fuck's sake. 'Grant. Not now. Priorities, eh?' We don't have time for this shit. We need to focus on the problem in front of us. Or, more precisely, the problem not in front of us.

'I think he might have had something to do with it.'

I spin round and stare at him incredulously. 'With what? This? Have you completely lost the plot?'

'I know you won't want to hear this. I know you two are—'

'And? Does that seriously bother you so much? Jesus, Grant. Get over yourself, will you? Grow up.'

'It's not that. I couldn't care less if you're banging the entire crew every day and twice on Sundays. Just hear me out.'

'Right. Go on then.' I fold my arms. He's obviously not going to shut up until he gets this off his chest.

'Jules came to ask if I'd pull a double shift, yeah?'

I nod. Is this what's bothering him?

'So, since we were on a line, I asked him to keep an eye on things for half an hour while I got something to eat and a shower. It was after I came back I noticed the *Koch* was missing.'

'What're you saying? That Jules did something to Proteus? Some kind of sabotage? Why the fuck would he do that? What possible reason could he have?'

'I don't know, Izzy. I've been wracking my brains for another explanation.'

'You are so full of shit.'

Grant sighs heavily and rubs his hands over his face then up through his hair. I feel like slapping him, or grabbing him by the shoulders and shaking him, but he looks so fragile that he might come apart in my hands. I remind myself that he's been awake for at least thirty hours, dealing with all this alone. More than most, I know sleep deprivation can play with your perceptions, put strange ideas in your head.

'Look, just go and get some sleep eh?' I make my voice soft. 'I'll get all this sorted by the time you come back and the world will look different then. Okay?'

'Maybe you're right,' he says, exhaustion weighing down

each word. 'Later then.' He heaves himself to his feet and shambles away.

I resume the hunt. Until I can either trace the *Koch* in Proteus' data banks, locate it on one of the display screens, or it magically reappears on the horizon, we're following a ship that exists only in our minds, as a memory. A ghost ship.

8 SHUTDOWN

To call it a sound completely fails to convey what it is. Sound is merely one aspect of it, and not even the first.

❯ • ❮

First is a stillness, a breath-held moment of the kind that precedes thunder. The stomach-dropping certainty that, whatever is coming next, there is no stopping it and this present moment is the last one that can ever exist before this new thing, this irredeemable thing, happens.

It is physical. A compression at the back of the throat, a tug of weight behind the eyeballs, pressure around the heart, a shift in the ears' understanding of balance. Something in the fit of the bones.

Then, only then, comes the sound and it is more terrible than anything that came before. From the north, where we assume the icebreaker must still be though we haven't heard from it or seen it in days, it starts and it grows, cleaving this moment from everything that went before.

Opening up endless oceans between one second and the next, it moves towards us.

No one speaks, I don't think anyone can, and the sound widens and spreads and washes over and around us.

Not a bang or a whimper but a rending, a tearing of this time, this now from everything that will follow – the infliction of a wound that can never heal. It is a sound to make you weep and fall to your knees, to pray to any god that might hear you to make it stop, to take you back, just a few seconds to where this sound is not happening. But knowing your pleas will not be answered. This is happening, this will always be happening and there will be no end to it.

We know without speaking that we are all touched by the dread that comes with the sound, indivisibly twined around it. To feel it yourself is one thing, but to see it reflected in the faces around you, the truth of it in other eyes, makes it undeniable. We move closer together on the bridge, drawn to human intimacy but at the same time locked mute in our own worlds.

> • <

I can't say when, or even if it stops but the sound is temporarily drowned out by a barrage of alarms sounding in unison from the equipment. A chorus of electronic bleeps and pings. Even the ship's klaxon goes off, still loaded with Ralf's gull-scaring file. A volley of barking and snarling breaks out and shocks us all into action, as if the dogs are on our heels.

Bjornsen strides to the main controls and starts shouting

into the ship's comm system. Grant unfolds his arms from over his head and stares at the red flashing displays as if seeing them for the first time, muttering *shitshitshit* under his breath.

The ship rises and shimmies from side to side. Jules crosses to the front observation window and I join him. Ragged fragments of ice are streaming towards the ship, bumping into our bow and twirling back into a shattered mess behind us.

'It's going the wrong way,' says Jules.

At first I struggle to grasp his meaning, thoughts tumble through my head in bits, chased by dogs. Can nobody shut that thing off? The edges of the channel are warping as the larger floes that made up the body of the pack-ice start to buckle. The space we were sailing along is filling up with broken pieces, all moving fast in the same direction. Then I realise. The ice is flowing against the current.

Bjornsen's voice cuts above all the noise. 'We must turn back. The ship will not survive this damage. The ice is too much, too fast. We need to lose the streamers.'

'Hold on,' Max shouts from his station. 'You can't do that. Have you any idea what all that equipment costs?'

'Ja. I know. We do it anyway.'

'This is madness, you can't—'

'We need to turn and turn fast. We either dump the streamers now or we end up sailing over them when we turn. They become tangled, they pull us down with them. Have you, mister company man, any idea what your life is worth?'

Max gulps. 'But surely. There isn't any other way?'

As his voice tails off something passes between the rest of us. No matter if he still objects, we aren't going to be paying any attention to Max.

Once the alarms have been turned off and the klaxon finally silenced, Jules, Bjornsen and I make for the streamer couplings on the back deck. A team of Russians comes with us. That terrible sound has mostly dissipated but its remnant clings, right at the edge of hearing. The sound of the world ripping open. We don't talk, but we stomp about clanging our tools and equipment louder than is necessary.

We don't see the bear until it's almost upon us.

PART TWO

AFTER **BEFORE**

I

Every morning I wake with that sound in my head and I want to vomit up my own bones.

That whispering tear, the nauseating echo of damage that follows me wherever I go, like a bloodhound, three paces behind. During the day I play the wind-up radio for background noise. Earplugs don't do it, that sound got inside my head and it's always there. It's part of me. The mornings are the worst. I wake dizzy, disoriented. Sometimes, for those first few seasick moments, I'm convinced I'm still aboard the *Polar Horizon*, adrift on a frozen ocean. Perhaps I am.

I've learned that if I lie still and try to focus on something, the feeling will recede enough for me to get up and move about without retching. I stare hard at a patch of damp on the wall beside my bed where sooty patches of mould bloom through the faded paper.

From next door, music surges and a voice-over cuts in. Its

tongue weighs as much as an elephant, its heart is the size of a car...

Attenborough lives on, through my neighbour's endless box sets. Nicola spends all her electricity credit watching them on a decrepit laptop then doesn't have enough left to boil a kettle. 'I can't help myself,' she said last time she was through cadging a cup of coffee. 'He's like a drug. I swear. I hear that voice and everything melts away.'

The walls between the subdivided flats in this building are thin so I heard plainly enough what she traded for the box sets and laptop in the first place. I can take a thousand reruns of the entire series of *The Life of Mammals* before I'd want to listen to that again. Although, it's the ones about oceans that Nicola seems especially obsessed with. Maybe there's a kind of escape there. I've heard them all so often I'm able to recite the next line, 'and some of its blood vessels are so wide you could swim down them,' in time with the soundtrack. What would the great naturalist have had to say about the state of things now? He doesn't seem the sort to say I-told-you-so but I bet he'd be thinking it.

Behind the stains and the constellations of mould, the wallpaper's original design of silvery green palm leaves is still discernible. The paper has started to bubble and peel away from the wall in limp tatters but I resist the urge to pull at them. There's nothing but cracked plaster underneath. I get up and go over to the window.

The haar hasn't lifted for days, it might even be weeks. I used to keep track of these things, take notes of when the winds came, when they went and the haar resettled, but I've lost the desire to map this reality accurately. I have become vague.

It's June, or July perhaps. I'm reasonably sure the year is 2045. That's enough.

The town, and the ever-expanding migrant camp surrounding it, is swathed in a thick yellowish-grey miasma of forgetting. Was there ever a time when it wasn't this way? They call it simply 'Avie' now. As the place has grown more crowded, the people are displacing the letters. More now being less. Avie, a vie. A life. Hanging by a few diminishing letters.

I question every day why I go on. Sometimes it seems I do so only to keep repeating the question. So then why? The only explanation is that stubborn, paper-thin faith in the possibility of change. It's still there, against all reason. Things could change. The idea isn't strong enough to be a belief, or even hope. It's a grudging admission that I can't disprove the theory. I try to think of it scientifically, logically, like that. But, no matter how I want to dress it up, my thinking is no different from religious faith, magical thinking, plain idiocy. Elsewhere in the Arctic, belugas are gathering in their thousands, Attenborough murmurs through the wall.

From the street below my window rise the stifled drones of electric mopeds, like drugged mosquitos, skimming around the harsh voices of the hawkers and the guttering of private generators. There's the sound of a scuffle, smashing glass. A young male voice very close by shouts, 'Give it here or I'll fucking gut you.' Footsteps stumbling, running, receding. This is as peaceful as it gets around here. The nights are worse. No one with any sense goes out at night. I was lucky to make it home in one piece.

> • <

I pull a blanket around my shoulders and shuffle over to the stove. My bag of dusty coffee is nearly empty but there's enough for one cup. I investigate the cupboards: one ancient tin of meat paste and something that may once have been bread. I'll pass. I need to chase down more work if I want to eat better. I don't want to scavenge, or worse end up back in Digs.

My most recent spell in a government-run centre in Cumbria near enough ended me. It got so bad I began to suspect that was the unspoken intention. It made a terrible kind of sense. Being half-starved and half-mad with lack of sleep, not to mention jumping with lice, I was ready to believe almost anything. Daniels came through for me just in time. He owed me a favour so signed me out and dealt with the necessary paperwork on condition I took over the programming on a big contract he had in the pipeline. I agreed. He could've asked for more and I'd have given it. His restraint was a kind of generosity that has become all too rare.

That's definitely the last time I end up in one of those places. No matter how bad it gets, I'm not going back to that.

> • <

My work detail had been preparing for the day's labour, half a dozen of us, scratching under our clothes and stamping our feet in already leaking boots. In Digs you work long hours doing whatever grunt work the government needs doing. Mostly, as the waters continue to rise, this involves shifting government buildings and offices to higher ground.

Construction works are under way on the highest mountain ranges, all of which require new roads. We were in no hurry to get started on another day breaking rocks, so weren't complaining at having to wait for our supervisor to appear.

Ash, a lanky ex-insurance broker I often worked beside, nudged me in the arm. 'Look,' she pointed over towards the security fence, 'we've got visitors.'

On the other side of the fence, a small group materialised out of the rain, pressed close together. A thin woman, clearly pregnant, leant into a bony-shouldered man who cradled a toddler, an older girl pressed into the woman's legs. They gazed up at the guard tower, their faces slashed vertically by the rain, diagonally by the wire fencing, their appearance fuzzy, as if barely coming through on a disintegrating signal.

The guard, perhaps thinking they were absconders, misunderstanding their trajectory, shouted, 'Stop right there. Where do you think you're going?'

'Here. We've come here. We want...' the man's voice broke.

The guard was silent for some time, wiped a hand down his young face. 'Wait here,' he eventually said and lifted the phone to the main building.

The man shifted the immobile toddler to his other hip, his wife stroked its hair. The child was so still, the woman's face so sad. Let it be sleeping, I thought, please let the child be only sleeping.

'Comes to a sore fucking pass when families are queuing to get in here,' said Ash.

'I hear they're turning folk away now,' said someone else.

There were murmurs of assent from the others. There are rumours. They could be true.

'Next they'll be charging people to get in.'

'Christ's sake.'

'Well who wouldn't want a piece of this?' said Ash, throwing her arm out to take in the muddy yard, the dismal, squat buildings. 'Five-fucking-star luxury accommodation.'

'Daily activities for all the family!'

There was some subdued laughter. Workers' Dignity Centres were originally set up as a way to house and feed the displaced population, while providing a workforce for the manual labour of relocation. Politicians talked about 'pulling together' and 'building a brighter tomorrow'. The reality doesn't have quite such a feel-good vibe about it.

Finally the gates scudded open and the family were led into the compound and stumbled towards admissions. They would be separated of course. I wondered if they knew this would happen. Those fit to work stay in low chicken coop-like dormitories. The very young, very old or very pregnant are bussed away and housed separately.

As we plodded towards the main gate, the door of the admission building banged open again. There was a scuffle. A guard was fending off the pregnant woman who was shouting and pleading, although I couldn't make out the exact words. The man tried to hold her back as she grabbed again for the large waste sack the guard had slung over his shoulder. I looked away, pulled my hood down low and fixed my eyes on the muddy path ahead.

That night, I didn't sleep but sat up filling in contact requests, ignoring the grumbles from my dorm-mates to turn out my bedside light. The only way out of Digs once you're in is to convince a sponsor to sign you out into paid employment. I put down everyone and anyone I could think of that might be in a position to offer me work. Some I knew but most I didn't. Daniels was the only one who responded.

>•<

I open the window to clear the musty mildew smell from my room. I'd closed it last night because of the wolves. Packs are thriving now in the hills and forests. Loosed from an abandoned reintroduction project further north they have multiplied and spread. They're not, for the most part, any danger to humans but the way their howls come loping down from the hills, stalk straight through town and slink under my window feels somehow personal. It sets off a chill in my bones.

I lean out and sniff the air. A mixture of wood smoke from people cooking on open fires, accumulated rubbish and overloaded sewers. Not exactly an improvement on mildew but at least it's a change. The faint pop of gunfire comes from the direction of the mountains. Could be any number of sources: army, hunters, gangs. No point worrying about it. I close the window again.

>•<

I'd worked for Daniels when I first left Seismic after the arctic survey. Friend of a friend. Some tenuous connection. I'd been given his email with a tip that he was always on the lookout for good programmers. His business dealings, while not technically illegal, usually skated close to the edge, but he insisted if there were in fact any crimes committed they were victimless: finding a way to skim the odd pence from mothballed bank accounts without anyone noticing; knocking a percentage or two off money transfers between businesses so rich that the loss was like a midgie biting a T-Rex. Later, as the old systems started to give out, he'd diversified. As had I, picking up odd bits of legitimate and not-so-legitimate work, wary of depending too much on one source of income. But Daniels was always my best client. While the internet was still at least partially functional, he needed programmers to help him wring as much data as possible out of its circuitry before it went down forever.

'Data is knowledge, knowledge is power, power is survival,' he used to say.

I told him, 'You should have that printed on mugs, or mouse mats or something, y'know? Catchy.'

Most of the other programmers were a little in awe of Daniels. With his block-like head and heavy brows he could come across as more than a little intimidating, but by that time I knew him well enough to know it was just a front. He spent his down time reading mouldy sci-fi paperbacks and lived with a cross-eyed stray cat he'd taken in and allowed to boss him about mercilessly.

'Yeah, you're laughing now, but it'll be me who laughs lastest.' Daniels had a way with words that was both painful and strangely endearing.

A year after he helped me out of Digs, he was dead. Bits of him turned up on a stretch of waste ground – where the rest went, nobody knows – and all deals were off. Since then I've been scraping by on short-term contracts, cash in hand, staying off the grid as much as possible and keeping my head down. What used to be a risky existence on the fringes of society has now become commonplace as the old systems and structures fray under pressure. The fringe enlarges as the fabric of society tears.

With thousands displaced from flooded coastal cities and unpredictable weather disrupting transport and communication across much of the rest of the country, it's hard to be sure who, if anyone, is in charge anymore. Central government is more of an idea than a verifiable reality. There's the feeling that local authorities, the individual police forces and army units are mostly improvising. The hardest part is tracking down work without falling victim to some scam or other. Everyone is doing whatever they have to do to survive. It's best not to be too trusting.

> • <

I sit at the kitchen table, rub my eyes and sink my head into my hands. Inside my skull feels every bit as clouded as the restlessly shifting fog outside the window. Not surprising. No better than poison, the gin they serve in Lachlan's. But it's good in the short term and sometimes it's hard to see past that. It was the shock of bumping into Grant after all these years. Must be, shitting fuck, twenty years? I shake my head but quickly still it again as my bruised brain protests at the movement.

I put the radio on low and twist the dial, searching for one of the elusive pirate radio stations that broadcast sporadically. The options are slim, random and often bizarre but anything is better than the Public Herald, the one clear and reliable station that comes direct from the government, or whatever's left of it, on radio and TV. When they're not broadcasting a stream of propaganda, they're playing perkily banal pop or insincere over-emotive charity singles. Some say there's no rationale whatsoever behind it and that the Herald is a collection of automated systems spewing out a stream of nonsense without human intervention. I don't believe any automated system could be quite so patronising. We're all in this together. Make it happen. Love can save the day.

The dial blips and I twist it back and manage to catch onto a station playing nothing but Jacques Brel. Fair enough.

〉• 〈

Lachlan's isn't exactly a private club, there are no membership cards or secret passwords. But you don't get in unless you're known. Maisie, the proprietor, watches her clientele and rarely has any difficulty ejecting undesirable elements herself. She's strong as an ox, her inked body gnarly with muscle. Pubs don't exist in the same way they used to back in the days of plenty. There's no prohibition, alcohol isn't illegal, but it's scarce and mostly home-brewed, so businesses tend to be small and inconspicuous, with a selective customer base. Passing trade is not necessarily what you want these days. Lachlan's patrons are a mix of freelancers like myself and medical staff from the nearby public health centre. If anyone needs a drink, they do.

Maisie poured my usual double and took the fistful of change I passed over. 'You're getting scrawny,' she said. 'You'd be better off spending that on a decent meal.'

I grunted in reply. She had a point, but the gin mutes the hunger better than a full stomach compensates for sober reality. I told myself I'd get my shit together tomorrow. Always tomorrow.

I surveyed the holiday postcards on the wall behind the bar. Maisie collects them and pins them up the way some pubs used to make a display of foreign banknotes. They're all of beaches and coastlines around the world. Each one a bright window into an unreachable past. The currency of nostalgia.

There was a new one. Looked like the Caribbean. Palm trees, white sands and crystal waters. The caption *Life's a Beach* printed in hot pink across the blue sky. That might well be true, but now the sand is streaked green and black, gangrenous, the sea viscous with toxic algae, sea slugs and jellyfish and a thousand slimy things. Around Northern Europe, the sea still looks like sea. It was always steely and uncompromising, but now it's more muscular and volatile. It might take one coastal town and leave another a couple of miles away standing. It might accelerate forwards several metres overnight in great gulping leaps. It might rise up and send a towering wall of water miles inland then retreat as if nothing had happened.

Maisie's wall of postcards is a mosaic of memento mori.

> • <

Jesus though. Grant.

Some state he was in. I didn't recognise him when he came over to my table and sat down uninvited. I wasn't in the mood for company and was about to tell this presumptuous stranger to sling his hook when he said, 'Hi, Izzy.' I stared hard, couldn't place him. He gave a small rueful smile. 'It's Grant. Seismic Systems?'

I sat back and tried not to gape. This wasn't the Grant I'd known. But then, none of us are who we were twenty years ago. Every cell in our bodies has been replaced, probably several times over, and the trade hasn't gone in our favour. Grant's a few years older than me so into his fifties now. His face was leaner than I remembered and lined, his hair salt-and-pepper and cropped unevenly. The last twenty years haven't been kind to many people but it looked like they'd kicked the crap out of Grant.

'What the holy fuck are you doing here?'

'Good to see you've not lost any of your natural warmth and charm.'

'Fuck off. Seriously. You can't just wander in and say hi. Like you were just passing? Or what?'

'Well, if I'd known you'd be this pissed off.'

'I'm not pissed off. I'm just… It's a shock, that's all.'

He made a show of getting out of his seat. 'I can leave if you'd—'

'Don't be such a twat, Grant. Sit.' I eyed the two glasses he'd brought to the table. 'One of them for me?'

'Now you mention it, no.' He knocked both drinks back one after another, cleared his throat and wiped his eyes. 'We need more of this shit,' he said, scooping up the empty glasses.

'So, how've you been?'

I snorted. 'Fucking phenomenal, Grant. Living the dream. You?'

He looked down at the table. 'Yeah, me too.' He wasn't laughing. 'Your family?'

'My dad went in twenty-nine, so he missed most of the fun. It was sudden. I wasn't there.'

'I'm sorry.'

'Yeah, well.' It hadn't been sudden, and I had been there. For all of it. Much good as it did either of us. I turned the glass on the table, watching specks of light catch the liquid within. 'Better off out of it eh?'

'Your brothers?'

'Last I heard they're all okay. None of them in Scotland. It's not like we made a great effort to keep in touch before anyway. And now, well. They have families of their own to worry about. What about you? Your folks?'

Grant sighed, shook his head. 'Thirty-seven.'

He didn't elaborate. Didn't have to. Thirty-seven had been a bad year, sudden leaps in sea levels, massive flooding along all the tidal inlets. More died in the chaos that followed the water than in the floods themselves. I vaguely remembered his folks had lived somewhere near Clydebank. All under water now. Grant silently raised his glass and we both drank.

'You being here isn't just a coincidence, is it?'

'Well, yes. No. Kind of. I've been working for some people up here but I'm taking a little time out. Then I heard you were living here so…' He reached out and put his hand over mine and squeezed. 'It's good to see you, Izzy.'

'Really?' I knew he wanted me to return the sentiment. But I couldn't. Seeing him again stirred up too many memories, none of them good. Sure, I'd wondered what had happened to him, but not all that often. Didn't give him much thought after I'd been discharged from hospital. I had my own shit to deal with.

'Do you think about it much?'

'Think about what?'

'The last survey. Don't you wonder—'

'No.'

'Oh come on. You must—'

'Ancient history, Grant.'

'Did you know the whole crew, everyone, left the industry? I mean straight away, right after the survey, before it all really kicked off with the floods and everything. It was like deep down everyone knew things were only going to get worse. Knew what we did up there had started something.'

'Bullshit, Grant. It was a job. We didn't do anything.'

'Didn't we?' He directed the question more towards his gin than me.

I stared at the ceiling, counted rafters. I didn't want a fight.

'That healed well.' Grant was looking at my throat.

My hand went to the faded white line of scar tissue. Another memory better left in peace. 'How'd you know what happened to everyone anyway?'

'I traced them all. The Norsemen. The Russians. All either dead or as far inland, away from the sea, as they could get.'

'Why would you do that?'

'Doesn't matter. Look, it all ties together.' He pushed one of his many crumpled pieces of paper across the table towards me. He had a whole pile of them he'd pulled from a stained rucksack at his feet.

'You found everyone?'

'More or less.' He rifled through pages and pages of hand-drawn maps of the Arctic Ocean, that familiar bald spot at the top of the world surrounded by a ragged asymmetrical monk's tonsure of coastline.

'Jules?' I'd thought more about him. At least in the early years. In a lush Pyrenean meadow, perhaps in a log cabin he'd built himself, growing vegetables and tending goats, like a sexy wholesome Man Heidi. Maybe on clear nights he would sit on a rocky promontory, smoke a pipe, and look towards the northern skyline on the same nights I looked to the south. I'd allowed myself that much self-indulgence, for a time.

'Eh?' Grant was absorbed in his maps. The Arctic Ocean swarmed with lines and arrows that snaked like serpents, mapping the various ocean currents and weather systems.

'Jules. Did you find him?'

'Back in France now I think,' said Grant. 'Those mountains in the south, on the border with Spain.'

'The Pyrenees?'

'Yeah. That's them. What are you smiling at?'

I shook my head and silently raised a toast to Jules, then another to his possible goats.

Grant laid out a series of drawings with dates and figures, a few lopsided graphs scribbled alongside. 'See this?' He pointed to a spiralling arrow. 'This is, was, the Beaufort Gyre. It collapsed soon after we were up there.'

'That's the other side of the ocean from where we were. You're not saying that was our fault are you?'

'But don't you see,' he scrabbled through his piles of paper, 'it's all linked, the currents, the drift of the ice, the wind force against the edge of the ice sheet. You push over one part of this and there are knock-on effects on everything else. Like dominos. The ice goes, ocean temperature climbs, weather systems go crazy, glaciers melt, sea levels rise—'

'I'm still not seeing what this has to do with us.'

'We were there. Right at the start of it all.'

'Come off it, Grant. The Arctic was in trouble for a long time before we got there.'

'You think it was a coincidence everything accelerated so quickly afterwards? A total fluke that all the ice was gone within a year of the survey?'

'Yeah. I do.' I stared him out.

'I don't believe you really think that, Izzy.' He reached again for my hand.

'Believe what you like.' I snatched up our glasses and went back to the bar. Of course I'd thought about it. Enough to know thinking was a waste of time. It wouldn't change a single thing.

He was still sorting through his scraps of paper when I returned. Moving them around like jigsaw pieces. He glanced up only long enough to pick up his glass. 'And then there's the biggest unknown factor.'

'And what's that, Grant?'

I felt a heavy wash of pity for him, for this deranged shadow of who he used to be. As the gin sloshed around my brain, this feeling was pulled into the great ocean of pity for everything that had passed. For myself. For the world. I was in danger of becoming maudlin and sat up a little straighter, trying to keep myself afloat.

'The *Koch*, Izzy. Where did it go?'

'Probably some breakers' dock in Siberia I would think.'

'But do you know that? How can you be sure?'

'Well it must be somewhere. It can't just disappear.'

Grant held my gaze as we both felt my words echo back through the intervening years. Yeah, so, what if that was exactly what I'd said at the time the *Koch* disappeared without a trace? I shrugged it off and looked away.

'We've no way of knowing what damage it could've done. After it left us, how much more of the pack-ice did it break up? Enough to set off a reaction that cracked the whole place open? Was that the noise we heard? Or what if it went down? It had two nuclear reactors on board. If they—'

'Jesus. I don't know! It's all academic now anyway.'

'Have you ever wondered if it could have been deliberate?'

'Why would anyone want to cause all this?' The idea is preposterous.

'Maybe they didn't mean it to go so far. Perhaps they just wanted to shake things up a bit, cause a bit of chaos they could capitalise on. But once it started, it couldn't be stopped.'

I've spent a long time and drowned a lot of brain cells in toxic quantities of alcohol precisely to avoid over-thinking all this shit. I wondered if I could get Maisie to throw him out.

Grant went back to his scraps of paper, muttering something about the polar vortex and arctic oscillation.

I nodded and drank and didn't listen too hard. A couple of times I tried to draw him into talking about something else but he looked at me blankly for a few seconds as if I'd just spoken to him in a language he hadn't heard before and carried right on where he'd left off. My head was swimming, badly. I stopped listening completely somewhere around the dipole anomaly.

I should've just wished him well, made my excuses and left. I was on the verge of doing just that when he mentioned the possibility of work, lucrative work, for people with seismic experience.

> • <

The coffee tastes like burnt paper but I drink it down to the gritty dregs, let it do its work. Feeling more alert, I remember the card Grant pressed on me when Lachlan's was finally closing and we were turfed out into the night. I find my jacket where I dropped it in the hall and search the pockets. There's something about running into Grant, picking at the scabs of old memories, that's put me on edge but I have to consider his offer. I turn the card over in my hands. How much longer can I afford to be picky about the jobs I take? It looks official enough: Northolt Research Facility, a logo of a green world with the sun rising behind it, latitude, longitude.

II

I hear voices from the stairwell and move to my door to listen, relieved to notice I must've bolted it when I came back last night. Brodrick's crow-like complaining and some other voices. The young couple from downstairs? The high note of desperation in the woman's voice, the supressed anger in the man's. All of them sporadically overridden by piercing shrieks from their baby. Is Brodrick evicting them? Demanding more rent? It wouldn't be the first time. He's a merciless piece of shit, exactly the sort that thrives when there are no laws to protect ordinary people, and no one to enforce them if there were. My hand hovers over the dead bolt. My own confrontation with the landlord only hours ago is still fresh enough to smell.

'You're late tonight.' Brodrick's long, cadaverous face had leered out of the dark as I made for the stairs.

'Didn't know there was a curfew,' I muttered back, tired and careless, realising too late that this was a mistake.

He stood on the bottom step, blocking my progress. 'You want to be careful,' he said, 'it's not safe out there at night.

Especially for the ladies.' He extended the vowel sounds of this last word and used the extra time this allowed to snake a proprietorial look down the length of my body and back up.

I made to push past him but his scrawny arm had a surprisingly strong grip on the banister. His other hand came up and brushed the hair back from my forehead.

'You're still a very beautiful woman, Isobel,' he croaked.

'I just want to get to my bed, if you don't mind.'

He stepped back as if giving way but gripped my arm as I passed and put his face close to mine. 'You'd do well to remember that, technically, it's my bed.' He grinned and darted his tongue out to lick the side of his mouth. His breath smelled of dog food. 'And you owe me two months' rent.'

I'd shaken his hand off and taken the stairs two at a time to the third floor, the sound of his phlegmy laughter crackling at my heels all the way.

> • <

In the bleak morning light my hand retreats from the bolt. I can't risk drawing attention to myself. I need to pay Brodrick off somehow, but it is not going to be on my back. The thought makes me gag. Nicola might not look tough but she has a far stronger stomach than me. I couldn't. Not him. Not ever. But things change. What if it's only a case of not yet? Everything breaks eventually. I need to find some other way before my options narrow that far.

Desperation doesn't make me anything special. We're all desperate, it's the new default setting. If we could figure out a way to parcel anxiety and sell it by the pound, we'd be laughing.

> • <

I plug the lat/long into the bike's satnav but it doesn't bring up the usual features. There's no option to zoom out or change view, no jump to destination, only a turn at a time, the display scrolling as I twist through the streets like a rat in a maze. The bike whines and jerks over the crumbling tarmac. Where the road surface is particularly bad I stand up on the foot pegs and take the strain on my thighs to spare what's left of the bike's suspension, not to mention my own.

I do miss the kick and growl of a petrol engine, but have developed a grudging affection for my little electric bike. With its DIY silver and red spray job and customised fibreglass faring, it has a wind-up toy quality about it. A bright speck of fun in a dark world. There's also the simple release of movement, even if it's at a sedate pace, the tension slips from my shoulders and falls to the road unrolling behind.

The satnav sends me north and uphill. As I clear the more densely populated areas, climbing higher, the houses get larger, farther apart and interspersed with offices. Higher still and there are government buildings, private clinics.

Still I have no idea where this route is leading me. If it doesn't get to the point soon I'll be running into the militarised zone that rings the high ground. Nobody gets above three hundred metres elevation without clearance. Nobody.

Society, if it can really be claimed any such thing still exists, has become stratified by metres above sea level. Survival depends on how well you can keep moving up as the water rises. The government and military top brass are highest up, those with enough money or influence to pay their way are next, then on a sliding scale of usefulness are the rest of us. What will happen when we run out of North, when we run out of up? The layers might compress, become denser. When that happens, when the rising sea finally has us cornered, the seaside is not where anyone would choose to be. I whistle along with the inane tune twirling drunkenly through my memory, *Oh I don't love to be beside the seaside, oh I don't love to be beside the sea...*

A sharp turn in the road takes me around a bank of gorse, then loops back to enter an area of close-grown woodland. The tarmac gives way abruptly to rough stone compacted into the earth. I slow the bike and, as the whine of the engine drops pitch, I hear the silence. It's in the air held between the trees, infinitely precious, preserved from another time. I drive even more slowly and with exaggerated care. I don't belong here. I am an alien presence, a pollution. I could break whatever has protected the silence until now.

The track continues to twist upwards. I must surely be in the militarised zone now. If I'm unlucky enough to run into a patrol I could end up back in Digs before the day's out. I feel dizzy and realise I've been holding my breath. I push air in and out through my nose, loath to disturb the atmosphere any more than necessary. I begin to wonder if this whole thing is some elaborate joke, or a plot to get rid of me by some business rival or disgruntled client with a grudge, or perhaps Brodrick has sold me to one of the gangs and found someone else willing to pay his ridiculous rent. There are plenty of possibilities. Take a number and join the queue.

The track winds its way closer into what is either a tight pass between two mountains or a deep notch in the side of one. From within the trees it's difficult to piece together the surrounding geography. Flashes of sky and mountainside flicker past, each one suggesting an alternative arrangement of sky and rock, light and shadow. Just when I'm on the verge of convincing myself to turn back, the trees thin and the track opens out into a wide clearing bordered on three sides by forest and on the other by a steep rocky escarpment behind which the Cairngorms rise and roll into the distance, green-brown to blue to smoky violet.

Dazzled by the sudden light and colour, I skid to a stop, kick out the bike stand and dismount. I crane my head back and turn a full circle staring up into the bluest sky I've seen in a long time. I haven't been this high in what feels like forever. The green of the forest shimmers against the intense blue of the sky. I take a deep draught of clean, pine-scented air and cough it out, my lungs not used to the purity.

On the far side of the clearing, almost lost against the escarpment, a small stone-built bothy looks to be in a state of semi-collapse. I check the satnav. You have reached your destination. Really? This is Northolt?

Fucking Grant! What was I thinking, listening to him? He's clearly deranged, and apparently I'm not much better. What kind of half-arsed setup has their headquarters part way up a mountain in the middle of nowhere in what looks like some kind of prehistoric pile of rubble? I stamp and swear for a while hoping I'll feel calmer, but that doesn't happen. Then I decide I'm not simply turning around and leaving again without the satisfaction of tearing whoever's in there a new arsehole for wasting my time. If there's anyone in there at all, that is. It looks deserted.

I stride out across the clearing, kicking at the clumpy grass and dirt that covers the open ground. It's good to stretch my legs at least, and the sky is still blue and the trees so intensely green; before long my righteous anger feels like a pointless waste of energy. I'm still curious about this place though. I look around at the horseshoe of forest and stumble over my feet. Perhaps I'm more tired than I realised. The ride up here must have taken a couple of hours. My cramped leg muscles are still recovering. I carry on but my feet tangle again and I stagger to the side. Something is definitely wrong, a weird seasick roll has taken over my gait, as if my brain is struggling to compensate for something my eyes haven't yet fully processed and my legs are paying the price. I stop in my tracks and shake my head, telling myself to get a grip. And that's when I see it.

Just past the edge of the rock, in the trees to my left, there's a pattern mismatch. A visual glitch. A fault line intrudes into the moving green mosaic of leaves, an unnaturally straight edge where the tops of the trees appear offset from their lower portions by just the tiniest amount. A light breeze ruffles through the branches and the effect dissipates. I stare hard at the patch of green where I thought I saw the abnormality and shake my head again. There it is. I'm giving myself a headache but keep the movement going long enough to trace the line right back into the mountain until it turns and folds down, creating a perpendicular crease in the rock face.

If this is what I think it is, this is something else. I clap my hands in delight and the sound startles a bird which breaks cover and flaps ten feet or so from the ground across the green background of the massed forest. I swivel and scan the trees on the opposite side. There it is. The same bird banks then climbs, the sunlight illuminating its orange-red plumage framed by darker wings as it clears the tops of the trees, flashing like a flaming arrow before disappearing. Which bird is real and which the reflection?

I've never seen an invisibuild on this scale before. And certainly not so flawlessly executed. The technology isn't new, having started up way back before everything went to shit, but it is expensive, which means few of them were ever built. They were mostly the preserve of the wealthy and 'eco-conscious' in the grandiose way that only the rich could afford to be.

These buildings could never work in urban environments, but in the countryside a single structure could achieve the promise of 'minimal visual impact on the natural environment'. Developments in solar tech enabled their mirrored surfaces to gather enough power to make the buildings self-sufficient. I'm surprised they're still being built, but perhaps this one was already in place from before. It's hard to make any judgement about how old it looks when looking is so cleverly deflected. I squint and tilt my head, crouch for a different angle but only catch glimpses of the building's structure, hints of the overall design. It seems to cover a large portion of the rock, irregular angled surfaces mimicking the geology, stone reflecting stone in asymmetrical clusters crusted all across the escarpment. It's impossible to pinpoint the line between the illusion and the hard fact of the mountain.

Trying to take in the dimensions of the larger building is making me queasy, so I focus on the only part I can be sure of. Constructed from pale grey local stone with a sagging slate roof and two drooping windows, the bothy looks ready to collapse. I wonder briefly if they've faked it up to look old or transplanted it from somewhere else, but it looks convincingly as though it has stood on this exact spot, possibly for centuries, gathering moss and lichen. On the weathered wooden door someone has stencilled the Northolt logo. I trace the shape of the world with a finger and a flake of green paint comes away. I push gently and the door swings in with a creak so cartoonishly ominous it breaks the tension. When I step inside I wait for it to slam dramatically behind me but the door rejects convention.

The interior is musty smelling and dark and it takes a while for my eyes to adjust. There's an open fireplace, a table, two chairs and a low palette for a bed. Basic stuff years ago but luxury for a lot of folk now. There are no signs of occupation. 'Hello-oh,' I call. I'm answered within seconds by a low grating noise from the fireplace, which I realise is moving with the whole chimney breast along the back wall.

Please insert your identification card into the reader, a bright, metallic voice directs.

Okay, if that's the way we're going to do this. I dig in my jacket pocket and retrieve my ID card. It's immediately spat out and the message repeats. *Please insert your identification card into the reader.*

Same thing again. This has never happened before. The card is one of the best copies I've ever had. It has got me through army checks, hospital visits, everything. It works. Even if I wanted to, I can't insert my real card as it's safely hidden behind the wardrobe back in my room. I never bring it out with me, too risky. I insert the card again and this time the voice changes tack.

Please wait. There are a series of rumbling noises from behind the wall. I take a few steps back, debating whether now would be a good time to leave. But it still has my card.

The rumblings are coming closer and before I can decide what to do the panel slides upwards revealing a pair of feet, trainers in plastic overshoes, followed by skinny denim-clad legs and a body wearing what looks like a doctor's white coat. The face is young, male and smiling. An open, guileless smile.

'Sorry about the machine. We've been having trouble with it lately.'

'It's still got my card.'

'Oops! Sorry about that. Hang on a mo. Come in, come in.' The guy hums tunelessly as he enters a code and an access hatch slides up. After a few moments of rummaging around he draws his hand back out clutching my ID card. 'Ta da!' He hands it over with a grin.

'Hi! I'm Clyde.' He extends his large bony hand in my direction. I stare at it, for a moment nonplussed. The affable manner, the boyish fringe and innocent eyes, are somehow unbelievable. Or perhaps I've forgotten what friendly looks like. I shake his hand. 'Shall we?' He raises his eyebrows and enters the corridor behind the panel. I follow and this time the door does close behind me, not with a slam, but with a sandy whisper of stone as the fireplace slides back into position.

> • <

The corridors are white, windowless and twisting. We've turned round on ourselves so many times I'm disoriented. I couldn't find north to save myself.

It must be deliberate. There can be no logical reason for either constructing or following such an elaborate route to wherever we're going. I stop, to see what happens. Clyde continues on for a few moments before he notices I'm no longer following. He walks back to me, head tilted at an angle, an expression on his face that could be framed and titled 'quizzical'.

'Look. I'm already lost, okay? You can just take me wherever we're going now.'

He nods enthusiastically. 'I know! These corridors are a nightmare, right? Honestly though, don't go wandering off. We might never find you again.' He laughs, for just slightly too long after noticing I'm not joining in. 'Sorry. We're nearly there. Promise.'

It occurs to me now that Clyde didn't ask for my name. He handled my card but I can't recall him looking directly at it, certainly not long enough to read it or check the photograph against the real person standing in front of him. Either the card reader got everything it needed on the first go, or they imaged my face and ran a match before I even entered the bothy. They're not short of places they could hide cameras.

'Here we are!' Clyde stops and presses a hand firmly onto the wall, a pressure sensitive door pops forwards and he swipes it to the side. He waves me in before him. I enter a short hallway, less clinical than the outer corridor, with a few coats hanging on hooks above a shoe rack, a series of framed Escher prints on the other wall.

I haven't seen a room like this in years. It winds me as effectively as a solid blow to the solar plexus. I could cry, if I remembered how.

A library.

The preservation of books was not held by many to be a priority in the great scramble northwards. Like excess weight from a labouring air balloon, humanity has, for the most part, jettisoned libraries with hardly a pang. But not everyone. The walls in this miracle of a room are lined with books, hardbacks and paperbacks mixed together, from floor to ceiling and the air is loaded with a sweet dusty scent. Two sets of sturdy stepped ladders on wheels wait, one on each side of the room, to provide access to the high shelves. Persian rugs with rich, intricate patterns are placed at intervals across the tiled floor. A golden light emanates from where the bookcases almost meet the ceiling and spreads softly across the high pale surface.

I glance at Clyde. He gives his widest grin yet. 'I know, right?'

We walk to the far end where the library turns ninety degrees to the right, making an L-shape. More book-lined walls and a collection of mismatched squashy sofas and cushions, books piled up on a low wooden table and a tall, broad-shouldered man pouring coffee, real coffee if I can believe my nose, into two pale green cups with gold rims. The man murmurs his thanks to Clyde who turns and leaves.

'Milk?'

I notice he has the real thing in a china jug, not the powdered substitute. 'Yes, please, a little.'

He pours and places both cups on the coffee table, gesturing for me to sit with him. 'Hello Isobel,' he says. 'I'm so glad you came.'

I study his face. About my own age? Maybe a little older. There are flecks of grey through his thick, dark hair and a small silver hoop in his left ear which gives him a vaguely piratical look. He's fit and healthy which in itself is unusual these days. It's generally a look reserved for the upper echelons while the rest of us become progressively pastier and more unwholesome. He blinks, his eyes dark and quick. He doesn't introduce himself, seems happy to wait for me to ask, a small smile playing around inside his neatly trimmed beard. I don't think Grant told me exactly what this lot are up to. For all I know, this guy could be some evil genius intent on destroying the world. He'll have to get a move on if he wants credit for that.

I take a sip of the coffee and can't help a groan escaping. 'Oh that is so good. Where did you get real coffee?'

'We grow it ourselves.'

'What? Here?'

'No no, we have other facilities.'

'Ah. Right.' I nod, digesting the implications of other facilities along with more coffee. We sit in silence for a couple of minutes.

'So,' I say, the silence finally breaking me down. 'Do I know you?'

'Not as such, not yet,' he says. 'But you will. I hope.'

'Okay. Before we go any further, you have to understand.'

I'm annoyed with myself. This is way too cosy, way too fast. 'I don't know what you've been told, but Grant — You know Grant, right?'

He nods and refills both our cups.

'Grant said you were looking for people with seismic experience. I have that, but it was a long time ago. I'm not sure how relevant it could be to you. My experience was mostly to do with the navigation software—'

'We have all the details,' he interrupts smoothly but without impatience. 'No need to go over all that now. We're sure you have what we need. The question is: do we have what you need?'

What do I need? That list has become a lot shorter lately. At one time I might have imagined I needed outlandish things like opportunity for advancement, travel, even job satisfaction. But now? Right now I'd settle for a decent meal and one more cup of this coffee. They can probably stretch to that.

'So what's the catch?'

'We want you to come and work for us exclusively. To live here for the duration of your contract.'

I sit and absorb this for a few moments. I don't like the sound of it. The idea of having a boss again is not appealing. When you're close to the bottom of society's pecking order, being pushed around by someone one station higher only adds insult to injury. At least dictating my own terms allows me some shred of dignity, no matter how illusory. I value my freedom to oppress myself.

'You mean I wouldn't even get out at weekends? I'd be like a prisoner?'

He looks startled. 'We'd think of you more as a guest.'

'A fine line you're drawing there.'

He frowns. 'How so?'

Has he honestly no fucking idea what it's like out there? Can he be so isolated, so removed from reality, or does he just not care? I don't know who I'm more angry at – him for being so cut off or me for envying him that. Part of my mind is already indulging in thoughts of a comfortable bed, clean water, food that doesn't taste like shit. All of these things should make me glad but I feel like either punching someone or screaming, or both. This guy sitting here in his plush little library, with his real coffee and his pretentious beard. Meanwhile, people are dying, actually dying, of malnutrition, of disease, and the rest of us are running just to stand still.

'You must know how bad things are now. So, you know I'll take your job, whether it makes me a prisoner or not. That's economic incarceration.'

'Look,' he rubs a hand across his forehead and sits forwards, 'much as I'd like to discuss the injustices of end-stage capitalism with you, maybe I could just show you around and tell you a little about what we're doing here? Then you can decide whether you want to be our prisoner or not. Yes?'

'I don't even know your name.'

'I'm so sorry,' he smiles. 'It's Alexander Forth. But call me Alex.'

> • <

At least half of the brightly-lit room is taken up by a gleaming white machine with a circular opening and a single bed-sized table on runners attached to the front.

'Looks like an MRI scanner,' I say.

'That's exactly what it is. But we've made adaptations. We're using it in a very specific way.'

Clyde, who has emerged from the partitioned office area at the other end of the room, hands me a sheaf of printouts that look strangely like seismic spectrograms from a survey report. In those, the shaded layers indicate where different deposits are stored within the rock, their properties, extent and density. Ultimately this knowledge was used to determine their monetary worth if dredged up to the surface. But that's all history now. No seismic surveys have been conducted for years.

They're both watching me closely. I feel like I'm in one of those quizzes where single squares of a picture are revealed one by one and you have to try to identify the image before the whole picture is revealed.

'And we have this,' says Alex.

He opens a drawer, pulls out a filing box and opens it. Inside is a bundle of printed pages, yellowed with age. It looks like some kind of technical manual. The instructions for this scanner?

'Of course, we've made copies, which we'll be working with. This is the original.' He turns the pages over in his hands.

Something contracts in my chest. Impossible.

'How did you...?' I have to clear my throat before I can continue. 'Where did you get this?'

The other side of the pages are covered in a close-written scrawl of handwriting.

Mine.

III

The noise, the claustrophobia: they were troublesome at first, but I got used to them. Like the thump of the acoustic guns on a seismic vessel, the bangs the scanner makes soon start to fade into the background and I don't consciously hear them anymore. As for the claustrophobia, it's a similar process, although it takes a more conscious effort to focus beyond the smooth white curve of the interior walls, until they fade away and I can see through them, to the frozen landscape of the far north.

The time it takes from going into the scanner to unhooking my mind from the here and now has gradually lessened from hours to minutes. Like anything else, it gets easier with practice.

The work, if you can call it that, is easy enough. I don't have to use my brain, I only have to lie still and let them use it. Life could be worse. I have comfortable quarters. I eat well and have a soft bed to sleep in at night. It's amazing how quickly it's possible to adapt, to begin to forget the life I had before. It's hard to imagine now. But I still try.

I picture my damp room back in Avie, probably no longer mine in any case. I think of Brodrick, the near perpetual haar, the way the piles of rubbish in the side streets rustle and twitch at night, animated by rats or by the human scavengers hunting the rats. The smells of blocked sewers and nameless rotting things, the stench of desperation and despair. I bring these things to mind from the safety of my pastel-coloured room.

I know that my time here at Northolt is limited, though I don't know exactly what that limit is. What I do know is that I'll have to go back at some point and I don't want to be completely out of touch when that moment comes. I'll have missed some new development, some new worsening of the situation. I can't prepare for that, but I can at least try to hang on to a sense of the reality I left behind. Increasingly though, as the days and weeks go by, I ask myself why I persist in putting myself through this recollection, this punishment. I haven't done anything wrong. It's like primitive religious self-flagellation. Why shouldn't I let all that go? Why not allow myself to sink into the rhythm on this new life and enjoy it while it lasts?

Northolt fosters a feeling of detachment. Outside of the tight confines of the lab work, I see no clocks or calendars. 'I find it relaxing,' says Alex when I ask him about it. 'The body and mind settle into their own rhythm when freed from distraction.' He's prone to making these frustratingly enigmatic statements. But he's also right.

I wake every morning without the aid of an alarm clock and report to the lab. Clyde is always there, with his puppyish enthusiasm, his floppy fringe and his readouts. It's impossible to get a decent conversation out of him about anything other than his work. He's completely wrapped up in it, and regards everything else as irrelevant.

❯ • ❮

It was a stretch to get my head around what they wanted from me at first. The readouts they showed me that day, although bearing a passing resemblance to seismic spectrograms, turned out to be nothing of the sort.

Clyde, wide-eyed and jumpy with energy, bounced on the balls of his feet, clearly thrilled by the opportunity to explain his work to someone with no prior knowledge of it.

'Memories have density, you see?' he said, nodding at me rapidly, willing my acceptance of this first point so he could race on to the next.

I made a non-committal *hmm* noise which was all the encouragement he needed.

'Different memories, formed at separate points in time have a signature. The brain actually date-stamps them for storage, in a way not entirely dissimilar to seismic data collected from a survey. So, you could think of what we're doing as a sort of exploration.' He walked me over to a series of charts pinned to the wall in a partitioned office area at the back of the lab. 'You see the layers here,' he pointed, 'and here the darker ones?'

I nodded. Taken as a whole, the patchwork of wavering lines looked like a primitive monochrome tapestry, a hobbyist's first attempt at a rag rug.

Clyde was running the tips of his long fingers along the lines with the concentration of a braille reader. 'It'd be great if we could find our way around all this in the same way we might analyse sedimentary rock, or study growth rings in a tree, but it's way more complicated than that. We're still learning how to navigate through it. There's so much we don't know.'

I was less interested in what Clyde didn't know than in finding out what my role was supposed to be. 'You want me to program some kind of navigation or processing software?' I hazarded a guess.

'No, no. It's not your software skills we're after,' he laughed. 'It's your access to the relevant data set. The raw material.'

I looked at him blankly.

He sighed, frustrated by my slowness. 'Memories.' He reached out and tapped the side of my head. 'Stored data.'

The head-tapping would've been intensely patronising coming from anyone else, and could well have resulted in physical harm coming to the fingers involved, but Clyde, I already appreciated, wasn't big on social skills. He only meant to point out the physical location of the data, in the most unambiguous way possible.

I stared again at the manuscript they'd given me, still gripped in my hand, still completely impossible.

Call me Isobel.

I couldn't tell yet if it was complete but it was definitely genuine, albeit written by a version of myself I no longer knew. She was no more than a ghost. Grant's haunted face surfaced in my mind, his obsessing over the survey. A feeling of unease was steadily rising around me, tugging at my legs, knocking me off balance.

'We're interested in that specific time and place,' said Alex. 'June 2025 between the Svalbard archipelago and the North Pole. We want to examine a particular chain of events that was set in motion there.'

I sat down heavily on one of the plastic chairs and put my head in my hands. So this was what Grant had been on about. Our place in some supposed chain. Would they stop me if I decided to leave right now? I looked up and saw the two men watching me. Alex came over and crouched down, placed both his hands on my shoulders and looked steadily into my eyes.

'The timeline of the *Polar Horizon* is only one of many we're investigating. It's one piece in a much larger puzzle. Possibly a significant piece, but by no means the only one.'

'But why? What good will digging all this up do? The past is in the past.'

'Ah! But what is the past? What's it made of?' Clyde waggled his eyebrows at me like he wanted me to throw him another stick.

I felt suddenly exhausted by Clyde's unstoppable enthusiasm. I ignored him and looked back to Alex.

He raised his shoulders and turned his palms out in a gesture that was perhaps only pretending to be apologetic. 'Science is a lot like driving in the dark along a twisting road. We can only see as far as the beam of our headlights illuminates. But we have to keep travelling forwards or we will never get anywhere.'

Or you'll drive into a brick wall, I thought.

I contemplated the shiny exterior of the scanner. 'What guarantee do I have that you're not going to turn my brain to mush?'

Clyde tutted. 'It's a non-invasive procedure. Perfectly safe. We've done this before.'

I thought I saw Alex shoot him a warning look and again Grant's gaunt, troubled face surfaced in my mind. 'Grant?'

'Yes,' said Alex. 'Your friend was very helpful but we weren't able to recover much. Unfortunately his memories were somewhat compromised.'

'Somewhat pickled in alcohol, more like,' Clyde muttered.

I cleared my throat. Best to give them fair warning. 'I'll be honest with you. I'm not sure I can remember much either. Kind of made a hobby of forgetting.'

'Which is where your journal comes in,' said Alex.

'We've never had anything like this before. It's unprecedented.' Clyde's gaze flitted between the sheaf of papers in my hand and the top of my head as he spoke, as if he was itching to get in there and start poking about.

My journal. That was the biggest question, but one I decided to keep to myself for the time being. Its presence at Northolt, the physical reality of the thing in my hands, was impossible. It burned a long time ago. The image was so clear in my mind, the heat of it tingled in my fingertips, the smoke nipped at my eyes and nose. I'd watched the pages smoke and curl then catch fire and burn red all the way through. I'd stayed as white flakes of ash caught and swirled in the updraft, like snow. I'd seen the charred remains crumple away to dust. It could not be here. But here it was. Could I have imagined or dreamed its cremation?

IV

'Stop right where you are.'

The man in the pale green overalls standing next to my bed takes a step back and clutches the bundle of sheets he's holding to his chest.

'Put them down. Now.'

'I… Um… Laundry service?' He points to a trolley parked in the middle of the room loaded with piles of folded sheets and towels. 'Shall I make up the—'

I can feel my face reddening. 'No, it's fine. I'll do it,' I mutter.

He grabs his trolley and wheels it fast towards the door, one of the wheels squeaking indignantly.

'Thanks,' I say, but he's already gone.

Back in Avie, people were pushy at best, more often aggressive and dangerous. The stresses of survival lent an edge to every interaction. That's missing here. Maybe I need some time to adjust.

> • <

There's a gym and I'm free to use the library. There's no alcohol in Northolt, a shortcoming that bothered me intensely at first, but not so much now. My liver could probably do with a break anyway. I don't leave the facility, as agreed, but there's a largish central courtyard open to the elements where I can get some fresh air if I feel the need. The warm sun and blue skies of the day I arrived have not so far reappeared. Most days the sky is either overstuffed with blurry clouds or scoured down to a pale grey nothing. And in between the shades of grey, the rain falls.

The food is good and I mostly eat in my room although there is a kind of mess hall. It's never full but there are usually a few groups of people dotted about at the long tables. From the preponderance of ponytails and politely distracted demeanours, I assume they're mostly other researchers, perhaps investigating those other timelines Alex mentioned. The maintenance and cleaning staff, easy to pick out by their pastel-coloured overalls, always seem to be on their way somewhere else, forever sliding out of view. Apart from the occasional murmured pleasantry, none of the other residents of Northolt try to strike up a conversation, which suits me fine.

The enigmatic Alex drops in to the lab every now and then but the timing of his visits is unpredictable. I know he and Clyde work together late into the nights analysing whatever they've retrieved from my head. They don't ask me to help with that.

'No offense,' says Clyde. 'It's not you. It's just the way it works. As far as we can tell, it's not possible for anyone to be objective enough to evaluate their own memories without distorting the findings in some way.'

I accept this without argument. Passivity must be habit forming. I'm relaxing into the non-event of life as a spectator, like sinking into a warm bath.

> • <

At first they tried having me silently read a projection of the text on the ceiling of the scanner, flipping pages by clicking a hand-held switch, but this method prevented me from slipping into the trance-like state needed to get a clean image. So Clyde has recorded me reading the pages of my old journal aloud.

The recording sessions happen in another room with a small soundproof booth. Clyde gives me a selection of photocopied pages and I read them into a microphone. He sits and nods at me from the other side of the glass and occasionally asks me to reread a sentence or paragraph, or to skip a page.

'Try not to think too much about the content. Pretend you're reading a story to someone else. Fictional. Nothing to do with you.'

Of course that's impossible. I can feel the old memories stirring. Dark shapes rising from the depths. They don't look exactly the same. They're changed somehow by the reading process, reshaped by the remembering. There are layers and folds. The original memory, the reading, the remembering, the listening. Multiple reflections, filters, distortions. Raw and processed data. Evolution and mutation.

In the scanner I wear earphones under the ear protectors. Still not sufficient to completely block out the banging of the machine but enough to push the noise behind my voice.

So what I hear is my own voice relating the story of the past. Except it's not my voice from then, it's my voice from now. Deeper, scratchier. Adding another layer.

It works best if I close my eyes and let it wash over and through me. It's hard to take any other approach anyway since the entries are out of sequence, both in the recording and the playback. At first I assumed this was a mistake but Clyde assured me it was intentional. 'We're trying for a closer emulation of how the brain accesses long-term memory. Non-linear, y'know?' He grinned. 'It might seem random, but…'

The scenes, although jumbled, are mostly from the start of the survey and the images become clearer with each session in the scanner. The endless frozen sea, the faces and voices of Bjornsen, Grant, Max and the others; even the flickering displays of the Proteus system are gathering definition and detail. I assume it's this data they're most interested in but Clyde encourages me not to ask too many questions in case I start projecting. Imagining rather than remembering. Adding yet more layers.

The more often a scene repeats within the scanner, the more solid the experience starts to feel until even my own voice slips into the background and I can inhabit the scene itself. It's all very real. Very present. The thrum of the engines, the drone and bleep of the hard drives, the navigation and trigger units. Bjornsen's growled instructions. Grant sighing and jogging his knee up and down as he works, the *snick snick* of his teeth when he bites his nails. But I can't touch any of it. I'm there but also outside of it all. There's a splintering of my perception. Part of it is looking out through my own eyes as they saw at that time. Another part is free floating, disembodied. It's more who I am now, my awareness now, and it generally stays close to the me of twenty years ago. Like I'm looking over my own shoulder.

The details start to fade as soon as I sit up and start moving around.

'It's like a kind of dreaming,' I say to Clyde one day as we're wrapping up. I've already removed the blood pressure cuff from my arm and am working on peeling the ECG electrodes from my chest.

Clyde as usual is hunched over his monitor. 'No it's not,' he says, without looking up.

'No?'

'Totally different process,' he says. Then with an air of having just remembered something, 'Alex is doing some totally batshit stuff with dreams. You should ask him about it.' He turns back to his screen.

I wonder what Alex would make of Clyde's use of 'batshit' to describe his work. Although Alex seems to be in overall charge of what goes on at Northolt, there's no real feeling of a pecking order. But still.

> • <

The next time I run into Alex, he's sitting at one of the broad desks to the rear of the short leg of the L-shaped library, surrounded by antique-looking hardbacks and rolled maps. He looks like a ship's captain from another era, trying to plot a course through uncharted waters. Or a pirate looking for something to plunder. I can't decide which role suits him best.

I draw up a chair and look at the map he has spread out over the table, weighted at the edges with leather-bound volumes to stop it curling.

'How are things coming along with Clyde?' he asks, looking up briefly from his notes but not putting down his pen. The map is yellowed, the ink aged to a mottled indigo. Frayed-looking coastlines are annotated in a language I don't recognise, the letters loaded with diacritical dots and circles. Perhaps some variety of Old Norse. The landmasses too are unfamiliar and populated with fantastical animals, bears with huge heads and exaggerated claws, seal-like creatures with gigantic tusks, packs of wolves with their heads low, following a scent.

'I think it's going okay,' I say. On the other side of the ragged divide between land and sea, winds with malevolent human faces drive the waves in all directions. Fish and whales, narwhals, porpoises, creatures from a dream menagerie, jostle for space with sailing ships drawn only slightly larger.

Alex lays his pen next to the lined yellow pad covered with his notes in the same indecipherable script as the map.

'I'm sorry I've not been keeping up with how you're getting on as much as I'd like. There's so much to do and never enough time.'

'It's hard to describe. But it feels to me like a kind of dreaming. Clyde disagrees.'

Alex smiles ruefully. 'Clyde does like precision. You might not see it, but for an empiricist, he's capable of some really astonishing imaginative leaps. He just needs to be sure where he's leaping from, and to have some notion of where he might land. Which is not unreasonable.'

'He said you were interested in dreams.'

'He did? Well, it's one of the areas I think bears examination. Too imprecise for Clyde. But all science starts as conjecture, fantasy.' Alex raises a hand and twirls it above his head as if trying to conjure the correct phrase. 'Airy nothing,' he says and smiles to himself. 'What I'm interested in is really only a proposition, a what if.'

'What if what?'

The map crackles softly like a low fire as Alex runs his palm over it, smoothing down the creases. 'We live on the land because it suits our physiognomy, and because of that we give it great importance. We even call the planet Earth when the vast majority of it is sea. It's an unjustifiable bias. Especially now, with the sea encroaching on all fronts. It's surely time we challenged our prejudices.'

I nod. I don't see what this has to do with dreams but I have time to listen.

'In the same way, we believe our waking hours are the important ones, that what we physically strive for and accomplish within them is significant. We assume that consciousness is where we find meaning and fulfil our purpose, assuming we have one. I don't think we can be so sure. What if the real work of being human, of being the particular human each of us is, is done while we sleep? Maybe our conscious lives are only fuel for the lives we lead while unconscious. Awake and dreaming are both types of consciousness. What if we're fixating on the wrong one?'

I suspect Alex is talking shite. I'm sure I've heard this idea before, or one very like it. Kids' comic. Or some old network sci-fi movie. Doesn't matter. I'm comfortably sleepy. He might be an idiot or a lunatic but it makes a reasonable bedtime story and I like the sound of his voice.

'Brain activity in REM sleep is exactly the same as when we're awake. Our brains see our dreams in the same way they see the physical world, despite the lack of visual input. All those hours we write off as wasted, only for recharging, as if we're no more than biological batteries. Also a very biased view.'

In seismic, all the instruments have a bias, a margin of systemic error of known magnitude to be accounted for in processing the data. Within the navigation software's calculations, bias is the difference between a predicted result and an observed one. It carries no baggage of right or wrong. It's a clean and factual measure of error. That said, screw around with the bias settings too much and the survey results become gibberish. Even a small amount will have repercussions.

My mind's still a little fuzzy round the edges from a long day's deliberate dreaming, or whatever Clyde would prefer to call it. I gaze at the creatures on the map. The ink used for the animals is darker and sharper edged than the land and sea, giving the map a layered, three-dimensional look. My eyelids droop. Alex's pen scratches across his yellow pad as he resumes his note taking. On the old map, a whale's back arches as it slides below the waves, a bear raises its foreleg and turns its massive head towards me. The winds carry the distant howls of wolves.

'Other animals must dream as well,' I say, sitting up straighter. I need to wake myself up, at least enough to make it back to my room. 'It can't only be us. Cats and dogs. They twitch and jerk in their sleep, like they're chasing or hunting or doing something.'

'They do,' says Alex. 'I should've said sentient, rather than human. We're not the only dreamers. Not by any means.'

I wonder what the dream-like creatures on the map might dream about themselves. Do fish dream? Do bears?

The thought is making me tired again and I stifle a yawn. 'I'll let you get on,' I say, pushing myself up from the chair.

'Sleep well,' says Alex, bowing his head to his work once more.

> • <

I slept well at Northolt. The first few weeks were tricky as I adjusted to a night-time routine that didn't involve knocking myself out with alcohol. But after that was dealt with, I slept better than I had in years.

That all changed when the bear reappeared.

It's not like I'd forgotten him. How could I? But the memory was a tamed thing, or at least contained. Going over and over those scenes in the journal, allowing their reality to germinate, was like opening the cage, giving the bear back his wildness. I thought I could handle it. It was only in my head after all. But now I'm not so sure.

I wake, several times a night. Where previously my sleep was one continuous expanse, now fissures and cracks appear and grow. My nights are crazed and broken. I'm more aware of my dreams, waking right in the middle of the action, clammy with sweat, heart thumping, adrenalin tearing through my bloodstream.

It's always the same. The white arctic light, the sound of splintering ice. Knowing I have to run but unable to make my legs move. Time has stopped for me. I'm paralysed while the seconds continue to flow in the world around me. Bjornsen yells something. Jules gestures wildly. The crew scatter. I can do nothing. All the time the bear is coming closer and closer, the feeling of impotent panic building until I wake, jerking up into the darkness, no longer sure of where or when I am, staring wildly into the darkness, the bear's breath hot on my face.

Reluctant to fall back asleep and risk a return to whatever nightmare woke me, whatever level of reality was trying to claim me, I get up and walk around. I pace the perimeter of the room, back and forth in tight circuits, but it isn't enough. It's as if measuring out the room in footsteps is shrinking its dimensions. I need more space. Far more than my quarters allow. I take to wandering the corridors of Northolt at night.

> • <

For weeks, I get nowhere. They must know what I'm doing but no one stops or questions me. I imagine the doors have sensors and my movements are being tracked. Maybe they have too much on their minds to be bothered with how I spend my nights, as long as I turn up each day and lie in the scanner.

Call me Isobel…

The corridors are no less disorienting than when I first arrived, if anything more so. Clyde wasn't deliberately trying to confuse me that day. The place is a maze, with so many dead ends and reversals it's impossible to get any accurate impression of the size of the building. This doesn't bother me when I start my nocturnal walkabouts. If I keep walking long enough, I eventually wind up back in the general vicinity of my quarters, even if the route makes no logical sense.

My aim isn't to get anywhere specific, it's just to keep moving. The corridor lighting is motion-sensitive, the overhead panels click on in front of me and click off behind. I can't help being reminded of Alex's analogy of driving in the dark. Just enough light to keep moving forwards, but not enough to know where I'm going.

Trying to figure out my route in advance doesn't work. Intersections are not always what they appear to be. What may look like a possible turning often is merely a reflection in one of the intermittently placed floor-to-ceiling mirrors of an opposite turn. Sometimes they're reflections of other reflections. It's hard to avoid the thought that what feels like a miles-long journey is in reality a tight circuit, a Gordian knot of corridors and mirrors covering little more ground than the room I left.

Eventually, I start to take more notice of the doors I'm passing. Those leading to private living quarters have a plastic bracket where the name of the present occupant can be displayed. Whether there's a name card present or not, I leave these rooms alone. Others I begin to try at random. Many are locked. Some turn out to be only supply cupboards or storage rooms, some are office-type setups with desks and monitors. One I stumble across seems to be a kind of records room, the walls lined with tall filing cabinets. I'm not surprised to see such an old-fashioned system. A lot of businesses and organisations went back to hard copy records long before the internet went flaky. Everyone knew it was impossible to guarantee the security of anything stored on a networked computer. This type of backwards migration became the norm.

I walk the length of the room, stopping every so often and opening a drawer. They're the heavy metal kind that labour out with a deep rumble and close with a satisfying whump. Labels on the front of each cabinet, drawer and internal file-dividers show a customised alpha-numeric classification system.

The papers I pull out at random are mostly the mundane records of any large organisation: requisition forms for equipment, duty rosters, maintenance schedules, that sort of thing. Others contain tables of figures impossible to decipher at a glance. They could be anything.

I've begun to lose interest when the code on a particular divider catches my attention. A simple enough series of letters and numbers but they draw me like a magnet.

PHRZ2025.

Polar Horizon. 2025. I take out a folder with the same code printed on the outside and glance over my shoulder. There's no one about. I scan the corners of the room for cameras despite knowing that just because I can't see them, doesn't mean they're not there. My skin is prickling with the sensation of being observed. Seeing a camera would at least justify the feeling.

I leaf through the contents of the folder. A heading jumps out at me. *SUBJECT : P.BJN* followed by a string of numbers and letters. Further down the page, *Subject resistant to drug trials. Non-responsive to regression therapy. Suggest inter-cranial electrode Deep Brain Stimulation.*

Another page offers, *SUBJECT : G.McL Subject continues to respond well to modified serum. Recreation of data set continues. Difficulty of verification remains to be resolved.*

Another, *SUBJECT : M.SMT Subject fully compliant, full response. Recovered data contains inconsistencies.*

P.BJN and G.McL could only be Bjornsen and Grant. The others I don't immediately recognise. I pull a sheaf of papers out. Words and phrases repeat – drug trials, deep brain stimulation, regression – and, at the foot of each page, a box labelled *Termination Date*. Some of these are completed, some not. The dates range from 2035 right up to 2044. My hands are shaking as I stuff the papers back into the folder. It's too big to conceal on my body. I stare at it dumbly, trying to weigh up the implications of its contents but it's too much to take in all at once. I need time to think.

I replace the folder and slide the drawer closed. Better to leave everything as I found it for now. I can always come back.

It doesn't take long, winding again through the endlessly disorienting corridors, before I begin to wonder whether that can ever be true.

V

Clyde is acting weird. Weirder than usual. He's chronically distracted. His chat was always a bit limited, but there's something else now, some new distance in our relationship. Not that I'd call it a relationship, or a friendship, more of an association maybe. These last few days he's been acting like he's never met me before.

When we're prepping for the day's work, him cueing up the audio, me attaching the ECG electrodes to my chest, he repeats the same precise instructions, like I don't know this stuff inside out by now and could probably do it in my sleep. Yesterday he started explaining that I might be aware of a banging sound while the scan was running.

'No shit?' I said.

He looked startled then laughed nervously. 'Well, of course,' he shuffled through his notes, like he was searching for some technical specification he'd overlooked, 'you know that, don't you?'

Perhaps he's got other things on his mind. I know nothing about his private life, had assumed he didn't have one. He's so absorbed in his work it's hard to imagine him outside of it. Or maybe, he knows about my nightly explorations around the building and is trying to figure out how to broach the subject. I can imagine how Clyde might shy away from such an unpredictable, direct conversation.

The day after I found those records I was ready to confront him or Alex about them, but I want to have the evidence in my hands when I do, so I've held back. Why didn't I pocket even one page when I had the chance? I haven't been able to find the file room again. I've spent I don't know how many nights attempting to retrace my footsteps, but with no success. I have found other record rooms, even ones I thought at first were the original but they all differed subtly in at least one aspect. Larger or smaller rooms, differently designed filing cabinets, some of them padlocked, arranged in various layouts, alternate systems of classification. The one feature they all have in common is that none of them contain files labelled PRHZ2025.

Miles of corridor unspool ahead of me and dissolve behind. Nothing is familiar but I can't help feeling I've seen it all before. The sense of déjà vu intensifies between the daytime scanner sessions and my nightly wanderings until it's like a constant alarm bell ringing in my head.

I wasn't sleeping much anyway, and now hardly at all. My brain feels as if it's stretched too thin, my mind strung taut and left out to dry, like the hide of some luckless animal.

VI

Clyde pulled me out of the scanner early today. I'd only been in for an hour or so and hadn't been able to release my thoughts in the right way. The voice-over of the journal was looping over a section about a workboat trip, then flipping to describe displays on Proteus. I tried to slip into the zone but couldn't quite let go.

Previously this sensation of letting go has been like sliding from the side of a boat into a river and allowing the water to take my weight, not so much swimming as drifting, going with the current, trusting it. Now it feels different, like the river itself has changed, become grasping and dangerous. There could be rapids, even a waterfall coming up. The river might suddenly empty itself and me along with it into some vast and unknowable sea. Or, and this is the worst possibility, the one that keeps my fingers clamped to the side of that boat, maybe the river's gone altogether and what's off the side now is a sheer drop into a fissure in the earth, a crack in reality. A space through which I'll never stop falling and from which I can never come back.

'I think that's enough for now,' says Clyde.

I notice with a start that he has a beard. Not a terribly impressive one, more of a straggly goatee thing, but it definitely wasn't there yesterday. He must need to shave several times a day if that's the speed it usually grows.

'Wow. Instant goatee. Nice. Is that fake? Or is it some kind of genetically modified super goatee you've grown in a test tube and attached to your face?'

Clyde runs a hand over his chin. 'Ah,' he says, 'well. Yes. Ha ha!'

I jump as he puts his hand on my arm. Clyde doesn't do touching.

'Look, Alex and I have been talking about this and we think maybe you need to take a break. We've been working with you longer and more intensively than we ever have with other subjects.' He looks into my face, actually makes sustained eye contact. 'Perhaps we didn't consider the toll that might take on you.'

'You said it was perfectly safe.' All this touching and eye contact, rather than being calming, is making me jumpy and cross.

He raises his hands. 'And it is. It is. But we think you're tired. A break. That's all. A few days, maybe a week or two would do you good. And you'll come back refreshed. Like any normal person would take a break from a normal job.'

'Normal doesn't exist anymore.'

'Well. If it did.'

I try to rein in my irritation. He has a point. Surely a break would be a good idea. Then why does it feel like I'm being sacked?

'So I can leave?'

'Ah,' Clyde tugs at a straggling tuft of his pseudo goatee. 'Leave Northolt? No, we'd prefer you didn't.'

'I—' I start to protest.

'We don't think it would be sensible,' Clyde interrupts. 'There's nowhere for you to go, and it wouldn't be fun. Believe me. Things haven't got any better out there since you left.'

'What's been happening?' Part of me wants to know, needs to. The other part wants to cram her hands over Clyde's mouth and stop him saying anything at all. I push my hands into my pockets.

Clyde shrugs. 'Just more and worse of everything. Riots. Gangs on the increase. More people, not enough food or shelter to go around. The government too stretched or too preoccupied with saving their own skins to do anything about it. Avie is a mess. Trust me, you don't want to go there. We'd rather you stayed safe. Here. With us.'

'You worried I might not come back?' The idea of Clyde missing me, personally, is absurd. But then, I'd miss him too if I never saw him again. In a way.

'Honestly? Yes. We need you in one piece to carry on with the work. If you go down there, you could end up in several pieces, fried up in some gang lord's curry. Not a lot of use to us then.'

'Right.'

'I mean, that would be just terrible. We don't have any naan bread for a start. Or mango chutney.'

'Yeah. Cheers, Clyde.'

'Oh, man, I miss mango chutney. Don't you?'

I slam the door on my way out.

> • <

So, I'm on sabbatical. It's not helping. I'm spending a lot of time in the library but I can't concentrate. I'm reading a biography of one of those old-time polar explorers and they're just about to freeze to death, or eat each other, when my mind wanders and the next thing I know, I'm reading a novel set in some future city. It's mostly underwater and full of massive lizards. There's one woman who wafts around being vacuous in a bikini, and all the others characters are men who keep trying to kill each other for no clear reason.

I keep hoping to bump into Alex. I've decided I need to ask him about those files, even without the evidence. I need to look him in the eye and demand some answers.

> • <

I haven't seen him for days when I unexpectedly stumble across him one night in the library. He's sitting cross-legged on the rug, hands resting in his lap. His eyes are closed and his face is as smooth and impassive as a marble statue. I wonder if his skin would be cool to the touch but don't dare touch him to find out. There's something peaceful about his expression, but also an absence, a vulnerability.

I do one of those polite little excuse-me coughs into my fist but he doesn't react. His body is absolutely still. I move closer and stare at his chest, trying to discern the rise and fall of his breath. I'm wondering whether I should try to take his pulse or find a hand mirror to hold under his nose, when he opens his eyes. For a second they appear entirely black and fix on me with a sharp, predatory quickness.

His nostrils flare. I start backwards instinctively. Then he blinks and immediately looks like his normal self. It was only a moment. I tell myself I imagined it. The light is low and the library is full of shadows that slip over and around each other. It is a room filled with ghosts.

For a long moment Alex looks right through me, as though I have no more substance than a shadow. Like when I'm in the scanner, haunting a scene from twenty years ago, I'm less than invisible. Am I even here now, or is this a memory too? I glance down at my own body, reassuring myself of its physicality while at the same time irritated by my own idiotic suggestibility.

'Hello, Isobel, what can I do for you?' He sounds exhausted. Deep lines have returned to his face, etching the years back in.

'I'm sorry. Were you asleep?'

'No. Not sleeping. I was thinking. Not thinking. Meditating.' He twirls his hand in the air, that mannerism he has when searching for the right words. 'Travelling. In a way. Exploring possibilities.'

'What? Like an out of body experience? Astral projection? Do you believe in all that stuff?' It seems incongruous for someone running a serious scientific research programme.

'I don't believe or disbelieve it. Belief is largely irrelevant. But I am open to the possibilities. There are many routes towards alternative levels of consciousness, many ways to transcend our limitations.'

Sounds like bollocks to me but I'm still curious. 'Does it work?'

He thinks about this for a while. Surely it's a yes–no answer? He's either experienced this transcendence or he hasn't.

'I'm not really certain. I'm fairly sure something is happening but it's difficult to recall the precise details afterwards.'

'Where d'you go though? You must have some destination in mind.'

'Not at all.' He looks mildly offended. 'That would be extremely controlling.'

'But—'

'Anyway,' he unfolds his legs, 'you didn't come here to talk to me about this.'

'No. I wanted to ask… I mean, I found…' How can he not know what he's doing? What's the point in doing it in that case? I'm trying to square the soft-edged vagueness of Alex's current attitude with the hard, clinical precision of the records I found. Maybe he doesn't know about them either. Now I come to think of it, they seem more like Clyde's style. Perhaps the two of them don't tell each other everything.

Alex stands up and stretches. 'Would you mind if we talked tomorrow? I'm tired.'

'Sure,' I say. Talking to Clyde about this first might be a better idea, if I can find him. At least he won't go all transcendental on me. I leave the library and venture once again into the labyrinth of corridors.

> • <

Each time I get a little more lost. I can't find Clyde. Sometimes I forget I'm even looking for him. The intelligent lighting is starting to spook me. My progress is no longer a journey of exploration, more a flight from what's coming behind. The darkness is catching up with me, like some great beast on my heels. I glance back over my shoulder too many times. I tell myself to stop. Who was it said something about the abyss staring back? I'd like to punch that person in the face.

The only thing worse than looking is not looking. I can feel the darkness gathering density, embodying itself as it gains ground. Alex's 'airy nothing' taking form, becoming something terrible. Sometimes I can hear it breathing. A deep huffing growl of exhalation, maybe two or three, one after another, coming closer. I turn and it stops. I continue and there's a new sound, something scraping on the ground, just beyond the last corner. Trailing along the walls towards me. A sound like claws.

> • <

I try to sleep during the day, which reminds me even more of my time on the *Polar Horizon*. This time I've got complete control over the light levels in my room but my body clock still objects, some primitive mechanism that sticks, cogs jumping teeth.

One afternoon I dream I'm being tracked through a labyrinth with high walls of ice by a gigantic naked man with the head of a white bear. After that, I decide I don't really need sleep anyway. Not much. I keep going as long as I can until the need is beyond negotiation. When I'm at that point, but never before, I lie down for a few hours of oblivion. There are no dreams. I get up as soon as my eyes open and do the same again. This way I'm staying one step ahead.

> • <

It's one of those nights when repressing the urge to run absorbs most of my attention, so I can't say how long I've been wandering or where in the intricate internal circuitry of Northolt I am when I stumble across the room. Unlike most of the other doors, this one is partially open and a dull green underwater lighting seeps into the corridor, dimming as I approach, bringing the invading glare of the overhead lighting with me. There isn't any question of not going in.

The room is dominated by a vast table, something like the bed of the MRI scanner but larger and with a full-length, semi-circular glass cover. It's like a scaled-up, high-tech version of Sleeping Beauty's coffin. The walls are lined with banks of processors, green and blue LEDs flickering, the low drone of machines at work. At first glance the coffin seems opaque. I put a hand out to touch and quickly withdraw it in surprise. The glass is coated in a crisp layer of frost. I brush a portion away and it drifts to the floor like crystalline sand. The glass is still foggy so it's difficult to make out what's behind it. I put my face up close and peer inside.

White fur jewelled with frost, glittering brilliant white. A series of images flash through my mind: the bearskin rug on the wall of Grant's cabin in Svalbard twenty years ago; the fake bears that occupied the office in Edinburgh; poor Mercedes, splayed on her rock; and of course, the towering ten feet of bear that boarded the *Polar Horizon*. The line of scar tissue across my neck twitches and my knees turn to water. I steady myself against the edge of the table. My view inside the coffin is limited to the small portion of frost I cleared. Using both hands now, urgently, ignoring the cold on my ungloved fingers, I work my way along the side. It's definitely not an empty skin. This is a body, lying on its front with bulk and bones and huge clawed feet.

When I reach the head end and scrabble away as much of the frost as I can, it feels as though the ice has slipped into my head along with the horror, through my eyes to close silently around my brain.

> • <

A polar bear's fur is not white. It's transparent and only looks white because the hairs are hollow and reflect light. Nobody knows what colour a polar bear is in absolute darkness.

A polar bear's skin is not white. Remove the fur and a polar bear's skin is black.

> • <

His cranium is shaved, the dark exposed skin studded with a skull cap of silver wires and electrodes. Bolts at his temples and another in the centre pierce the skin and drive into the bone. Tiny lights blink decoratively. His eyes are closed but the lids puckered in a way so redolent of grief and loss that the emotion hits me in the chest.

Stretching back from the base of his skull, a six inch wide channel of fur has been shaved following the course of his spine. More wires and bolts protrude from the black skin, locked into the vertebrae. I can't help thinking of the Proteus system, its long streamers of sensors collecting data. His jaws are held open, the formidable teeth resting on plastic tubing. It looks like—

That sound, so low and so very slow it has been absorbed into the hum of the many machines, divorced from its meaning. It flows back and forth in shallow waves, with long pauses between each reversal. I struggle to interpret its meaning, to hear it for what it is.

Breath.

PART THREE

TODAY ? REBOOT

ARCTIC OCEAN

JULY 2025

All I can do is lie here and breathe. And wait. Now I'm in a position to sleep as much as I want to, I can't. Not properly.

I doze disconnectedly. Each time I wake, my memory returns like a series of blows. That terrible sound, the shifting ice, disconnecting the streamers on the back deck, the bear.

The bear.

> • <

The wound is more than superficial, but less than profound. It's already beginning to heal and it itches as the skin knits together. There will be a scar. 'A real beauty of a scar,' said Ralf, who doubles as our medic. He's not a doctor, has no medical degree, but assures me this is only a technicality. He knows his shit, so he says.

I have a rough line of stitches, which I mercifully don't remember the sewing of, a sore arse-cheek from the tetanus injection, and a supply of painkillers. 'Don't get too fond of them,' says Ralf, 'they can get a bit habit forming.'

I can't see that happening. The pills don't reduce the soreness of the wound all that much, never mind give me any type of pleasurable high. All they do is put distance between me and the pain. It's a point on my map, but remote. I keep thinking of that line from *Lawrence of Arabia*. Peter O'Toole, his devastating china-blue eyes on the shifting horizon, his airy voice: 'The trick is, not to mind that it hurts.'

> • <

Since we ditched the streamers, and Proteus took a vow of silence, we are sailing more or less blind. We still have the basic ship's sensors but compared to the bristling array of equipment used during a survey, and with ship-to-shore communication still down, we've gone from super-high-definition 3D-vision to shuffling along in the dark like a sleepwalker navigating the depths of a dream, our hands stretched out in front of us.

In fact we have Hannes out in front. The big Swede is on iceberg watch, up in the crow's nest. A navigation method so low tech it's really no tech, but reliable, within the limits of human vision. We're taking the only route open to us, following our original path back south.

The ice, however, has its own ideas, a geometry of thought that does not align with our own. Parts of the channel have narrowed considerably. The broken path has acquired angles and slews drunkenly from side to side. Some of the movement is natural, a consequence of the perpetual motion of the pack-ice, but now there are strange unpredictable currents and sudden rushes of movement, maybe the after-effects from whatever happened, how long ago? How many days? I've lost track. I've asked Ralf to remind me enough times for him to look at me sharply, clearly questioning my mental capacity. So I've stopped asking.

> • <

We're no longer even trying to dodge the small floes. Anything the hull of the *Polar Horizon* can deflect without coming to serious harm we nudge out of our way without adjusting course. The sporadic thuds and booms of impacts set off a strange kind of percussion that travels through the hull to reach me in my new cabin, providing a counterpoint to the thrum of the ship's engines. Slabs of ice scrape along the length of the ship. I think of those drifting statues, sense them reaching, limbs straining, fingers scrabbling for purchase on the sheer slope of our hull as we pass through their frozen galleries. Their faces sinking below the water in our wake.

Under normal circumstances these collisions would be considered unacceptably reckless, but we're racing against time now, balancing how much damage we can take against how badly we want to survive. Even if we successfully retrace our path and make it into open water we won't emerge back where we started at the Svalbard archipelago. But once we're free and clear we can find our way back from wherever we end up. Or that's the idea.

Without the icebreaker, our options are limited. Forcing a more direct route through the unbroken ice is out of the question. We'd either hole the hull and sink or, like so many other ships strewn across the centuries, become trapped in the ice. So we move forwards the only way we can, picking our way back through a trail of damage, sailing along a healing scar.

> • <

News of our progress is mostly relayed to me by Ralf, who checks in regularly. Jules, apparently, is not keen on being in command but with Bjornsen out of commission he has little choice. Ralf tells me Jules has looked in on me but I was sleeping at the time.

I nod when he tells me this. An instinctive movement, hard to supress, for which I'm rewarded with a jagged stinging sensation across my neck.

'That wasn't too clever, was it?' says Ralf, impatiently. He leans over and gently wipes away the watery blood pooled in the hollow at the base of my throat. He takes the opportunity to examine the wound again. Its positioning and extent seem to fascinate him. 'I swear, that bear must have been a surgeon in another life. It's like he was trying to make sure you would live.'

I want to say something to the effect that, maybe it would've been best in that case not to tear my throat out, but I'm under orders from Ralf not to talk, just in case there's some internal damage he can't see. I can breathe and swallow without too much trouble, but no talking. I content myself with a short splutter of disbelief.

'He managed to avoid both external jugular veins. Right across your throat and he missed them both by a bee's dick. It looks so deliberate. Just weird. A bear like that could kill a person with a single slap.'

I roll my eyes at Ralf.

'Anyway, it's looking good. You'll be up and about in no time.' Ralf's bedside manner, when he remembers he's being a doctor and therefore should have one, is punctuated by spikes of excessive breeziness.

I ask him, with a pantomime combination of hand gestures and facial expression, when I'll be able to talk again.

'Oh, I dunno about that. Might be ages. But, y'know,' he grins, 'I kind of like this new silent version of you. Quite restful to be around. Definitely less sweary and sarcastic.'

I make an unambiguous hand gesture.

He laughs, enjoying my frustration more than I think is fair. 'Soon, honestly. See if you can get some more sleep. That's when the body heals itself so the more you get, the quicker you'll be back in the land of the living.'

> • <

I have the strangest sensation when falling asleep. Everything is inverted. I no longer fall. It feels more like rising, swimming up towards unconsciousness not sinking down into it. My lungs feel tight, like I'm holding my breath even though air still moves in and out of my body. There's a sense of building pressure and light-headedness, like oxygen deprivation, a tiredness in my limbs as I pull and kick for the surface, finally breaking through, mouth open like a fish, the shock of cold air on my face telling me I'm alive, wholly alive in a way my conscious existence can't allow. It feels as though dreams are the only place I can really breathe.

> • <

I doze after Ralf leaves and wake an unknown time later. I brush the tips of my fingers along the row of stitching and am reminded by some nettle-sting jags not to touch. I wonder how the scar will look in the future. Will it fade to a thin white ghost of itself, only visible to whoever I allow close enough to see it? Or will it make itself hard to ignore, imposing itself on strangers? Will they stare or look away? Will it matter to me? I can't say. I'm finding it as difficult to imagine myself in a real, solid future as to reassemble the order of recent events.

My memories of the last few days are disjointed. Ralf tells me that for the first twenty-four hours I didn't regain consciousness. They weren't sure I would. Probing my memory of being on the back deck, uncoupling the streamers, trying to start from there and move forward, it's like I'm gathering together pieces of a jigsaw, searching for where the jagged edge of one piece might fit another, where a bulge matches an indentation. It's a painstaking process. Often disrupted when I pick up one particular piece and the visceral jolt of it makes me drop all the others so they once again become scattered and meaningless. I'm left holding a fragment, not wanting to examine it too closely, but knowing I must if I am ever to put together the whole picture.

> • <

The bear raised to his full height on his hind legs towers over me, his breath hot on my face, the stink of it nearly knocking me off my feet. The smell so strong it nearly suffocates the fear, but not enough to stop me pissing myself. It runs hot out of the bottom of my waterproof trousers and steams over my boots. The bear grins, licks his black lips, and opens his jaws wide to show me the spikes of his teeth. I can see his throat vibrating with a roar that detonates like thunder in all directions out across the endless monochrome world.

Sweat beads on my forehead as I force myself to relive this moment.

He raises one massive foreleg and a flash of clawed white slices across my vision so fast I wonder if I saw it at all. Then I feel my blood splash down from my throat onto my chest, staining it black, and the empty space between each beat of my heart expands and stretches, out and out and out, until I can't feel it anymore. The sun begins to slip from the sky and sink into the sea. Darkness returns, but it is not the darkness I longed for. It is not kind. It does not forgive.

The sun is still there, or so Ralf tells me. I'm in a different cabin now, this one below decks, close to the medical room. It's smaller but much the same in layout and with the same dismal grey decor. I can have darkness if I want it, but it isn't the same, doesn't satisfy the need for true night. I have artificial darkness, artificial light. Night is a story I was once told and am no longer sure I believe.

Finally, it is the fact of the sun that allows me to move forward. Its presence proves that part of my memory is false. The sun did not sink into the sea. It's still out there. Still circling us. Still hungry.

> • <

Something hits the bear on the shoulder and clatters to the deck, taking his attention away from me. He turns and drops to all fours with a low growl. He is hit again, this time on the head and a heavy wrench skids past my feet. Someone is throwing the contents of a toolbox at him. The bear shakes his head then hunches down and springs, cat-like, throwing himself with a snarl towards the source of this outrage. It's Bjornsen and he's shouting something at me. I can see his mouth opening and closing but it takes time for the sound to reach my ears. The air is thick with seconds, minutes and hours. Finally a single word reaches me: 'Run!'

> • <

The edges of dreams and memory fit together too readily. How much of what I think I remember happened in reality? How much of what I assume I dreamed is in fact real? Or was. Time is water. Ice is memory.

Slipping and sliding in my own blood and piss, I turn and run. I haul open a door, throw myself along a corridor, around a corner and down another, pinballing through the ship but the bear is coming after me. The only thing that keeps me ahead is grabbing the handrails and pivoting myself sharply around corners while the bear, carried forward by the momentum of his own weight, skids past the openings and has to double back. More corners, more corners are what I need. In a straight run he'll be on me and I'll be finished. I hear a voice, shouting, 'This way!' It's Bjornsen again. I charge towards the sound of his voice and realise it's coming from above. A hatch, a ladder. I jump and climb as it's pulled upwards. I lose a boot. Please let it only be the boot. I wiggle my toes to check the foot is still there. Bjornsen slamming the hatch closed. The bellow of the thwarted bear below. That's all I remember. I must've passed out after that.

> • <

When I came to I was lying on the bed in this cabin, a figure leaning over me, woozily coming into focus: Ralf, our jug-eared third officer, and, unknown to me at the time, my nurse and main companion for however many days to come.

There are more blanks and breaks in my memory from that point. I think I resurfaced and went back under a number of times before trying to get up when Ralf would push me gently back down. 'Don't try to talk,' he said and stacked a pile of pillows behind me so that I could at least sit up. Where did he get all those extra pillows from? I tried to ask and a strange rasping croak came out of my mouth accompanied by the sensation of a sticking plaster being ripped off the inside of my throat.

'I said, don't.' Ralf shook his head at me. 'Okay. This is the situation.' He related the highlights like items on an itinerary, counting them off on his fingers. 'You're hurt but you'll live. The captain is badly injured. I'm not taking any bets on whether he'll make it. Jules has taken over command of the ship and we're heading for home as fast as we can. The icebreaker's location is unknown.'

I made the universal sign for paper and pen and pointed Ralf towards the desk.

Bjornsen? I scrawled.

'Not good. I think one eye can possibly be saved if we get him to a hospital in time, but the other is just gone. Nothing even a surgeon can do about that.' Ralf sighed heavily and looked at his hands, as if blaming them.

I jabbed the pen on the paper to snap him out of it.

What happened?

'Of course, you wouldn't know. So, after you were clear, and I was patching you up, they tried to flush the bear back out, get it off the ship, but it wouldn't cooperate. They decided if he wouldn't leave then he had to be contained. But that is one smart bear. It was like he figured out the plan and even knew the layout of the ship. They were barricading doors and passageways and he came out of nowhere and took a pop at Bjornsen before he could get out of the way. He's lost a lot of blood but is more or less stable for the time being. I don't know how long that will last. Blood poisoning is my main worry.'

My own injury paled into insignificance. No more than a scratch really. Nothing in comparison to losing your sight.

How did you get rid of the bear? I wrote on the notepad.

'Oh. We didn't. He has deck four all to himself. We cut him off from the outer passages so he can't smash through the windows, and we've secured all the other possible exits. For the first day or so he raged and smashed around. Now he's quiet as a church mouse. Perhaps he ran out of stuff to trash. Or he's found the kitchens and is sleeping off a gigantic food binge. Or he's dead. Or just bored and waiting for something to happen. We don't know. I tell you one thing though, no one is going to open a door to satisfy their curiosity.'

The pen fell from my fingers, rolled off the bed and onto the floor.

10 RECONFIGURATION

ARCTIC OCEAN

JULY? 2025

I think about Bjornsen, sightless in his quarters, me voiceless in mine. The bear confined between us. There's a terrible symmetry there, a pattern that refuses to reveal its meaning.

The sounds of our progress through the ice drag slowly through my waking hours and I find myself listening for the bear on the deck above. Is that dull thudding the sound of his footsteps overhead, between the engine noise and the ice scraping past, or is it my own heartbeat?

With deck four given over to the bear, those personnel who previously had quarters there have been hastily moved down to deck three. The corridor outside my room is noisy with voices and footsteps, doors opening and closing, even music playing. Michael Jackson? Of course. Of all the many things that could be responsible for our situation. Let's blame it on the bastarding boogie.

> • ‹

Grant comes to visit and sits awkwardly on the edge of the bed, looking at me then away as if he can't stomach what he sees. I know I'm no oil painting but I could do without him rubbing it in. I grab the pen and paper.

Think we'll get double time for this? I scrawl on my notepad. Typical of Grant that even in these circumstances he's so preoccupied with his own thoughts he doesn't think to ask how I'm feeling and it's up to me to cheer him up.

The smile I earn in return for my effort is hardly worth it. More of a grimace. I'm wondering if there's a diplomatic way to phrase piss off and come back when you're not being an arsehole when the grimace buckles in on itself and Grant buries his face in his hands, sobbing in great snot-laden gulps, his shoulders shaking. What the fuck? I sit there stunned and let him carry on for a bit then slap his arm and hand him a tissue.

He honks into it noisily and reaches for another, filling that too before speaking, his voice clogged with emotion. 'I never meant for any of this to happen, Izzy. I'm so, so sorry.'

It's probably a good thing at this point I can't talk. Him taking the blame for things that aren't his fault is just another way to make this all about him. A new way to feed his ego. I picture it blind and gaping, like a baby bird.

Grant dries his face with a third tissue and clears his throat, readying himself for something. 'I need to tell you. Jules didn't cause the problems with Proteus.'

I make a tell-me-something-I-don't-know face. And then he does.

> • <

I'm not sure what my face is doing now, but whatever it is Grant directs the rest of his speech to the floor.

'I uploaded some code to Proteus. But it wasn't… I didn't think… None of this was supposed to happen! It was only supposed to adjust the data, to make it look like there was nothing down there. I… There's no easy way to tell you this so I'm just going to tell you it all straight out. I guess it's a good thing you can't talk right now.' He gives a limp attempt at a smile.

I cross my arms and glare.

He focuses on the floor again. 'You remember those guys that occupied Niall's office dressed as polar bears?'

Is he trying to be funny? He's still not looking at me.

'They approached me, online, chat room, doesn't matter how. They sent me some stuff they'd found out about this survey. All things we sort of knew but hadn't acknowledged. I think we both suspected something was dodgy from the start, if we're honest with ourselves. We didn't have the necessary permits, we weren't fully crewed, the state of this ship, all of it. But as usual, we kept our heads down, too worried about keeping our jobs. Just following orders, eh?

'I guess they knew I was already sympathetic to their point of view. Coming up here, fucking with a whole ecology we don't really understand? One that's already on the brink of collapse? They were persuasive, but I told them I was thinking about quitting anyway, or at least finding some reason I couldn't do this survey. So they changed tack. They didn't threaten me but they mentioned that they'd traced the big money to a collection of shadow corporations, multinational interests, impossible to pin down. Some seriously scary people. The sort who don't think twice about dealing decisively with anyone they see as a problem. They said it would be unfortunate if these people were to come across my name in that context.

'They gave me a flash drive. I was to upload the program from it onto the system and—'

I can't believe what I'm hearing. Grant winces at the sound of my hand slapping the covers.

'And it would scramble things up just enough to create a smokescreen of errors while it falsified the data sets. That was all. Just enough to convince everyone that the whole idea of drilling in the Arctic would be an expensive waste of time.

'I did that. But the errors were way bigger than they should've been. I don't know why. I tried to uninstall the program but it wasn't where it should've been. It had migrated to the base code and embedded itself. I couldn't get it out. I don't know if it was even responsible for all the shit that was happening, or if it was just bad luck and coincidence, or a combination. And then Max ordered that course detour. He's the only one saying the course deviation came from head office. He's the only one communicating with them. How do we know he's not making it up? Or taking his orders from someone else? I saw him talking to that Ilia guy, the one that skippered the workboat when you and Jules went out. Whatever they were talking about, it looked pretty intense. I don't trust Ilia either. There's something about him. What could those two possibly have to say to each other?' Grant hunches his shoulders and sighs heavily. 'God. I don't know. It's all fucked up.'

He turns towards me, his story finally told, and reaches for my hand but I snatch it away. How could he be such an idiot? Why didn't he tell me any of this sooner? Trying to implicate Jules to cover his own stupidity is just low. And now he's casting aspersions on Max. And Ilia. That's easier to believe, but it's starting to look like Grant will try to pin responsibility on anyone who happened to be standing in the same room as him when things went wrong. How can I trust anything he says now?

He stands. 'I guess you'll do whatever you have to do. Just please believe that I never intended for this to happen. It's like everything combined in the worst possible way. No one was supposed to get hurt.'

When Grant leaves, I lie there staring at the ceiling, everything seething around in my head. It takes a while, but eventually I calm down enough to be absolutely clear on two things. Firstly, whether I believe Grant's story or not, and whatever I think of him, the only thing that matters in the short term is getting back to civilisation, and a hospital for Bjornsen. Secondly, I don't care what Ralf says, I can't stay cooped up in this cabin any longer or I'll go completely stir crazy.

> • <

Someone, Ralf I presume, has changed me out of the clothes I was wearing at the time of the attack so I'm now wearing an outsized set of men's striped flannel pyjamas. They stink of sweat and confinement. I manage to get into clean trousers but stall at how to get anything over my head without aggravating the stitches across my neck. Ralf has left a box of medical supplies in my cabin and I root around in it until I find a roll of gauze, which I wind carefully around my neck, over the stitches, to protect them and tie it at the back. I manage to pull a jumper over the pyjama top. Good enough.

I drink a glass of water and decide it's time I try out my vocal cords. The first thing that pops into my head is don't blame it on the sunshine, but that makes me laugh and the sound that comes out of my mouth doesn't sound like a laugh, more like a snarl.

❭ • ❬

On the bridge, Grant is nowhere to be seen, probably skulking in his cabin. Fine. Proteus' screens are running with rivers of error messages. I rattle the mouse as I pass the control station but nothing registers. The system is preoccupied with itself and pays no attention to me.

Jules is outside on the narrow deck that runs around the bridge room. I go out and join him, glad to feel the wind on my face again, even though it's so cold it nips my skin and makes me strangely aware of the wet feel of my eyeballs turning in my skull as their surface temperature suddenly drops.

Visibility is poor. The wind comes in sporadic gusts carrying flurries of snow and moving patches of fog around without clearing it away. A stuttering, agitated kind of weather. The sun is a distant magnesium flare.

The channel we're attempting to sail is cluttered with a rubble of moving ice. The ship batters through it all. How much more of this can she take? Jules and I both hold onto the railing as a chunk the size of a family car careens off the starboard bow. His hand covers mine and his eyes go to the bandage round my neck.

'Should you be up?' he says. He looks haggard, about ready to drop, doesn't register the irony of his question. The wind lifts his hair and blows it back. At his temples and around the top of his forehead is a heavy frosting of white hair which I'm sure wasn't there before. Have the responsibilities of command aged him so quickly?

I put my mouth up close to his ear, not wanting to strain my voice by raising it above the wind. 'What can I do to help?'

He raises a hand to touch my face and I flinch involuntarily at the movement, even while noticing it seems slowed, his arm floating towards me, his hand already cupped, his nails long and dark. He usually has such beautifully clean hands. I look up. Perhaps it's the light, that silvery wash over everything increasing the contrast in my vision. Jules's dark eyes are darker than I remembered, the irises enlarged, heavily flecked with black. His expression is both tender and fierce. His lips are also dark. They part, the point of a tooth showing.

> • <

I wake with a jolt back in my cabin, encased in shades of grey. Was I even on the bridge with Jules or did I dream that? I sit up and rub my temples. Time is water. Memory is ice. I swing my legs over the side of the bed. The floor is cold on my bare feet.

A soft but deliberate scraping noise is coming, I realise with alarm, from somewhere inside the room. I reach for the bedside lamp and blink through the burst of light. A figure is sitting at the desk with their back to me.

11 DATA RECOVERY

ARCTIC OCEAN

SUMMER 2025

By the set of his shoulders and the way the light draws glints of dark gold from his hair I know it's Jules. I'm pleased to see him and this feeling is so uncomplicated that it isn't hard to push aside my initial confusion as to whether I really saw him on the bridge earlier or not.

'What are you doing?' I ask.

He holds a short silver knife with a thin tapered blade the shape of a willow leaf. At first it looks as though he's carving away at his own hand and then I realise there's another shape following the contours of his fingers into the hollow of his palm, across the pad at the base of his thumb and finishing at his wrist. He's carving some kind of figure. It looks primitively human.

'A poor copy, I'm afraid,' he says. 'I can never quite capture the expression of the body, the fluidity, the sense of power and movement you see in the originals.' He holds the little figure up for me to see. It's a bear, neck stretched forwards, forelegs sweeping down along its sides, rear legs straight back, toes pointed so the whole body is streamlined. It looks to be flying, or perhaps diving. The forward tilt of its head and the flatness of its body also remind me of the polar bear rug pinned to Grant's cabin wall in Svalbard.

'Ancient peoples in the northern parts of the world carved them out of walrus ivory, caribou antler or local stone. They were symbolic of a shaman's ability to leave their body and travel in the spirit world, astral plane, whatever you want to call it, with the spirits of helper animals. The polar bear was considered a very important helper, or companion.'

My recent experience of bears hasn't been exactly helpful or companionable.

'They would travel together to the moon or perhaps to the bottom of the sea, where they would talk over matters to be resolved. And sometimes they would dance. Here,' he hands me the figure. 'I carve them from wood, much easier to handle, but perhaps if I had the patience and took the time to carve from the proper materials, my work would be better.'

I turn the figure over in my hand. It's warm to the touch, smooth on the underside, ridged on the back with the shape of a skeleton: vertebrae, ribs, pelvis, it looks very close to human bone structure.

As if reading my thoughts, he says, 'It's the same basic design. Having it on the outside of the carving like this was to show how the shaman and the bear could share characteristics. The shaman in bear skin. The bear within the human form.'

I go to hand it back to him.

'Keep it. It's a gift. Perhaps it'll bring you luck.'

I sleep. Or at least it seems as though I do. I lie with the carved bear nestled in the dip of my palm, examining the grain of the wood flowing and swirling around the bones of the skeleton like a current, like time. The way it changes speed, grows thin and loops back, different points touching, making and breaking connections. Time splinters us into all the people we have been and will become, passing each other in a hall of mirrors.

My name is Isobel. I am eight years old. This is my bear. His name is Snowball. He is a very old bear. Look. You can see his fur is white but if you pull it apart and look underneath, his skin is black. He has proper eyes. They are dark orange. Very dark. With black middles. See? My dad bought him for me in a shop where you get to pick the colour and the clothes and they make the bear for you right there while you wait. I chose white fur and no clothes. The lady tried to get me to pick a ballerina outfit, or a party dress, but I stared at her until she stopped talking. When they've put all the stuffing in, they leave a gap in the front and give you a little red satin heart to kiss and make a wish on. Then they shove the heart in and sew it up. I kissed it and I wished my wish then I made the lady push the heart up into Snowball's throat so that he could talk to me. And he does.

Time flows forwards again, pooling in the present where I am half-awake and someone in another cabin is definitely watching *The Little Mermaid* with the volume turned way up. The sheets feel wet. I have far too many pillows and throw a couple to the floor. The soundtrack is reassuring, coming from a safer, less complicated time, but that too gets caught up in the conflicted currents we're sailing through, another fragment spinning unpredictably in a shattered sea.

> • <

I am horrified to find I am a ballerina, complete with pink fluffy tutu and sparkly tights. I watch the material float and shimmer as the water moves around my legs and realise I am dancing under the sea. Not ballet. A waltz perhaps. The music changes to some kind of old-fashioned jazz crooner. My partner, the bear, now played by Peter O'Toole (he will win an Academy Award for this, surely) is a superb dancer. Fish swim around us. The shadows of whales pass overhead. Ribbons of seaweed flutter decoratively at the edges of the dance floor. We spin and dip, then stop at the bar for gin and tonics. When we talk, bubbles come out of our mouths.

'Darling, of course we all need to survive. You lot have done jolly well on that score. I can't argue with that. But surely you can see you've gone too far now?' He gestures with an olive on a cocktail stick before popping it delicately into his mouth and swallowing. 'Coming here was a mistake. This place is not for the likes of you. We put up signs. Can you not read? The place is frozen solid for goodness' sake, could we have made it any clearer?' He sighs, world-weary. 'Of course, we all heard you coming long before you appeared.

You do make such a racket, all that banging. Bloody annoying. Can't hear myself think. And the noise frightens everything for miles around. Admittedly, initially that was a spot of luck for me. It doesn't take much to distract a seal, not exactly towering intellects, more like animated blubber with eyes. Damn tasty though and an excellent bulk food. Sticks to your ribs as my mother used to say.'

He takes my hand and we take to the floor again. I tip my head back and he leans in and rests the side of his face against my neck. His fur is warm and soft as feathers, and I can feel his breath below my ear. Flakes of light fall all around us, scattered from glitter-balls made of sea ice, as we spin and rise and we're out of the water and then above the Earth, which shrinks to a blue-white marble below us. We're out of the atmosphere and the points of light are stars and moons and planets. We twirl around them, further up, faster and faster until the points of light stretch into concentric circles through which we pass as if in a tunnel of light, north, always north towards the centre, the golden point of Polaris.

❯ • ❮

Jules is here. I don't remember him arriving. 'Are you okay?' he asks, gripping my shoulders, a little too hard. 'Talk to me.'

'What time is it?' Everything is jumbled, out of sequence.

He looks at me with an uncertain concern, which annoys me so much I clamp his face between my hands and kiss him on the mouth to get rid of it. It does the trick. His pupils dilate and he kisses me back. We press our bodies together in a close embrace, chest to chest, and set off in a slow tango, counterclockwise around the cabin, which is much bigger than it seemed before. The grey walls recede and glitter with a capillary network of silver veins, like granite shot through with quartz. Our legs brush against each other with every step, the strength and tension in our bodies a mutual resource, a sensuous shared musculature. We pause together, turn as one and stalk towards the bed.

> • <

This is not my body. It can't be. Since when did I have so much skin? It collects in useless folds all over me. It's as heavy as a survival suit but is somehow the opposite of that. The heaviness is inside as well. I am so fucking old. I can feel time on my bones, like limescale. I am wearing striped pyjamas. They smell appalling. There is a bear sitting on the edge of my bed. 'Snowball?'

> • <

'That's it, come on now, wake up. You can do this.'

Someone is bending over me, his ears like jug handles. I would grab on to them if I could find the energy to raise my arms. But maybe not. He seems kind. I open my eyes fully. Ralf, of course it's Ralf.

'How many of these did you take?' He shakes the yellow pill container, making a rattling sound like maracas.

'Only a couple.' I feel fragile. Everything is too loud and too bright. My mouth tastes like something died in it and my voice is a hoarse growl.

'You're talking!' Ralf sounds more pleased about this than me.

'Yeah. Just take them the fuck away, will you. I don't think they agree with me.'

'You sure?' His gaze rests on my wound. 'That's got to hurt.'

'Well, I don't mind it so much.'

'Okay, your decision.' He pockets the pills, looking slightly deflated.

I know he means well. 'I'm sorry, I don't mean to sound ungrateful. Thank you for looking after me.' I grab his hand and give it a squeeze. 'I really appreciate it.'

'Not a problem.' He smiles and blushes a little.

'How's Bjornsen doing?'

Ralf's expression darkens. 'I wish I knew.'

'Still unconscious?'

'In and out. Not making much sense when he's awake. He's either delirious or totally unresponsive. I don't have the equipment on board to monitor his brain waves, so I can't really tell what's going on. He's running a low-grade fever and his pulse is all over the place. If we could just get out of this ice.'

12 DIAGNOSTICS

ARCTIC OCEAN

STILL SUMMER 2025

The open channel is almost completely gone. I can just about make it out from the bridge deck but have to question whether I'm fishing too hard, throwing out a line of wishful thinking. Whenever I look away and back, it's briefly there, like an after-image on my retina, then gone again.

The arctic light plays tricks with distance and perspective. A moving bank of blue-grey fog obscures the horizon to the east. While I watch an enormous berg looms out of it, travelling at speed, seeming to hesitate before rotating and spinning off back into the fog. Closer to the ship the light is hard-edged. Brilliant white ice shapes slide over black water, in complex chess-like movements. I'm sure I've almost figured out the logic of it when a rapid clattering startles me out of my trance.

A black cloud streams towards the ship, growing swiftly in size before splitting at the last minute and flowing around us like a river. Hundreds of madly flapping black guillemots, flying flat out. Matt black bodies, red legs tucked up tight underneath. A stream of blasted embers. There are no cries, only the rattling of wings and the thrashing of air as they plummet headlong into the distance ahead of us. When the last one passes I walk around the deck and scan the distance behind. There's only ice and water and sky and the longer I look the less I can tell one from the other. I see nothing following us, but I can't shake the feeling that something is.

> • <

'No magnetic compass is any use up here because of the weak magnetic field. We can't trust the gyrocompass: it hasn't settled from all the course changes, and without satellite data to correct the deviation we don't know how wrong it is. We've no radar thanks to that damn bear and we can't navigate by the stars because it's daytime, all the time.' Jules is too tired to hide his impatience. 'Look, Isobel, I appreciate your input but, believe me, we've been through all of this already.'

'There must be something. Surely we've at least got an old sextant knocking about?'

'We could take a reading from the sun,' says Ralf, 'but that's only so much use if we're not sure what time it is. We know we're close to the summer solstice since the sun's holding a steady elevation but that also makes it hard to be precise. Everything digital went nuts after the...'

He pauses while we all look anywhere but at each other. We haven't yet come up with a word to describe what happened before the arrival of the bear. The sound, the sensation, the incident, the thing, the whatever that was. No one wants to be the first to use a word like disaster or catastrophe. After all, most of us are still standing and breathing, so surely those words are too strong? I'm not going to be the first to voice the feeling that they're not nearly strong enough.

Ralf clears his throat and continues. 'We've all got different times, nothing agrees.'

I don't wear a wristwatch. Onshore the time is everywhere you look: on phones and computers, tagging every message and post, television and radio stations constantly reciting the numbers, all exhorting us not to waste a second of productive time.

Here we're being reminded of the luxury of being surrounded by such annoyances. But surely someone on board must have an old-fashioned clockwork watch? Apparently not.

My stomach growls. Since the kitchens are now in bear-occupied territory, the food supplies still within our grasp are strictly rationed. Apart from a seemingly inexhaustible supply of salty instant soup powder, mostly what's left is meat. A couple of freezer units full of the stuff. Nothing to go with it in the way of fruit or veg or even rice or bread. Just meat, boiled in a kettle. And not much of that. We don't know how long it'll take to get back to shore so we have to be careful.

We watch as another iceberg overtakes us, ploughing through the ice, turning it over and opening up a furrow of open water in its wake.

'We could tuck in behind one of those bergs and follow it all the way out,' says Ralf. 'It'd make an efficient icebreaker.'

The berg runs up against a thick ridge of ice and a thick slab breaks off the back. The sound of it cracking, like the report from a gun, reaches us and the slab topples into the water with a crash. We watch in silence as the sea sucks it down then spits it back up sending out choppy waves that crackle and splinter through the surrounding floes.

'Then again,' sighs Ralf.

'Hannes has been up in the crow's nest for hours,' says Jules. 'He's probably going snow-blind by now. If you want to help, why don't you go and take over from him for a while?'

There's not much I can do with Proteus still gibbering away, locked in some loop of digital insanity, chewing on its own tail. I eye the crawling green lines of code swarming across the screen like lice and scratch my head. 'Yeah, that might not be such a bad idea.'

I pick my way through the debris from the felled communications mast on deck, the geodesic globe that housed the big radar antenna caved in like a deflated football. Apparently, before they managed to contain him, the bear enjoyed a thorough rampage about the ship and this is only some of the damage he managed to inflict.

Ship design has thankfully moved on since the days of a barrel strapped to the mast. The crow's nest on the *Polar Horizon* is an enclosed metal box, about the size of a public toilet cubicle, with windows on all four sides. It's only big enough for one person so I rap on the glass and stand to the side of the door while Hannes edges out.

He pushes his hood back, his blond hair fluffing out with static around the huge pair of copper-tinted snow goggles he's wearing. He pulls them off and hands them over. 'You'll need these,' he says, squinting as the unfiltered light hits his eyes, ringed with red pressure marks from the rubber seal. He looks tired and distinctly rattled. 'Don't worry too much about the pack-ice, we don't want to go too deep into any big solid areas. It's the bergs you need to look out for. Radio down best estimates on position, direction and speed for anything bigger than a double bed.'

'Right,' I say, 'got it.'

'And don't look too long in the same direction, keep your eyes moving. This light is weird. It can play tricks on you,' he says, blinking repeatedly as if to clear an unwelcome mental image.

'What sort of tricks?'

He shakes his head. 'Maybe I'm just losing it. It's nothing. Forget I said anything.'

'No, really. What?'

'Have you heard of the fata morgana?'

I turn the words over. There's something there but I can't pin it down. 'No, I don't think so.'

'What about the Knights of the Round Table?'

'Sure.'

'That's where the name comes from. It's a kind of optical illusion, like a mirage. People used to think it was witchcraft. Something to do with the angle of the light passing through layers of air at different temperatures.' He pauses, closes his eyes and presses his thumbs into the sockets. 'Yeah, must've been that.'

'What did you see?'

'It's not just me,' Hannes says, defensively. 'It's a well-documented phenomenon. What I saw… Well, it looked like a city. Out there. Towers and spires in a huge bank. Really high, like, I don't know, fifty storeys? All shining in the light and solid. I mean, really there.'

'The whole area's been charted. Even if we're really off course, there's no land, and definitely no floating cities out here.'

'I know, I know. It was just really freaky. It looked so real. But the thing that got to me was…' He looks at me carefully for a moment. 'Okay, this sounds totally nuts but, honestly, it looked like…'

'What?' This hesitancy. It's not like him.

'It looked like it was on fire. Like all the buildings were burning. And then there were these sounds, like wailing or moaning. It was… like I say, it was really freaky.'

'Probably birds.' I try to sound reassuring, as much for my own benefit as his. 'I saw a big flock of them earlier.' I don't mention that they weren't making any sound other than beating the air.

'Yeah, something like that. So, anyway,' he laughs unconvincingly, 'if you see Manhattan in flames, don't worry. It's not there. Try to concentrate on what is there. Yeah. That's your mission.' He gives a mock salute as he climbs backwards down the ladder.

> • <

I shut myself into the tiny space and try to get comfortable. The increased height and length of vision don't reassure. There's no end to the ice – I watch it moving, rising and falling, like the flank of an animal, breathing. Perhaps in other circumstances this would be peaceful, but here and now the breathing is ragged, the animal wounded, cornered and dangerous. Leads open and close far too fast, sheets of ice push up against each other forming new pressure ridges or ride up over each other then collapse into the water under their own weight. I think about Hannes's burning city. How we came up here searching for what we believed to be hidden, but now cannot believe what we find in full view.

The hours pass in a trance. A few bergs prowl close to our heading and I radio the details down, trying to keep us away from the biggest hazards, feeling the slight sway as Jules makes careful course adjustments and the occasional jolt of impact from the smaller dangers we now accept as manageable.

A shape looming at the side window and a sharp knock mean someone has come to relieve me. I'm surprised to see it's Grant. He avoids eye contact when I hand the snow goggles over and give him the brief. I don't mention the fata morgana, reasoning that since I haven't see it myself, I have nothing to report. But a part of me hopes Grant does see it in all its terrifying eeriness and shits his pants. Not very charitable, but there it is.

'Grant. About—'

'Yeah?' He looks at me hopefully, almost meeting my eyes, his gaze hovering somewhere around my left ear.

'Whatever you did, whatever happened or didn't happen with Proteus, we need to work together, okay? We need to get home.'

He nods into his chest and finally meets my gaze. 'Okay.'

'Good. But see when we get there? I'm going to tear your arms off and beat you to death with the soggy ends. Just so's you know.' I turn and climb back down the ladder, leaving him to wonder whether I'm joking or not.

13 PROTOCOLS

ARCTIC OCEAN

2025

I head for Bjornsen's room, one of the larger cabins on deck seven, directly below the bridge. Not that I can do anything to help him, but I feel I should at least drop in. He must be getting hellish bored there on his own, with only Ralf stopping by now and then to take his temperature. I arrive in the short corridor between the two rooms just as Max, who has the other top-spec cabin, is closing one of the doors.

He raises a hand in a fake-friendly greeting. 'Hey there, you!' Max has clearly forgotten my name. 'The captain's still sleeping,' he says, adding, 'ah geese,' just when I think he might not.

I realise it was Bjornsen's room he came out of, not his own. Max has never struck me as a particularly caring type. 'Right. I'll just pop in, all the same.' He steps out of my way as I move towards the door, then pause. Since he's there, I ask, 'Have you managed to contact head office yet?'

He hesitates a split-second too long before replying. 'Ah, no. No luck with that yet. None. Whatsoever.'

'So we're still completely cut off?'

'For the moment, yes.'

He hums tunelessly and shuffles sideways. He couldn't look or sound more shifty if he tried. I remember Grant's insinuations. I hadn't paid them much attention at the time, too preoccupied with feeling furious at him for being an idiot. But maybe he hadn't been simply casting around for someone, anyone, to share the blame. Maybe there was something there.

'Can I try? Might be something in the settings.' I reach out, trying to prompt Max into giving me his mobile.

He stares at my hand and compresses his lips into a line, but makes no move to take the phone out of his pocket.

'Have you tried switching it off and on again?'

I'm partially joking but he looks affronted. 'I've tried everything. Anyway, there's a strict protocol governing use of the mobile. I can't allow anyone to mess around with it.'

Just when I think Max can't be any more of a dick, he surprises me. 'Are you kidding? We're stuck out here, fuck knows where, surrounded by ice, with a critically injured captain, a fucking polar bear occupying deck four, and you're worried about protocol?'

'Well,' he sniffs, 'perhaps if your software had been fit for purpose we wouldn't be in this mess.'

I don't appreciate the slur. There's nothing wrong with Proteus, or at least there wasn't before Grant screwed it up. But I don't want to get into that. I'm not about to tell Max about Grant's little adventure into industrial sabotage. 'Or perhaps if you hadn't forced an unplanned course change. What was that about anyway?'

'Protocol—'

'Fuck protocol.'

'I don't have to listen to this.' He tries to walk away but I block his path. 'You need to calm down,' his tone turns patronising and his top lip curls back as he looks down his skinny nose at me. 'You're getting hysterical. Women really aren't suited to this kind of environment, ah geese.'

I couldn't say whether it was the blatant sexism or the geese, but five seconds later Max is flat on his back in the cabin passageway and I have a knee in the centre of his bony ribcage and my hands around his windpipe. My other knee is pinning his left arm to the deck. His free hand is scrabbling, trying to prise my fingers away, but that's not going to happen.

Well, this is interesting, I think, observing his nostrils flaring, the veins at his temples visible through his thin skin. His mouth opens and his eyes protrude more than usual, becoming bloodshot. He aims some ineffectual flapping punches at my head and body. Spit flecks the side of his mouth.

I'm holding him with no effort whatsoever. He's trying to speak but I'm just watching him, more curious about his efforts than whatever it is he's trying to say. I've hated everything I've ever heard come of out his mouth; I'm not very interested in letting him speak. I wonder at how calm I feel. Wouldn't murderous rage be more the thing? But I don't feel that at all. I feel practical, capable, matter of fact. Part of my mind is already calculating how much Max weighs and how hard it'll be to move his body.

We both blink when a red dot suddenly appears on his cheekbone, rolls across his face and down towards his ear leaving a vivid trail. Another drip falls near his lips and he splutters and spits some more. I realise the blood must be coming from my neck. I forgot about the stitches, again. Max is now arching and twisting like a landed fish. I feel vaguely offended that he seems to be more upset about getting my blood on him than he is about me strangling him to death.

I take one hand off Max's throat and grab his flailing arm by the wrist, relax my grip around his neck sufficiently for him to breathe. He sucks in air and starts to speak. I shake my head and tighten my grip a little again. I'll let him live, but listening to his whiney bullshit I'm not so sure about. His skin is returning to a normal colour and his eyes are less desperate. He stops struggling. I experimentally release the pressure on his neck again, and this time he doesn't try to talk.

'Right, good. Now, perhaps you'd like to clear a few things up for me?'

He twitches his head in an approximation of a nod.

'Who are you working for?'

'Pilgrim—'

I shift more of my weight onto the knee on his chest and lean my face down close to his. 'I'd like you to consider your position here and remind yourself that I am a fully hysterical woman, and as such it is quite possible that my ovaries will compel me to do something rash if I think you're not being a hundred per cent honest with me.'

'I don't know,' he gasps. 'Honest—' He squirms underneath my weight. 'If you'll get off me.'

I eye him warily.

'I swear. I'll tell you what I know.'

I take my hands off and sit cross-legged beside him.

He lies there for a while, making a big deal of breathing, then pushes himself up to a sitting position with his back against the wall before making an even bigger deal of clearing his throat.

'The course change,' I interrupt his little pity play. 'Where did that idea come from? Exactly?'

'I'm just a tiny cog in a big machine. I have no influence.'

I give him a hard stare.

'Okay. The icebreaker. It was all about the icebreaker. I don't know why they want it, and you know what? I don't care. The course deviation was a cover to explain the loss of contact while they increased speed and headed through the ice in the opposite direction. I don't know the exact heading they took. What happened afterwards,' he rolls his eyes, 'your guess is as good as mine. I've no idea. All I needed to know was that we would be able to find our way out without them. There was supposed to be a pre-broken route in the ice. All we had to do was follow it out.'

'That's not what happened.'

'No, it's not. But it should have. It was all planned. Checked and double checked.'

'But Pilgrim supplied the *Koch* in the first place, didn't they? Why would they want to steal their own icebreaker? It doesn't make any sense.'

Max spreads his hands. 'Who knows? Pilgrim is huge, bigger than you think. There are parts of the organisation—'

'What parts?'

'I don't know who they are exactly. It's more like a network. Global. Plenty of room for differences of opinion, I imagine.'

'Sounds like a massive fuck-up waiting to happen.'

'I'm pretty sure none of them envisaged this. Look, I have no idea what's going on. I want to get out of this as badly as you do.'

I don't trust the series of expressions flitting across Max's face and can't decide what parts, if any, of his story I believe, so I stop looking at him. My gaze rests on the door of the cabin opposite. 'How much did Bjornsen know about all this?'

'Nothing. As far as I know. That's what I was trying to find out. I thought perhaps he could shed some light.'

'And?'

'He's not making a lot of sense.' Max rubs at the mark my hands have left on his neck. We sit in silence for a time.

'What I'm not getting is what's in this for you? I mean, how much are they paying you? Do you really need it badly enough to risk your life, to risk all of our lives?'

'It was never supposed to come to that.'

'Amazing how many people say that right before other people get hurt.'

Max looks puzzled. 'Who—'

'You're like children. Never think through the consequences of your actions.'

'I—'

'I mean, fuck's sake, what goes on in your heads? Anything? Anything at all? Or is it really all just wide fucking open space in there?'

Max shrinks against the wall as if he wants to pass through it to a place of safety on the other side.

'Never mind,' I sigh. I'm wasting my breath getting angry. I close my eyes for a couple of seconds and make a partially successful effort to let it go. 'Out of interest, what do you need the money for? Your family been kidnapped by terrorists? Baby brother need a life-saving operation? What?'

'Possum farm.'

'I'm sorry?'

'Back home. Get a nice spot in the country on the South Island. There's a big market for possum wool. It's niche, but growing.'

'Are you for real?'

'Absolutely. Possum, or possum-merino blend, is a high quality product, very durable, outstanding heat retention. And it feels amazing next to the skin, softer than mink. Here,' Max lifts the edge of his jumper revealing some white fabric underneath. 'Feel.'

Half in a daze I reach over and rub the material between my fingers.

'The possum is a major ecological pest in New Zealand. It's been killing native plants and bird life since its introduction in the 1850s. As well as being both luxurious and practical, possum wool is also very much an eco-friendly product. This isn't a joke—'

Once I start laughing, I'm not sure I can stop. There's something scary but liberating about giving this feeling the run of me. I'm not sure how long I would've gone on if it wasn't for the door from the deck opening and Hannes sticking his head in. He glances between us but doesn't stop to ask questions.

'You pair might want to come up and take a look at this,' he says, and disappears again.

14 SYSTEM CRASH

ARCTIC OCEAN

-

The mood on the bridge is as tense as a rocket launch countdown. We hardly breathe; the ice has opened up ahead of us. Great slabs are swinging off to either side like doors opening onto the possibility of freedom. We stand at the threshold, sick with hope, as our future grinds on its hinges.

Ralf punches the air. 'Yes! Come on!' he yells, like his team has just scored.

Hannes slaps Jules on the back, grinning from ear to ear. Jules looks shell-shocked. He meets my eyes and we share a hesitant smile.

The radio crackles and Grant's voice comes through from the crow's nest where he's still on lookout duty. 'Are you guys seeing what I'm seeing?'

Hannes grabs the mike and whoops into it like a wild man, loud enough to clear the wax out of Grant's ears. He throws down the handset and starts hugging anyone in range. I can hear Grant still talking and there's something about his tone, even fuzzed with static, that snags my attention and sounds a warning bell in my chest. I can only catch fragments of what he's saying 'Fast… Out of the way… Impact in five…'

'Hey!' I shout as loud as I can to the room. 'Quiet!'

'Two.'

We're all slammed to the floor as the ship lurches forward. I try to push myself up but am thrown backwards as the deck cants precipitously. Everyone tumbles down the incline, thumping into units and each other, grappling for handholds. The ship's stern pulls sharply to starboard, the bow lowers and the iceberg heaves into view.

It's almost as big as us and its shape weirdly echoes our own with a pointed bow, raised front section and long low back, like it's taking the piss. Having done its work it now glides innocently away as if the resulting chaos has nothing to do with it.

We pick ourselves up. Jules has a split lip, a thin red dribble running down his chin. Hannes is rubbing his shoulder and swearing under his breath. Our bruises will surface soon enough but otherwise we all seem to be more or less intact. Which is more than can be said for the ship.

Jules and Ralf scramble onto the deck and round to stern. When they come back their faces are set and grim. 'The back deck has taken a heavy impact. Someone get down to the engine room. Check everyone's alright, see how bad the damage is.'

'Ah shit. No no no.' Hannes's negatives run into each other and blend into a groan of dismay. But he isn't bemoaning the damage to the ship, he's looking outwards.

The ice is moving again. The wake of the passing berg, or the shifting currents, or a combination of the two has changed the direction of drift.

Jules issues terse orders to the crew in an attempt to manoeuvre the ship back towards the closing exit, but at least one of the rudders is damaged. Grinding and clunking noises rise up from below decks and the engines are labouring. The ship wallows and shimmies and pulls to starboard. Within half an hour we are trapped in a long leaf-shaped lagoon, ice-locked in a sliver of open water, in the pupil of an eye intent on closing.

We kill the engines. If one of the rudders is fouling its propeller, using it might cause more damage. In any case, there is nowhere we can go.

We are taking on water in one of the lower holds, slowly but surely. It has been sealed off from the rest of the ship so we shouldn't sink, which no one even mentions as it would mean acknowledging the possibility. The ice will move again, or someone on shore will start asking questions and another icebreaker will be sent to free us.

Hours pass and stretch, time drifts, and a torpor descends on the crew. There's not much conversation. The initial burst of activity has died down to a punch-drunk slog. We all retreat into ourselves. The isolation of this place, of our predicament, creeps between us. We're each of us alone, hermetically sealed in our skins.

The ice growls and rumbles and cracks its knuckles, readying to crush us. Jules and I stand on the bridge deck taking turns with the binoculars, searching for any hint of an end to the ice. Our eye-shaped pool is one in a series of openings along the length of what looks like a fissure but is in reality a poorly executed meeting of edges, miles long, extending to the horizon before and behind in both directions.

The sun leers down at us from a baby blue sky, flecked with wisps of pastel pink clouds. I breathe through my mouth. Something in the ship's innards has ruptured, releasing the stench of raw sewage that hangs in the air like a curse now that the wind has dropped.

A flurry of movement in one of the gaps of open water catches my eye and I train the binoculars on it, twisting the focus to get a sharper view. A surreal cluster of spikes breaks the surface and churns the water. My mind throws up the absurd possibility of a monstrously huge sea urchin bobbing and rolling just under the surface, but the spikes are crossing and clashing, their angles at odds. I gradually become aware of dark shapes jostling under the spikes and an assortment of sounds drifting back to us. Peculiar squeals and squeaks intermingle with sudden blasts of air. I pass Jules the binoculars.

'Narwals,' he says after a few moments.

'What are they doing?'

'Dying, probably. Depends whether the ice moves again. This happens, even under normal conditions. Leads open and close in the ice. Sometimes animals become trapped too far from open water. It's called a *savssat*. A gift to hunters, in the right place and time.'

We stand there for a while listening as the high-pitched sounds of distress provide a counterpoint to the deep grinding of the ice. It's now only thirty feet away on either side of the ship and closing.

'This ship is strong enough to withstand ice pressure, isn't it? If it closes in on us completely?'

'Normally, yes. But with these currents,' Jules gives a lacklustre version of one of his Gallic shrugs, 'with the ice moving so unpredictably, and with the damage we've already sustained, nothing is certain.'

> • <

The electrics give out. A short in the system caused by the water we're taking on. No electricity means no heating or below decks lighting, leaving us to negotiate the darkened corridors with torches. The bear, at least, will be more comfortable with the drop in temperature. Frost blooms throughout the ship's interior, coating everything in a nap of crisp sparkling white.

With no power, the remaining meat in the freezers can't be cooked anymore. I haven't brought myself to eat any of it yet, but most of the others have, gnawing and sucking at frozen chunks, their lips and teeth dark with blood as the meat softens.

The battle with the rising water in the hold still goes on, but we are reduced to a rota of manual bailing out after losing the electric pumps. It's becoming clear we're not winning. Slowly, slowly, the ship is beginning to list in the water.

We are sinking.

The elements are competing to see which of them can finish us first, the ice or the water.

> • <

With no noise from acoustic guns or engines, there's only the ice and the animals. The narwhals were only the start of it. More have followed. Each in their own *savssat*, singing their own songs of death, there's whale, seal, walrus. Everything that could live here is dying. At the outer limits of my hearing another sound makes the hairs on the back of my neck rise reflexively. It must be some freak acoustic effect caused by the wavelengths of the combined animal cries refracting through the ice, but it sounds like a pack of wolves. Howling.

Even in my cabin I can hear that terrible music through the walls. Still wearing my coat and hat, I wrap myself in blankets and concentrate on writing. No one will ever read this account but I keep making entries anyway.

Sometimes I imagine I can hear a bassline of heavy footfalls under the higher notes of the dying animals. The trapped bear on the deck above, pacing back and forth. Paw prints in ice. The bear stops directly overhead where I lie on my side, cradling these pages. The click and scrape of claws so close through the ceiling as he lies down and curls on his side to sleep. His shape mirroring mine. My breath echoing his. Our dreams drifting down like snow and settling in stratified layers.

PART FOUR

VIII

I barely touch the ground. Adrenalin propels me along the corridors, and I'm hardly aware of the turns I take or even my own footsteps. Somehow I find my way to the library.

The atmosphere blankets itself around my shoulders as soon as I enter, calming, consoling. I fight against the effect. I don't want to be lulled once again into passivity. But I do need to calm down, at least a little. My heart is battering against my ribs and I doubt I can string a coherent sentence together, let alone ask Alex the right questions to figure out what's going on. The bear, the records of the *Polar Horizon* crew, my journal. How do they fit together? Does he even know?

I force myself to pause, sit on a step of one of the tall, wheeled ladders and try to slow my thoughts. I focus on the memory of the bear's breath, slow my own until it matches, the two rhythms interlocking. The bear breathes in, I breathe out.

> • <

In the short leg of the library's L-shape, Alex and Clyde are seated with two other men, one with a ponytail, one with a carefully trimmed moustache, both in worn black T-shirts. Probably researchers. All four are intent on some apparatus on the table between them. Alex glances up as I approach.

'We need to—' I start.

He raises a finger, a polite appeal for silence, then smiles and gestures for me to sit.

I stand behind an empty chair. 'Look. I—'

'Please,' he says.

'But this—'

'This won't take long.' He turns his attention back to the table.

I sit, feeling about six years old, interrupting the grown-ups, furious with myself for going along with it but reasoning that snapping that imperious finger, while certainly getting Alex's attention, might not make him very forthcoming. The others hardly register my presence. I fold my arms. I can wait, for a while.

I look more closely at the object on the table. Some sort of game. A circular chequered board is held in a bracket, like on an old-fashioned cartographic globe. Within the bracket are two copper hoops etched with symbols and scales – phases of the moon, others I don't immediately recognise. Pieces are arranged on both sides of the board. Must be magnetic. One set of squares are dark, the iridescent blue-green of oil on water, the other a bright red-yellow like the face of the sun. Set in the centre is a yellowish white four-pointed star.

Clyde makes a tentative humming noise, reaches out one of his long hands and moves a piece from one side of the board to the other, then turns a small brass wheel which pivots the board. As it turns, the squares also move, sliding around each other, taking their pieces with them: wolf, owl, walrus, seal, fox, all carved from a pale bone-like material. One set is a cream colour, the other dark with a reddish brown stain gathered in the grooves. Each one bears a skeleton carved in relief on its back.

Whenever I think I understand the rules of the game someone turns the wheel to set all the moving parts in motion and I'm lost again. The two researchers take notes. There are a few human-like figures in amongst the animals, carved in the same style and from the same material. One looks as though it's praying, another dancing.

I've watched long enough. I wait until the board is static, then reach in and lift one piece out. All eyes turn towards me at once. I turn the figure over in my hand. Apart from the material it's carved from, and the addition of a circular base allowing it to stand upright, the bear looks exactly like the one Jules gave me on the *Polar Horizon*. Focused, fluid, ready to fly.

Is this all a game to them? Arsing around with their theories and experiments, calling it 'research'. Northolt, the whole facility, nothing more than a toy: the corridors that reconfigure themselves overnight, revealing new puzzles and new pieces, all of it part of a larger apparatus, taking in Avie and beyond. All those high places where life scrambles desperately upwards, the sunken ones cluttered with the bones of the drowned. Everything spinning in decaying orbits while this lot study the wreckage, count the bodies and take notes.

I push down on a wave of vertigo and pull my thoughts back in, clenching my fist around the carved figure. 'I think it's time I had some answers.'

The circle of faces, their blank white detachment, repels me. But what makes my own passivity up to this point any more excusable? Right now it feels uncomfortably like collusion.

'Which questions, specifically, would you like answers to?' Clyde sounds amused.

'All of them. I want to know the plan. If you have one. I've gone along with everything up until now. I just assumed you knew what you were doing. But do you? What exactly are you trying to do? Are you just,' I look at the apparatus on the table, 'playing?'

The men exchange glances. 'Don't be silly,' says the arsehole with the ponytail. 'As Einstein said, "God doesn't play dice with the universe".'

I eye him coldly. 'God help us all if it turns out God is you.'

Ponytail's smirk curdles.

'Are you going to tell me what's going on or not?'

'We were wondering when you'd ask,' says Clyde.

That smug look really doesn't suit him. I resist the urge to remove it, maybe along with some of his teeth.

'You've been here long enough.' He smiles at me blandly. 'Your natural curiosity must've been blunted, I guess.'

That stings. 'It's not easy out there. Curiosity isn't always useful.'

'Just doing what you're told?'

'It's not like that. It's just... Trying to stay alive.'

Alex intervenes. 'Of course. Please, don't take Clyde's comments personally. He can be incredibly tactless.' He gives Clyde an exasperated look.

The note-taker with the pedantic moustache is scribbling on his pad, turning his head back and forth between us, spectating. Alex clears his throat. 'You two probably have work to be getting on with.'

The two men look disappointed but gather their things and leave the table, heading obediently for the exit. When the door clicks closed, Alex turns to me again.

'We didn't give you the whole picture initially because, firstly, to most people it sounds highly improbable. We didn't want to scare you off. Secondly, even if you'd still agreed to take part, too much knowledge about the hoped-for outcome could have affected the results.'

'A little knowledge being a dangerous—'

'Like in the uncertainty principle,' Alex cuts Clyde off, 'the act of observation affects the result. Could even be said to cause it. We needed to preserve your uncertainty. And, thirdly,' he pauses, staring into the mechanism of the game, 'we don't yet have the full picture ourselves.' He strokes one of the copper hoops sending it gliding in an arc. It makes a soft whispering noise as it passes over its twin. 'Understanding comes in stages, not all at once. Sometimes it takes great leaps but mostly it's a process of inching forwards, keeping an open mind, and waiting.'

An open mind? I think of the bear, the crown of electrodes and twisted wires bolted into his shaved skull. 'Where does the bear fit into all of this?'

'Shall we go to the lab?' Clyde asks Alex, who nods in response.

> • <

The route is much shorter than I remember. Is it possible that Northolt's corridors really move? Or maybe Clyde and

Alex are following a more direct route than the one my own wandering took me in.

Before long we come to the place where that deep sea-green light seeps around the edges of the door. Clyde ushers us in. Not being alone this time doesn't prevent my body from releasing a conflicting cocktail of chemical and emotional reactions. Topmost is a basic, primal fear at being in close quarters with a large carnivore, no matter how incapacitated, but under that is a strange sort of horrified sympathy. An ache. The two responses jostle for position, churning up my already messy internal landscape.

The bear's glass coffin – I find it hard to think of it in any other way – is there, a solid fact, not, as I'd begun to fear, a figment of my imagination or some lurid detail from a dream. Clyde flicks a switch bringing on the overhead lights, which burn away the shadows but lie flatly over the domed glass, obscuring the occupant completely. He pulls a chair up to one of the terminals and begins typing rapid-fire on the keyboard. A screen flickers into life with a scrolling command line interface, apparently loading a program. Green lines of code flow upwards, the right-hand edge looking like a ragged coastline on a map, complete with headlands and bays. The shape of it reminds me of the initial boot-up routine of the Proteus system. Cold washes around me in waves. Twenty years. I've spent twenty years drifting on the dark ocean between those two shores.

'These are some of the readouts we've been collecting from you,' says Clyde, pulling a sheaf of papers from a file and handing them to me.

I leaf through the familiar images of lines and shaded bands like layers of sedimentary rock which Clyde claims represent the laying down of memory. What are my results doing in the bear's lab anyway?

'And these are what we've collected from Snowball.'

'Snowball?' My mind jolts. The sudden trespass into my childhood. I never gave them permission to go rifling through my private memories. My heart seems to be beating in my throat. I swallow it down, telling myself it's only a coincidence, not wanting to show I'm shaken. 'Did you say Snowball?'

Clyde grins. 'Some of us felt the bear should have a name. Ursus Maritimus seemed a bit formal and constantly referring to him as the bear seemed, well, cold.' Clyde's breath steams in the air as he speaks. 'And given the world's descent into what some might call hell…'

I don't take the bait.

'Anyway, if you look at these readings, you'll see that the temporal component is entirely absent.'

I take the pages. There are the same lines and bands in shades of grey but instead of being compressed in layers on top of each other they swirl around the page in loops and circles. One section looks like eddying water, another like smoke, a few concentric circles are reminiscent of the growth rings in a felled tree. The notation under the images means nothing to me. The more I look at the readouts, the more patterns and associations I see, entirely failing to bring into focus the absence Clyde seems to think is visible.

'Meaning?'

'Meaning, in animals, or at least in this animal, there is no such thing as memory because there is no construction of linear time. Everything is now. Everything that happened, is happening, will happen, is always happening. It's fascinating, don't you think?'

I nod, but it's a reflex.

'Obviously, with Snowball, we don't have the benefit of verbal communication and, as far as we know, he has never kept a journal.' Clyde gives a little self-indulgent chuckle. 'So, to start with, we had to build up a pattern we could analyse. Let me show you something.'

Clyde gets up from his terminal and slides open a deep drawer, containing a rack of white plastic trays. Thick vapour spills out and slinks to the floor in slow curls. He pulls out the top tray and rummages through a collection of labelled freezer bags, eventually selecting one that contains something dark and bloody.

'Seal,' he says. 'Of course, we can't smell anything when it's frozen solid like this, but Snowball here has a far superior olfactory system. Watch. This is so cool.'

He goes to the head of the glass coffin, beckoning me to follow, which I reluctantly do, and presses a button under the table. There's a hiss of compressed air as a portion of the enclosure slides back, just enough to expose the bear's muzzle. Clyde takes hold of the breathing tube with both hands and pulls it out. It makes a wet sucking noise and the bear's teeth clack together. 'It's fine,' he says, 'he can breathe without ventilation for short periods.' He places the frozen lump of seal meat directly in front of the black nose. Nothing happens. He goes back to his terminal and rattles at the keyboard. A series of lights twinkle in a complicated Morse over the bear's skull. A nostril twitches. Or did I imagine it? Both nostrils flare wide, sucking in air. I take a step back.

'Don't worry. It's perfectly safe,' says Clyde.

I stay where I am. Perfectly safe my arse.

A snort of breath shoots two dragonish jets of steam into the room. I tilt my head for a better view without moving any closer. A ripple runs along the bear's black lips and they start to shine with moisture. A well of viscous drool collects in his lower jaw, then flows between his teeth to gather in a puddle under his chin.

I swallow, suddenly aware of too much saliva in my own mouth, slimed around my gums and teeth, coating my tongue. It feels thick and cold and tastes foul. I can't stand to watch anymore. 'Stop!' I shout. 'Stop it.' I feel sick.

Clyde looks at me quizzically but removes the meat from the enclosure, takes a handful of paper towels and mops up the puddle of drool, roughly pushing the bear's jaw from side to side as he does so.

A printer on the other side of the room clicks into life and begins spouting paper. Clyde douses his hands in sanitiser and rubs them together. I think about washing my mouth out with the stuff. What purpose could possibly be served by that twisted Pavlov shit?

'If you look at the readings you can see the response here.' Clyde points to a jagged spike among a forest of lines. 'We've collected hundreds of stimulus-response readings and—'

'How?' I stare at him. 'How many times have you done that?'

'Oh, lots.' He looks pleased with himself. 'We've got all the different species of arctic seal. Ringed, bearded, harp, hooded and ribbon. We also have walrus, beluga whale, that was a tricky one to source, shellfish, fish. Then there's the possible land-based food sources, muskox, reindeer, small rodents, waterfowl, eggs, kelp, berries. And that's just the hunger response. There are plenty of others. We provide the stimulus, as you've just seen, and record the result. If we collate and compare—'

'What sort of stimulus?'

'Well, hunger you've just seen. Then there's pain. Obviously. Sexual arousal. That's a complicated area for Snowball. Although to all intents and purposes he is male, having the overall physical bulk and being in possession of testicles and a penis, he also has a vulva and what appears to be a rudimentary vagina. But lacks the internal plumbing. Uterus, ovaries, fallopian tubes, all that lady business.' Clyde's gaze drops to my midsection. 'Ha! Of course, you'd know all about—'

I hold up a hand to silence him. 'Moving on,' I say.

'One response we've had particular trouble with is fear. The polar bear has no natural predators. We tried the scent of another mature male but that stimulated aggression more than fear. We think.' He scratches his head. 'Anyway, we've built up a pretty comprehensive model which has allowed us access to something far more interesting. We've had some extremely encouraging results with psilocybin.'

'So as well as doing all this hunger, sex, pain and fear stuff, you're simultaneously pumping his brain full of hallucinogenic mushrooms?' I gaze at the bear and feel a fresh surge of pity. What must it be like inside that head?

'Astonishing stuff,' says Clyde, 'lights up the brain like a Christmas tree!' He grins at me, then sighs when I fail to mirror his enthusiasm.

My mind is whirling and I'm glad of the silence so I can try to put my thoughts in some kind of order, but it's hard to know where to start. Alex comes and sits next to me. He pulls his chair close so our knees are almost touching.

'I know it seems barbaric,' he says quietly. There's genuine regret in his voice. 'But what we're trying to do is forge a connection. One that has never been made before. If we succeed, it could change everything.'

'The end justifies the means,' I say, my eyes on the bear's coffin, not intending Alex to take it as a serious question.

'Yes,' he replies immediately. 'Without a doubt.' It's clear he absolutely believes what he's saying. 'Our conjecture—'

'Your conjecture,' Clyde interrupts from the other side of the room, without turning around to look at us. 'Don't lump me in with your batshit ideas. I'm a scientist. A proper one. With a white coat and everything.'

'My conjecture,' Alex continues, ignoring Clyde, 'is that the animal mind, in both its conscious and unconscious states, is capable of a kind of time travel.' He closes his eyes against a derisory snort from Clyde's direction then goes on. 'A way of handling time, navigating through it, that the human mind, with all its over-engineering, can only achieve in dreams. If we can find a way to take the temporal blueprint we've been able to gather from your sessions and filter it, desequence it, through the model of Snowball's mind, then we can do what humans have always dreamed of being able to do, what we now must do. We can change the past.'

At this, Clyde makes no comment.

> • <

Back in my room, I lie on my bed and study the figure of the bear. I found it in my pocket when I returned from the lab, the carved bone warm from my body heat. The shape of it, the lines catching the exact point of flight, the moment between the impulse and the act.

I remember reading that in everything that flies, machine or animal, flight is an emergent property. Nuts, bolts, feathers, bones – none of them can fly on their own. But put them together in the right way...

I run the pads of my fingers over the bear's raised skeleton and try to imagine what I know, what I've been told and what I saw in the lab fitting together like that.

IX

It takes a long time, and it often feels like I'm going the wrong way, doubling back on myself, looping in meaningless circles. Then, around one more corner when I've almost given up, there it is. The way out. A flat panel set into an ancient stone wall, the flipside of the fireplace in the ramshackle bothy leading out of the main Northolt complex, and from there the outside world. The real, present world.

The card reader I used, or tried to, on the way in is inaccessible on the other side. I scan the walls for a lock or control mechanism and find a keypad tucked into a gap in the brickwork. I try a few predictable patterns, then move on to more specific guesses – the first six digits of pi, the date the *Polar Horizon* sailed from Svalbard – but soon come to stabbing in random sequences. I could keep going for years and be no closer to finding the right combination. I don't even know how many digits are needed. I kick the wall in frustration and a fist-sized lump of stone comes loose and clunks to the floor. Sometimes brute force is the only way. I pick up the stone and bring it down hard on the keypad. Sparks fizz from it and the door panel scrapes up a few feet then stops. I scramble through the narrow opening underneath, thanking Jules for the memory.

The stone fireplace beyond the panel hasn't slid back the whole way either but I wriggle sideways into the gap, trying not to think, as my tip of my nose brushes the rough stone, what would happen if it closed before I got clear.

Safely through, I peer around the small bothy, breathing in the mixture of old stone, earth and wet wood. There's a dark shape hunched against the wall near the door. I stay very still while my eyes adjust to the darkness. Whatever it is, it's covered in dustsheets. I pull at the heavy, dirty material. A glint of chrome, a handlebar. My bike. Someone must've brought it in from where I left it standing in the clearing. I drag the rest of the dustsheet off and wheel the bike out of the door.

The sky is clear, the first faint suggestion of morning lightening the sky to the east. I check the battery charge: nearly flat. The way back to Avie from here is almost all downhill. I can coast for most of it, and in any case I'm not leaving my bike behind. I close my eyes, offer up a silent prayer to the void, and press the ignition button. There's an excruciating second of nothing but then my heart lifts on the rising hum of the engine coming to life.

The trees whip around in mute alarm. Real trees or reflections? It doesn't matter. I accelerate across the clearing, towards the access road. Can I retrace the route without the satnav that got me here? Will anyone try to follow me? Take me back against my will? If I make it back to Avie, I've no way of knowing what'll be waiting for me there. It's unlikely to be good.

I'm getting ahead of myself. For now, neither the point of departure or arrival matters. All that matters is to be in motion.

I plunge between the trees, shift my weight to one side, drop my knee on the other and lean the bike into the first bend. Dirt and stones spray in a high arc from my back wheel.

X

I can smell the camp and the festering town at its core before I see them, a sulphurous miasma stretching its stinking tentacles up into the treeline. Everything is the same, but worse. Dirtier, smellier, more run down, more hopeless. I pass through the layer of industrial units and office buildings. More of them are now derelict, perimeter fences torn down and flattened, windows smashed, the flickering glow of campfires from inside.

The main camp has grown since I passed through it on the way up. I sink into the yellowish fog, pockmarked with weakly burning lights. There are more rickety shelters, cobbled together from whatever materials are available: salvaged wood, sheets of corrugated iron, flapping sides of canvas and plastic. Muted sounds of human occupation swirl in the vapour: a baby crying, voices raised, someone singing drunkenly, a barking dog abruptly silenced.

In the old centre, the stench is excruciating. I've lost my immunity to it but I know if I stay even a day or two my mind will filter it out again. The thought irritates me. What if I want to keep smelling it? What if I don't want to forget how bad it is?

I steer around a pile of rotting timbers in the street, the debris of collapse from one of the many improvised loft extensions that sprouted over the rooftops in recent years. Scraps of humanity are caught between the splinters. A rag of floral cloth, a wad of mushy paper that might once have been a book, a pink plastic comb with missing teeth.

My chances of finding somewhere safe to stay are slim to skeletal. Brodrick will have long since let my old room to someone else, or subdivided it and doubled his income. I might find a corner in one of the warehouses on the east side of town but even those unsafe spaces are usually stacked to the rafters with people with nowhere else to go. Perhaps I'll be able to scavenge some pieces of tarp and make myself a shelter. Or, I decide, picking over my options, fuck all that for a game of soldiers.

I brake hard, dig my boot heel into the cracked tarmac, haul the bike round in a U-turn and take the sharp left that leads up to Lachlan's. I still have some credit there and a sudden strong desire to reconfigure the contents of my head. There's far too much junk in there, big ugly things that I didn't even put there intentionally myself. I want to break them down, smash it all up, throw the pieces out the window, set fire to what's left.

I bypass the car park. Leaving anything there is as good as hanging a sign on it saying 'steal me'. I bump over the rough ground to the back of the building and slide in behind the bins where I chain the bike through both wheels and the frame to a set of railings.

Inside is quiet, some low mumbly music playing, the click of pool balls from the table in the side room, muted conversations and half-hearted laughter from a few groups scattered around the main space. Maisie is behind the bar. She raises her eyebrows when I walk in, but reaches for a glass and fills it before I reach her. I nod thanks and knock it back. The raw burn of it rips down my throat and brings hot stinging tears to my eyes. Jesus fucking God, it's terrible stuff. I've missed it so much. I gesture for a refill. Maisie pours but keep her eyes on me.

'What?'

She reaches over, puts a gnarled hand under my chin and has a good long look at my face, rubs a strand of my hair between her fingertips. 'Where've you been then?' She grabs my shoulder and squeezes. 'You look different.' Her fingers dig into the flesh on my upper arm. 'All clean and healthy looking.' I laugh at that, long enough and hollow enough for Maisie to leave off prying. She sighs, shakes her head, picks up the broom leaning against the wall and goes back to attacking the dusty floorboards. I take my glass, and the bottle, and find a table in a shadowy corner.

> • <

The television is still hanging lopsided, the Public Herald still showing old reruns of reality shows, which are now a peculiar form of fantasy, so far removed are they from any reality currently experienced. At intervals the familiar letters PHUK spin onto the screen one by one to unite in a little twinkle of stardust.

I ignore the screen and concentrate on drinking. It's not working. I take another gulp and wait. Nothing. Could Maisie be watering the gin down? It tastes the same way it always did: petrol mixed with raw alcohol and a dash of pine toilet cleaner. But the effect is missing. I need that familiar door to open, that loosening warmth to expand through my brain, softening the edges, gradually liquefying whatever's bothering me, but fuck all is happening. The door remains closed. I stare into the glass, as if the drink itself can offer an explanation, or an apology. We were close, spent years together, doesn't that count for anything? I need something I can rely on and this should be it. How can it abandon me like this? And now, when I need it most. The bastard.

The liquid flickers, orange and red splinters of light shimmer from the surface and climb the edge of the glass. I close my eyes for a couple of seconds then look up and realise it's only a reflection from the TV screen.

PHUK still broadcast what they laughingly call 'news' programmes between the dross of reruns. There's no way of knowing if the news is current or even remotely factual. The stories always have a spin on them in any case. When the boreal forests burned a year ago, in a great conflagration that scorched across North America and Siberia, they spun that into a good news story. The official version had it that nature was somehow working to get things back in balance, that the burning would replenish the soil, promote new growth, ultimately bring the water levels down. Some people even believed it, unwilling or unable to face the alternative.

Because even the news programmes are rerun at intervals,

weeks or months apart, I assume the flames filling the screen are an old programme. I stare glassily at the sheets of flame and try another shot of gin. Still nothing. Nada. Zilch. This sucks balls. Has all that messing around in my head they did in Northolt somehow removed my ability to get shit-faced?

The television cuts to a wide-angle shot and pulls back. Above the tops of the flames are towers, not treetops – blackened posts of twisted metal and glass ringed in smoke and fire, their bases disappearing into water.

'Can you turn the sound up?'

Maisie, wiping down tables nearby, doesn't look up. 'Nah, speaker's still bust.'

'Where is that anyway?'

She straightens up, her back giving an audible crack. 'You haven't heard?'

I shake my head.

Maisie glances at the screen. 'That's Canary Wharf. Old news. It burned for a week solid. They said there was no one in it, been out of use for years. But I dunno about that. Electrical fault started it apparently, winds spread it. Nothing to worry about, they said. But don't they always?'

I lift the bottle and glass for her as she bends to wipe my table, working the wet cloth with a circular motion, laying down a shining pattern of overlapping scales across the dark wood.

'Even they can't expect people to swallow that,' she says.

'What?'

'The coincidence. So many different places all over the world, all of a sudden, all having trouble with electrics that've been cut off for years.'

I've not heard about any of this. I feel a twinge of sadness at how little this further disintegration surprises me. 'What other places?'

'Well, I heard the Azerbaijan Tower went first, along with everything else on the Khazar Islands, but who knows? The Burj Kahlifa went up like a roman candle, the Shanghai Towers, Moscow City, Manhattan of course. They say the One World Trade Centre is still burning. 'Course, they don't show everything on our very own Public Herald, but word gets around. Always does in the end. You want another one of those?' Maisie's looking at the bottle on my table, which I'm amazed to see is almost empty. It wasn't full to start with but that's still way too much alcohol in too short a time. Or it would be if it was having any effect whatsoever.

'Yeah, go on,' I say, biting back a comment about maybe bringing me the un-watered-down version this time. Maisie can be quick to take offense, and quicker to act on it. And given that I can't think of anywhere else I want to be other than her bar, I really don't want to piss her off. Plus I'm kind of hoping she might let me sleep here tonight.

I watch the flames rage across the lopsided screen, the charred sticks of skyscrapers like guttering black candles. What's left of the former world having a deathday party. Make a wish and blow.

Where have I seen this picture before? There's something about the image. Is it something I've seen with my own eyes or did I dream it, or read about it? Is it the idea of it, of tall buildings rising from water, engulfed by flames, that calls out to a matching image already stored somewhere in the recesses of my head? Like that memory game of pairing up picture cards. I used to be good at that.

I open the new bottle Maisie left without comment on my table, pour a couple of fingers and knock it back.

If I was blowing the candles out on the world's birthday cake, what would I wish for? If wishing wasn't the most futile and childish thing I could do, I could wish the world back to another time, before it all went to shit. But what time would I pick? Before the breakup of the ice and everything that followed, or further back to when the North was still an impenetrable mystery, or further still to before humanity decided mysteries were there to be solved, exterminated, the last of them hunted past the point of extinction. Or to before we burned the first tree, putting our warmth above its life. Before we got so hungry.

There's no single point that would guarantee the whole mess wouldn't happen all over again anyway. Wind the hands of a clock back, let them go and they'll eventually catch you. Doesn't matter how fast you run. I could wish for a different kind of time. I take another drink. I wish I didn't care.

> • <

When I open my eyes I'm looking at a field of flowers. Against a jade background, garish multicoloured daisies, tiny pulsating suns and stars, open and close like eyes and every time one opens there's the sound of something breaking and each small sound adds to the deafening song of destruction as the world shatters.

'Izzy? You awake?'

The shape of someone's head and shoulders partially blocks out the flowers and reduces their volume. My immense gratitude for this act of mercy somehow comes out as, 'Ngaah'.

The shape moves away. I groan, roll onto my side and turn my head into the pillow. Everything hurts. Every part of my body is trying to get away from every other part. My muscles twist and cramp. I squirm and shudder like a salted slug.

'I hope it was worth it,' says a voice that sounds familiar but that I can't even attempt to place right now.

> • <

Time passes. Universes expand and contract. Flowers open and close. Worlds flourish and wither. Perhaps they do neither, or both at the same time. Then there's that same voice again. 'Here, drink this if you can. It'll help.'

I open my eyes a crack and see a chipped enamel mug steaming on an upturned plastic beer crate. The tea is bitter and scalds my throat on the way down but I don't mind that.

'Better?'

I look up, the white noise in my head beginning to clear. Where the fuck am I anyway? I sort through the jumbled images in my mind. The last thing I remember is sitting in Lachlan's, watching everything burn, drinking. Drinking a lot. And it not working.

My host is humming and busying himself over a camping stove set up in the middle of some kind of shelter. A framework of timber and metal, blankets and sleeping bags stretched out and nailed to walls and ceiling, bubble wrap and plastic sheeting visible in the gaps. Pinned directly above the bed is a blanket patterned with flowers so luminously bright they look radioactive. I'm sitting on a low cot-like bed made from wooden pallets. Some scraps of mismatched lino are laid over a flattened dirt floor. The figure turns and smiles.

'Grant? What the fuck?'

'Lovely to see you too,' he says and hands me a plastic bowl filled with some kind of soup. 'It's okay, I'm not trying to poison you. You had a good enough try at that yourself last night. If you can survive that, you can survive my cooking.'

'But how—'

'On you go,' he gestures for me to drink up. 'Found you under the pool table at Lachlan's last night. Out cold. Maisie was not best pleased. Said you went on a mission, something about making a map of the stars with pool balls, then started a fight when nobody wanted to dance with you. Cracked some poor guy over the head with a pool cue just before you passed out.'

I remember none of this. I chew a lump of something unidentifiable and swallow. Maisie will get over it, she's dealt with far worse. 'Was the guy okay?'

'Don't worry about him. To be fair, he was a total dick. You'd probably have done the same thing sober. And if you hadn't, someone else would.'

'I was sober.'

Grant laughs. 'Izzy, you drank a bottle and a half of Maisie's gin. It's a wonder you're still alive. You definitely weren't sober.'

He's probably right but I can't remember anything between feeling extremely annoyed that I wasn't drunk and then waking up here. It's not as if I've never blacked out before. But usually there's the fun part before that happens. Some memory of feeling expansive and uninhibited, or even at least the cringe of suddenly remembering some incriminating detail of whatever actions this feeling might've led to. This time there's nothing. I feel cheated.

We sit in silence and finish our soup. Grant takes the bowls outside and there's the sound of splashing water from a standpipe then his voice raised in greeting. A woman's answering voice, laughter, the babble of a young child. Further off, the whump of a football and a scuffle of small feet running. I stand up carefully and stretch. I don't feel half bad now. Grant is still smiling when he lifts the flap of heavy plastic sheeting that stands in for a door and comes back in.

'I should go and get my bike.'

'It'll be safe enough where it is for now.'

'I don't want to put you out. Thanks for the soup and everything but I should get going.'

'Don't be daft. Sit down. Relax. Or are you late for some important meeting?'

'Well, no I suppose.' Truth is I have nowhere else to go and no idea what I'm going to do when I get there. This itch to be moving is probably a way to avoid thinking about that too much. I sit back down on the edge of the cot bed. The relaxing part is going to be more difficult.

'What happened to the job then?'

'Job?'

'Northolt. You took the contract right?'

Job. Contract.

My time at Northolt went so far beyond those words and the sane, ordered world they imply, that they seem incongruous now. Ballet pumps on a polar bear. I wonder how much Grant knows about what they're doing up there. He was part of their work too, albeit an unsuccessful part. Now I've left, will I also be included in that category? Just another write-off, a botched experiment. Alex would probably say something unhelpful about failure being more valuable than success. For the first time since I woke up I really focus on Grant. He's shaved his hair.

He sees me looking, runs a hand over the stubble and grins ruefully. 'Lice. What can you do?'

'Suits you,' I lie, resisting a powerful urge to scratch my head. When he'd leant forward I'd seen something. 'Looks like grey suede. Give's a feel.' I reach out and he obligingly tips his head forwards again. I wasn't imagining things. There are three perfectly round bald areas, each a little bigger than a cigarette burn, at the back and sides of his head. The skin within the circles is pink, uneven scar tissue. An image of Snowball's shaved cranium, his crown of electrodes appears in my mind. I touch one of Grant's scars, cold pins and needles prickling across my own scalp.

Realising I'm not just examining his haircut, Grant sits back, evidently catching the look of shock on my face. 'They didn't make me do anything I didn't fully agree to up front,' he says. 'The scars look worse than they are. It wasn't such a big deal at the time. Didn't even hurt.'

'But they… I mean, how could you let them?'

Grant laughs. 'Honestly, Izzy, it was fine. I got paid, not to mention a few months' board and lodging out of the deal. And you've got to admit, it's pretty cushy up there.'

I shrug grudging assent.

'But I would've done it anyway.'

'Seriously?'

'Yeah. Seriously. I don't know how much they told you—'

The door flap bursts open and a caped bowling ball rolls into the shelter and throws itself at Grant.

'Well, if it isn't Captain Chaos,' says Grant, lifting the child up onto his knee. The boy pushes his scuffed swimming goggles up to the top of his head and stares at me with serious blue-grey eyes.

'This is my friend, Izzy,' says Grant. 'She's come for a visit.'

Captain Chaos jumps down from Grant's knee, strides over and prods me surprisingly hard in the arm. Is he checking I'm real? I poke him back, just as hard, and he considers this for a moment then breaks out a gap-toothed smile. He's small and wiry with dirty blond hair, patchy like scythed corn. An ancient lime green minimo is strapped to his wrist, the inch-square screen lifeless. We trade a couple more wordless pokes and pinches before he tears off out of the shelter again.

'So, Izzy,' says Grant, laughing, 'what do you want to be when you grow up?'

My face flushes. I'd always thought of Grant as the childish one. I rub my arm and make a face. 'That'll bruise.'

'He's a good kid. Lost his folks a couple of years ago but he's doing okay. The older kids mostly look out for the younger ones. Well, we all look out for each other. Have to, really.'

I don't know what to say to that. The silence stretches out between us.

'Will you stay for a while?'

The idea appeals but it also feels like a distraction. The sense of having forgotten something important I should be doing instead buzzes around my head like a trapped insect.

'I'm not sure, I—'

'Stay. A few days. Get your strength back. We don't need to talk right now.'

I'm surprised by how relieved I feel to hear Grant say this. I thought I wanted to know everything, to understand it all. But do I really? I'm no longer certain of anything. 'Okay.' I heave a sigh. 'Thanks.'

'Great. Now,' Grant stands and claps his hands together, 'no offense, but you smell like a pickled shite. Come on, I'll show you where you can get a wash.'

XI

The communal howff, a five-minute walk through a maze of ramshackle homes, is much bigger than Grant's shelter and more permanent looking. The bones of it are tree trunks and hefty branches, sanded smooth and cleverly locked together and there's a proper planked floor inside. A pan is bubbling away on a pot-bellied stove sending aromatic puffs of steam swirling upwards towards a vent in the ceiling. There are people of all ages, a dozen or more, most of them busy either preparing food or laying the table. A few curious glances come my way but no one asks questions. Something within me starts to relax and uncurl in response.

'Who's been sleeping in my bed?'

The smallest children squeal and giggle as Grant raises his arms and lumbers, stiff-limbed and growling, after Captain Chaos and a couple of others. They scramble up a ladder onto an elevated platform and dive under a pile of blankets, their shrieks becoming muffled.

Two older kids are setting out chairs, their movements fluid and accommodating of each other in a way that makes them appear older than their biological age, which looks to be around twelve. They have that difference, a certain composure common to those born after. For one thing, they don't use before and after as shorthand. They weren't there. The distinction doesn't exist in their minds the way it does in older people. They have instead a kind of grace, even if it's paid for by their inability to miss what they never had.

We all sit together.

The table quickly becomes noisy with talk and I allow myself the luxury of a back seat, carried as a mostly silent passenger on the animated talk and laughter around me. Someone hands me a bowl of orangeish lumpy stuff, fried mushrooms, green leaves and a hunk of dark bread on the side. Everything tastes delicious. When I lived in the centre of Avie, what seems like a lifetime ago before my stay in Northolt, I kept myself to myself and had assumed life in the camp to be even rougher, more dog-eat-dog, than in town, but perhaps that's not necessarily true. Maybe it depends on the company you keep.

Captain Chaos is perched on a stool opposite, swinging his legs and having a conversation with someone on his minimo. Although he can't be. Even if he had batteries and was able to charge them, the mobile networks have been down for years. I strain to hear what he's saying but it doesn't sound like words, not in any language I've ever heard. A series of low hissing sounds, hums and clicks, like a radio tuner searching through static.

To my right, a lanky boy I'd initially taken for elderly because of his white hair, leans closer to me. A fine white down covers his upper lip. His eyebrows and eyelashes are also white but he's not albino, his eyes are cornflower blue.

'His old man rigged a couple of them up to work like walkie-talkies. They used to play with them all the time,' he says.

'Does he think he can still…?'

'Who knows. Hey, maybe he can eh?' He laughs affectionately. 'Who fucking knows. Keeps the wee bastard occupied at least.'

After the little ones are put to bed, the talk takes a more serious turn. It's disappointing, but not exactly a shock that the atmosphere of peace and security is a fragile thing after all. Raids by organised gangs are becoming more frequent and destructive, tearing through the edges of the camp without warning, like freak storm fronts, leaving wreckage and bodies in their wake. The raiders take anything they can use: food, materials, people. The young they can employ in all manner of ways, women too have their uses. Men, along with the old and the sick, are more trouble than they're worth, and are either left battered but alive or killed on the spot depending on exactly how troublesome they prove. Some of the residents have set up a watch rota and warning systems to give people time to get out of the way or hide when a raid is imminent but organisation is difficult amongst such a transient population and these efforts fail more often than they succeed.

I'm grateful for the company, for the distraction from the way my thoughts keep being dragged magnetically, like a compass needle, back to the hills, back towards Northolt, always north.

It's much later, pushing into the early hours of the morning, a cold fog snaking close to the ground, when Grant and I make our way back to his shelter. We wrap blankets round our shoulders. Grant lights the stove and puts a kettle on to boil.

'So, are we going to deal with the elephant in the room now?' he asks, handing me a cup of his earthy tea.

'I think it's a bear. Don't you?'

Grant gives a soft laugh. 'You going to tell me what happened with you up there?'

I turn the question back on him. 'First tell me what happened to you.'

'Me? Oh,' he runs a hand over his scalp, as if checking the scars are still there, 'didn't work out. Didn't have the right kind of brain waves or something. I didn't really understand what that lanky bloke—'

'Clyde?'

'Yeah, him. Didn't understand what he was on about half the time. He seemed pretty disappointed my results were so poor. So was I. I'd been working for Alex for quite a while by then. Was sorry to let him down.'

'What were you doing for them before you got,' I stare at the crown of his head, 'perforated?'

'This and that. Whatever needed doing. Supplies. Information. You know I traced the rest of the crew for them.'

'You said you'd tracked everyone down. Don't recall you mentioning you were doing it on Alex's payroll though.'

'Didn't I? Well, I wouldn't have kept that from you intentionally. I'd no reason to lie. Shit, Izzy, we drank so much that night I don't know that either of us can be absolutely sure what was said. It wasn't a great time for me. I'd lost...' he looks down, digs one of his boot heels into the ground and makes a messy gouge in the hard-packed dirt. 'I'd lost a friend. Someone that mattered to me a great deal. I was a fucking mess, drinking far too much. You know how that goes.'

'I do.' We sit in silence for a while. I'm not going to pry into his loss. Everyone has their wounds, no need to stick your fingers in them. I think of the incriminating paperwork I stumbled across at Northolt. I'd left before asking either Alex or Clyde about that directly. 'Do you know what happened to them afterwards? The rest of the crew?'

'Much the same as me, I think.' Grant frowns. 'Went back to whatever they were doing before. Or moved on elsewhere.'

'Are you sure about that? Are you still in touch with any of them now?'

'No. What are you saying? You think something happened to them up there? Come on, the folk at Northolt are the good guys, Izzy.'

'You really think so?'

'What they're trying to do, it's not for personal gain or power, they're genuinely trying to help, to put things right. I know it all seems a bit nuts, and I'm not going to pretend I understand it all, but at least they're trying.'

A big part of me wants to share Grant's certainty, but it's too simplistic, an almost childlike faith. The F-word has always struck me as a trick, a self-deluding intellectual sleight-of-hand. Fair play if that works for you, but I've never managed to convince myself to fall for any variety of it. Good and evil? Nothing is that clear cut. 'Who's behind them? Northolt is vast, all the labs and equipment and the people working there. Who pays for it all?'

'Nobody that's aware of it.' Grant smiles at my puzzlement. 'Remember your friend Daniels?'

'Don't be ridiculous. Daniels wasn't—'

'Not him personally. I mean people like him, with the skills to siphon off resources when things broke apart. Plenty of stuff went missing in all the confusion. Scale that idea up to government and corporation level, companies and organisations. Like Pilgrim, for example.'

'They are definitely not the good guys.'

'Even they can't keep track of everything these days, although they certainly profited in the short term. The whole industrial-capitalist system is a burst sieve, pissing money from a million holes. Northolt have people who know how to collect it, and no one is any the wiser. And even if they were, what are they going to do about it? Take them to court?'

'You make them sound like some kind of Robin Hood setup.'

'Is that so hard to believe?'

'Yes, Grant, it is. Robin Hood's a fucking story. Fantasy. Shit like that doesn't happen in real life. And even if it did, I seriously doubt the merry men were ever into torturing animals.'

'They weren't torturing him.'

'Looked that way.'

'One bear, Izzy. What if one single bear could save the whole world from drowning?'

I stare sullenly into my empty mug. I won't answer that. It's not a real question about a real situation. It's just some stupid fantasy drama with a growly American voice-over Grant has allowed himself to believe in because he can't handle reality.

'And since when have you been an animal rights activist anyway?'

'It wasn't only that. It was everything, the whole setup. It all felt wrong. I dunno. I needed to get away.'

'So you quit? Without finishing the work?' Grant's tone changes. 'Shit, Izzy. I can't believe you were that short-sighted, that selfish.' He bangs his empty mug down on the beer crate, stands up and paces around as much as the cramped space will allow. He keeps turning towards me, about to say something then stopping himself and resuming his pacing, like he can't find the right insult.

'Fuck's sake, Grant. This isn't a comic book. We do not have twenty-four hours to save the Earth. The world's already fucked, and we're all fucked along with it. That's not my fault and it's not yours.'

He strides back towards me, pointing a finger. 'That,' he jabs the finger again, 'that right there is exactly the kind of self-serving crap that landed us all in this mess. Nobody's prepared to accept that their own actions matter. It's always somebody else's fault.'

'You can't take responsibility for the whole world and every mistake, every wrong or bad thing in it. It's not practical and it doesn't help anyone.'

'Maybe not.' Grant sits down heavily. 'But floating along like none of it has anything to do with you is fuck all use to anyone either, is it?'

Stalemate. We fall silent and avoid looking at each other.

After a few minutes Grant lies on the bed, drags a gutted sleeping bag over his body and turns his back to me. I put my empty mug down, reluctantly letting go of the memory of warmth it held, and tug the edges of the blanket tighter around my shoulders.

I watch the flickering candle and listen to his breathing until it slows and deepens. The temperature drops and the wind picks up outside making the shelter creak and rustle. I know he's right about the bigger picture, but can't see how that changes anything. We are where we are.

When I can't stay awake any longer I slide into bed next to Grant. He grumbles sleepily but shifts over to make room and doesn't object when I fit myself close into the shape of him.

XII

In the days that follow, I help out around the place, lending a hand at repairs and maintenance of the shelters. This work is endless. The camp residents hammer and fix each day with a dogged refusal to accept utter collapse. It's a welcome change. Fetching and carrying, useful physical tasks with obvious and immediate benefits to people who are right here, who I can reach out and touch. No mind games. No past or future. Only now. I work all day, and drop like a stone into a well of sleep at night. There are still dreams. I still wake several times each night, frantically grasping for some point of reference to tell me where and when I am, but to be sleeping at all, sometimes for two or three hours at a stretch, feels like a gift. The scattered pieces of my mind are putting themselves together again, cogs and springs easing back into place, the mechanism gathering, reaching for a memory of itself, of how it's supposed to be.

❯ • ❮

Food supplies arrive sporadically on trains run by the government but there's never enough to go around. Some days I leave the camp on foraging expeditions with Adam, who reverts to his civilian name when not wearing his cape. Nobody can be a hero all the time.

We walk south-east out of town, past Colyumbridge, being careful to stay out of view of the Hilton, now occupied by members of one of the less menacing gangs. They're a mostly harmless bunch, bikers and drinkers who generally exercise their violent or destructive tendencies within their own number, but there's no need to present ourselves as alternative targets.

The old logging path twists amiably towards the Lairig Ghru and the mountains. Summits crowned with snow rise up against white massy clouds making it hard to tell where the mountains end and the sky begins. Periodically, the sun breaks through an opening and falls on the land, lighting up the snow cover that clings to the descending ridges, brilliant white flaring along the bones of the dark grey-green mountains, displaying the skeletons of those hunched and slumbering beasts. The animal in the land, the land in the animal.

We skirt yet another encampment of shabby trailers, vans and tents and enter Rothiemurchus forest. Gnarled branches twist this way and that at weird angles, gloved with a pale grey lace of lichen to the tips of each twig. The forest floor is strewn with fallen limbs and trunks, sinking with unobservable slowness into the hummocks of vegetation to be reabsorbed. The scent of decay is thick enough to taste.

Adam darts here and there, light-footed, finding hidden patches of blaeberries, stuffing sticky handfuls into his canvas bag. I'm less sure of where the snares and traps laid in the dense undergrowth are and tread more carefully, scanning for the yellow of chanterelles. Adam runs back, a grey blur in his hand, and holds it out proudly. It's a squirrel, most of a squirrel, three quarters maybe. The tail and one back leg is missing, the bone a broken white pencil protruding from darkened flesh. Adam is grinning and nodding that I should put it in my bag.

'Really?'

He frowns and tilts the squirrel's body sideways then knocks it lightly off a nearby tree, showing me it's still stiff so relatively fresh.

'Okay, fine. I'll take your word for it.' I hold the bag open for him to drop it in and make a decision to avoid the stew tonight.

The old forest gives way to a patch of commercially planted pine. The uniform rows have been haphazardly hacked into for firewood and timber so daylight comes down in vertical spotlights through the bald patches. Elsewhere the trees have grown huge and closed their canopy fifty feet above so the trunks stand in pools of shadow like doomed office workers trapped shoulder to shoulder in a broken elevator, forlornly gazing upwards, praying for it to transport them on.

Adam's running silhouette flickers between the black bars like a sequence of pictures in a zoetrope, shedding dimensions, his little body stuttering and impressionistic as a dream, or a memory. So many children were born after the change. Few of them intentionally. Reliable contraception became harder to get hold of and, given the proven correlation between the shitness of circumstances and the amount of sex people need to compensate for that, the results were predictable enough. Always felt like too great a risk to me. Doing without has been a fair price to pay for certainty.

At the edge of the pine forest the view to the mountains opens up again. There's the iron ladder of the funicular railway laid against the flank of Cairn Gorm itself. Grant said the government are building some kind of stronghold up at the old top station. They commandeered the funicular and it runs constantly, transporting staff and materials upwards. A good choice of location, surely unassailable either by man or by nature. I don't envy them their safety though. If the sea rises enough to justify the move, they'll end their days presiding over a submerged world, waiting to run out of food, to starve or drown just like everyone else. All their power will buy them is a little more time to watch the sea claim the mountain passes, as the peaks become islands, the whole range transforming into a vanishing archipelago.

Adam tugs at my sleeve. He has more pressing concerns.

'Okay, you're right, time we were getting back,' I say. 'This squirrel isn't going to cook itself.'

> • <

The old Grant would've sulked for days after our disagreement about Northolt but this new version is more pragmatic. Nobody has time for such self-indulgence now.

It's late. The stars are hidden by cloud and darkness presses down on the camp. Grant and I huddle around a small fire at the entrance to his shelter, and the talk turns to Alex.

Grant got to know him a lot better than me, learning how he'd gone from environmental scientist to activist, and his interests in shamanism and quantum physics. Over the years he collected a menagerie of disparate disciplines, cross-breeding them like a theoretical Doctor Moreau. At this thought there's a growl and a flash of teeth from the bear that's always at the back of my mind, pacing behind my thoughts. It reminds me that Alex experimented with more than just abstract ideas.

'He's your original polymath,' says Grant. 'And he doesn't rule anything out.'

'Or he just can't make his mind up what to believe.'

'He'd say he does his best to avoid that.'

'He probably would.' I still can't decide whether I find this inspiring, infuriating or terrifying.

'Do you remember when we got back to Ny Ålesund?'

'Kind of.'

That day was never written into my journal so hasn't been re-recorded, digitised, filtered, replayed. It exists only in the neglected remnants of my fallible organic memory. It's always had a quality of avoidable risk about it, like a partially frozen pond.

> • <

That last day on the *Polar Horizon*, we'd woken to an eerie silence – the cries of the dying animals, the groan and crack of the ice as it closed around us, all of it had simply stopped. The silence drew us like an enchantment towards the bridge.

The open sea shone like silver. No animals. No ice. No one spoke. Nobody wanted to break the spell. I wondered if it was a dream, if we were all dying in reality, each of us still alone in our respective cabins, all having the same dream.

Two things happened at once. Proteus hummed back into life, hard drives chattering and lights flashing as the screens activated and pulsed with data. Jules raised his arm and pointed straight ahead. 'Look.'

I double checked on the now fully operational helmsman display. We were back where we'd started, near as damn it. The Svalbard archipelago lay dead ahead on the horizon.

We didn't talk much as we approached Ny Ålesund. A persistent skin of unreality clung to everything, a feeling of having crossed an invisible boundary and that the world we returned to might not be the world we'd known. Perhaps we'd find a race of sentient bears running the show and, as the only humans left, we'd be the ones to be tagged and studied, experimented upon, dissected.

The shapes moving around on the dock looked human enough and as we drew closer we began to loosen up, to accept we were really back. Whether the world was exactly as we'd left it was a question for later.

Bjornsen was stretchered off the vessel, still delirious, shouting something in Norwegian. From sitting with him on the ship I'd begun to recognise certain words that kept repeating. *Tid, kart, isbjorn, brutt* – time, map, ice-bear, broken, as one of the other Norwegian crew told me. But when I asked what exactly Bjornsen was saying about these things the sailor averted his eyes and shook his head. 'It doesn't make sense,' he muttered. 'I think he's really lost it.'

The chief officer at the facility, a short muscular woman with steel-grey hair and a don't-fuck-with-me demeanour, took one look at Bjornsen and issued concise orders for the plane that had been about to take off on its return flight to Longyearbyen to get clearance for the longer flight to Tromsø. Ralf's objection that Bjornsen needed medical care as soon as possible and should be taken to Longyearbyen hospital was met with a flat refusal. 'They don't have the facilities for something like this. He can't be here. Dying is not permitted on Svalbard. That's the law.'

'I've got him this far. No bloody way he's carking it now,' said Ralf, but the chief was clearly not someone given to changing her mind. 'Right. Fine. But I'm going with him.'

We watched the plane carrying Bjornsen and Ralf as it shrank in the sky before we turned to the next problem.

Even the unflappable chief took a double take when we told her about the bear. Once they'd swallowed their incredulity, the scientists more or less took over, led by the Russian team who were already tagging and studying the local bear population. Killing it was immediately ruled out. We had to find a way to get it safely off the ship alive.

'Why not just let it go and make its own way back into the wild?'

'Unwise considering how disoriented it's likely to be. And hungry.'

'We could put tranquiliser gas through the ship's warm air heating.'

'Too difficult to calculate the right dosage.'

It was eventually agreed that one of the exits from deck four would be unblocked and when the bear came out, the chief would shoot it with a tranquiliser dart. It would then be transported to an uninhabited part of the island, tagged and released. A helicopter was on its way from Barentsberg.

I'd seen the scientists, in their brightly coloured waterproof jackets and warm hats, as a homogenous group, not as individuals, but now I examined the memory more closely, tried to separate them out. That one. Those dark eyes.

> • <

Grant adds a few more fragments of broken up snowboard to the fire. They hiss and crackle, letting out a thin acrid smoke as they catch. Shadows shift at the edges of our circle of light. The familiar face comes into sharp focus in my memory. That curious expression balanced between intensity and detachment, no beard but a thin silver hoop in his left ear.

'Alex was there?'

'He was only a junior researcher at that time. But yes, that's where it all started.'

Another thought is stirring in the shadows, drawing closer to the light. 'The bear wasn't released, was it?'

'No. But that wasn't Alex's doing, initially. It was taken to an animal research centre in Siberia. A few years later the Russian government decided to close down that facility and all the animals were supposed to be destroyed. But by then Alex had started to form ideas of his own. He somehow managed to get the bear moved to his private lab.'

The thought steps forward out of the darkness and into the light. 'It's the same bear?'

Grant nods.

'But it can't be. That was twenty years ago and that bear was already older than it should've been, even if Bjornsen was right about it being the same one that attacked him and his brother years before that. It's just not possible.'

'And you're so sure of what is and is not possible?'

'No, but—'

'Izzy, you have to let go of the old ways of thinking.'

'If you mean common sense and logic then, nah, I think I'll hang on to them, thanks.'

'Folk used to be sure the earth was flat. Sense and logic change. We have to change too.'

I scratch my head. I can feel all the thoughts and memories crawling around my mind, making my brain itch.

'Don't ask me for the science of how they did it. Some kind of partial cryogenic suspension. Clyde said something about how they'd slowed cellular aging within the bear's body to such a reduced rate that they had, to all intents and purposes, removed it from time.'

My brain is jammed up like an overloaded hard drive, hundreds of gigs of data firing in different directions, conflicting lines of code generating error after error. The itch is maddening.

'Stay still.' Grant's eyes are focused on my hairline. He reaches forwards.

'What is it?'

He holds something pinched between his thumb and index finger. 'You're not going to like it.' He drops a dark speck onto the palm of his hand and holds it out for me to see. It lies there on its back, legs waggling in the air.

'Fuck!' I hunch over, dig my fingers into my hair and shake it from the scalp. Several crawlers fall at my feet. 'Shit.'

'Only one thing for it,' says Grant, kicking dirt over the fire. 'If madam would care to take a seat?' He sweeps an arm towards the shelter.

> • <

He uses scissors first, a big old rusty pair more like shears, chomping chunks of hair off as close to the bone as he can get without scalping me. The auburn coils pile between our feet. Every now and then a louse attempts to crawl out of the pile and I take a petty satisfaction in stamping on every single one, making little bloody smears on the lino.

Grant sits back and admires his work. 'Takes years off you.'

My ears feel absurdly vulnerable and my neck naked. I run my fingers across the remaining uneven tufts.

'Not done yet.' He gets up and returns a minute later with a bowl of water and an old-fashioned shaving razor which he sets on the beer crate.

'Only way to be sure.' He presses his lips together, trying to look serious. 'Plus, you look like a French collaborator after the war.'

The feel of the blade rasping over the bones of my skull sends pins and needles fizzing under my skin. When the hair is all gone, Grant brushes his fingertips from the back of my head, 'occipital,' over the crown, 'parietal, frontal,' down and back, 'sphenoid, temporal.' His thumbs exert a smooth pressure from my temples and around my ears. He repeats the motion and I close my eyes and bite back a gasp as the surging electric sensation increases. My head feels like a Van de Graaff generator. After a few minutes the pressure decreases gradually until Grant takes his hands away.

I open my eyes and the world floods back in. I feel lighter and hyper-aware of each tiny current of air in the shelter as it swims around my head. All of my senses feel cleaned and sharpened.

Grant takes my hands and pulls me to my feet.

'Where did you learn how to do that?'

'A little something Alex taught me.' Grant's smiling. He plonks a woolly hat on my head and pulls it down over my ears.

> • <

A few days later coming back through town with Adam, there are more people on the street than usual, singly and in small groups, all heading purposefully in the same direction. There must be a train coming in. Maybe food. I tell Adam to head back to the camp without me. Even before I went to Northolt, the handouts were starting to get ugly.

Distribution of supplies was originally based on a ticket system, something like rationing. When that broke down, they put soldiers on the trains to herd people into rough queues and discourage riots. But you had to get there sharp and be prepared to defend your place. I'd preferred to barter on the black market but that takes time. Right now I like the idea of returning to camp with a solid contribution. Something to pay my way. A sack of rice or flour, some tinned veg. Something more substantial than a bag of berries and a rigid squirrel.

The platform is crowded, people already jostling for position before knowing where the soldiers will set up the line. We hear it before we see it round the bend, the slow labouring engine, the grind of metal on metal, the clank of covered wagons. Goods trains are all heavily armoured now. The plating on the front of this one has been messily vandalised with red paint. As the train rumbles closer the mess resolves into the shape of a mouth, a wide clown-like leer, crowded with tiny triangular teeth. Wisps of mist cling and trail from it like smoke. The windows above are black slits.

People shove each other to the far end of the platform when they realise the train hasn't slowed enough to stop squarely. I don't think it's going to stop at all. The doors on one of the rear covered wagons roll back and a few sacks are thrown out onto the platform but the train keeps moving, picks up speed and is gone.

From behind where the sacks landed a loud 'Jesus fuck!'

The sacks aren't rice. Or flour.

We lay the bodies in the waiting room. The driver, an engineer and four young soldiers. All with their throats opened.

> • <

'Train didn't stop,' is all I tell them back at the camp. Someone else will fill them in on the details soon enough, then everyone can speculate on who was responsible: gangs, mercenaries, a rogue army battalion. No amount of debate will change anything, will make it not have happened. I don't want to talk about it. Don't want to think about it. My hands won't stop shaking. I go to bed hungry.

My dreams are jagged, icy, full of teeth. I'm in the library at Northolt. In this version of it, the book-lined walls stretch ahead out of sight. I'm looking for Alex but can't reach the place where the room turns. The books rustle and whisper as I pass, muttering to each other. They don't want me to reach him. I try to run but only go slower. So many books. And not one of them made any difference. Added together all they amount to is humanity's elaborate and over-long suicide note to itself. The words twitch and crawl blindly over each other in their dark cages.

I know Alex is there, just around the corner, I feel an urgent need to tell him something. Or is it a question I need to ask? I can't remember which but tell myself it will come back to me if I can only reach him, if I can see his face. The room narrows and the books begin to bleed shadows from between their pages and blend into each other, their spines blurring and merging until they smooth over into flat walls which close in, tighter and tighter and then I'm hurrying along a corridor, a narrow passageway that rocks under my feet.

Animal skins are pinned on the walls. Or at first I assume they're animal. But they're not. They're human. Split down the middle, peeled and flattened out, displayed like bear skins with the heads still attached, hair combed down their backs, faces tilted up, mouths open showing their teeth, and quietly at first, then louder and louder, comes a terrible screaming.

XIII

I'm in Grant's shelter. In the camp. None of that was real. So why I am still hearing the groan and crash of breaking ice, the desperate cries of trapped animals? I sit up and press my feet to the ground, try to anchor myself more firmly in the present, but the sounds won't go away. They come closer and push against the walls of the shelter. I look around: no Grant. Red light flickers at the gap of the doorway and I can smell smoke. I hastily tug on my boots and pull back the sheeting.

The place is in chaos. People run in all directions, several shelters are on fire and a there's a thick smog that makes my eyes stream. I wipe at them with the heel of my hand and squint into the dirty orange haze. Looming huge against a sudden bloom of flame, two men, faces streaked with black, dismantle a shelter with clubs and kick over the wreckage, presumably looking for anything of value. The wave of destruction is rolling in this direction. I move away from Grant's doorway and duck into the shadows, hoping the men haven't seen me. Someone is fighting with them now, trying to protect what's left of their home. The larger of the raiders grabs the much smaller figure by the head and gives an abrupt twist. Unbelievable that such a small sound should travel so clearly across the rest of the mayhem but I hear the snap with absolute clarity. The raider flings the body aside and starts tearing apart the remains of what their victim had been trying to guard. Finding nothing, they move on, closer to my hiding place. I keep low and go north, as quickly as I can between shadows and wreckage until I'm out of sight.

> • <

Where the howff should be is instead a mass of splintered and twisted wood. It looks as though it exploded from the inside. Some of the main beams are still upright but bent outwards like the bones of an enormous empty ribcage. How did I manage to sleep through so much destruction? Debris is scattered all around and trampled into the dirt. I scan the wreckage, don't see any bodies.

A faint sound tugs at the edges of my hearing and I strain to focus on it through the pandemonium. I eventually trace it to a soot-streaked tarpaulin and gently lift the edge. The boy with the white hair is curled on his side, holding Adam tightly to his chest with one hand. The blade of a knife flashes in the other. I step back, raising my hands, open-palmed. Recognition flickers in his eyes and he lowers the weapon. Adam doesn't look up but continues with his strange stream of static, delivering it into his minimo, held close to his mouth.

'Is he hurt? Are you alright? What happened?'

The boy ignores my stream of questions, as though the answers have no relevance. 'I'll take care of him,' he says flatly, and I don't doubt that he will. But I can't just leave them.

'You better come with me.'

'Why?'

'We could find somewhere safe...'

We both know there's no such place.

'We'll stay here until they're gone. You should go.' He tugs the tarpaulin back over their bodies, gently shushing Adam. The whisper of static lowers in volume but doesn't completely fade out.

I take a couple of steps, then turn back. It feels wrong to walk away but he's right. Why come with me? What do I know that he doesn't? What use am I?

I pick my way through more wreckage. There must be something I can do, some way I can help. Where the fuck is Grant?

After hours of searching the ruins, dodging groups of raiders, I finally recognise a pair of boots sticking out from under a pile of collapsed wood. I drag the smouldering planks away. He's lying face down, one of his arms twisted away from his body at an unnatural angle and his legs trapped under a heavy beam which, after a lot of tugging and straining, I manage to shift to the side. I help him turn onto his back and sit up. His blood-and-dirt-encrusted face is a grimace of pain and blood dribbles from the corner of his mouth.

'Ah, shit, Grant. Are you okay? Can you move?'

He coughs and a fine spray of blood flecks his lips. 'Been better,' he winces as he takes a shallow breath. 'Few broken ribs maybe, and I think my shoulder's dislocated. How's your first aid?'

'Um. Not really up to—'

'Shh. Just hold my arm straight and pull.' He looks up at me impatiently. 'Come on. I can't do it myself.'

'What if I break it?'

'You won't.'

I lift Grant's arm by the wrist and straighten it out to the side.

He groans through gritted teeth. 'Right, now, brace your foot against something and pull.'

My hands are starting to slip when I feel the bones pop back into place.

'Ah ya bastard,' Grant barks.

When he gets his breath back I tell him about Adam.

He nods and gets to his feet, pressing a hand to his ribs. 'I'll go back for them. You better clear out.'

'No, let me help, I can—'

'Izzy, listen to me. If those animals come back, they'll probably kill us all, or worse. Best thing you can do is get as far away from here as possible.'

'But I don't… I mean, where? I've nowhere else to go.'

'Yes you have,' says Grant. He's about to elaborate when we hear voices and the sounds of destruction coming our way. We don't have time to hide. 'On the ground,' he says, 'play dead.'

I flatten myself into the mud and Grant lies across me. Footsteps pass close by. Two sets, maybe more. There are raucous shouts and laughter and between their noise I hear a miserable whimpering. I open one eye a tiny crack. They have a girl with them. They've bound her wrists and are dragging her along behind them. I must've given some physical sign because I feel Grant pressing his weight down on me more firmly. The group moves on and we stay there with our eyes closed, hardly breathing until we're sure they're far enough away.

Grant gives me a brief, clumsy hug, gasping in pain as his ribs shift. He stares into my eyes. 'You have to go, Izzy. Go now. Run.'

XIV

It's not fear. Or the will to survive. It's a blind animal drive that overtakes both of those to reach something absolute and utterly without consideration. I pass through the camp, through the cries of the wounded and dying, through the splintered remains of homes, through the smoke and fire and ruin. Everything is burning. Even in town, orange flames dance in the bay windows of the old stone buildings. I weave through the clusters of people who reel in all directions through the streets, hefting bags and children, dragging hand carts.

I don't stop, I don't think. Blood pounds in my head in time with each footfall. I don't break stride until I'm back in the old forest.

> • <

The air has a sour taste and smoke blown in on the wind drifts across the undergrowth in ragged, cobwebby nets. I bend over with my hands on my knees, heart battering hard against my ribs as though demanding to be allowed out. I cough and spit. Gluey saliva hangs from my lip in an unbroken thread to the forest floor, until I spit again and break the connection. My legs are shaky but I set off at a fast walk, scared that if I don't keep the muscles moving they'll give out altogether.

What's happening back there is more than some opportunistic raid. The scale of it. I sort through possible explanations as I walk, no single theory fitting any better than the next. The dominant gangs could've somehow combined forces and decided, for their own warped reasons, to torch the whole region and take over, take all the remaining resources for themselves, along with control of the railway line. Or the burning started first in the same way the fires took hold of the world's skyscrapers, nature reclaiming the planet, and the raiders responded in the only way they know, by attacking those weaker than themselves. My suspicion of the government, or whatever splinter of it is operating locally, surfaces. Perhaps this is their doing, backed by army or militia. Now that they have their stronghold up on Cairn Gorm, they could've decided to clean up the area, get rid of all those troublesome huddled masses camped at its foot. I wouldn't put it past them.

I wipe sweat from my forehead with my sleeve. My clothes are sticking to my skin so I stop and pull the jumper over my head then tie it around my waist. Through the twisting lichen-covered branches the light is fading, the short day already retreating. Against the darkening sky, the pale tree canopy sways like a bleached and calcified coral reef.

The noise of human turmoil is far behind but the forest is not silent. There's a low groaning coming from the trees themselves. I put my hand on the cracked bark of an aged birch. It's warm to the touch and a distinct vibration travels from the tree through to my palm. I crouch and lay a hand flat on the path. This too is unnaturally warm. Feverish.

Exhaustion is beginning to catch up with me but I keep going. The ground climbs steadily upwards in a series of ridges with long ascents and shorter descents, the rise and fall of it like waves sweeping me along. Over the next crest and down into a wide plantation of cultivated pine. The ground here is softer, dry earth matted with pine needles. Small clouds of dust, or is it smoke, puff out from under my boots at every footfall.

As night closes in around the trunks, the temperature is rising. Red glints from between the trees. Something nearby is burning. Then I realise what I'm seeing between the trees is only more trees, their trunks veined with a red glow pulsing from the cracks in their bark. The trees are heating up from the inside. I watch, mesmerised, as a snake-like tongue of flame slides out of one of these fissures and licks across the skin of the tree making it shudder and shed a spray of desiccated needles. Instead of life-giving water and nutrients, the trees are drawing up fire, helplessly feeding on their own destruction. It's unstoppable. Because that's how they're made. Because that's how their roots work. They can no more choose to do otherwise than fly.

> • <

I head for open ground, hoping for cooler air, and emerge from the treeline at the same time as a pair of red deer break cover to my right. Their heads turn in my direction, a young stag and a hind, silhouetted against the sky. The glow from the forest gilds their flanks and outlines the stag's antlers with red, giving him a fiery crown. There is a long moment of stillness as we regard each other then, at some invisible signal, they take off together, leaping across the hillside, vanishing into the night.

I scramble clumsily over springy heather and gorse towards a lone pine and lean against it. Its gnarled roots clasp over a rocky outcrop before disappearing into the soil. So far it seems uninfected by the fever that grips the body of the forest. I lower myself into a natural cleft in the rock and sit with my back supported by a huge root, my head resting on a cushion of moss. The golden pivot of the pole star turns the sky above me, the other constellations only occasionally visible through breaks in the low smoky clouds. Scatterings of ashy flakes drift and spin in the wind. Debris from the fires. Funereal snow. In the distance I hear the cawing of rooks and jackdaws displaced from their roosts.

I sink further into my hiding place, as a deep weariness settles into me. I'm heavy enough to sink into the ground and be swallowed up right now and I don't care, I wouldn't have the strength to fight it. Everything is over. Everything is too late. I'm so tired of all the damage. I close my eyes. Let it all fucking burn or drown. Let it be over, finally. Make it clean.

If only it could be that simple.

> • <

When I wake the morning is already well advanced, but it's still dark. The meagre sunlight can't penetrate all the smoke in the atmosphere and the hillside broods in an unnatural twilight, lit from below by the bruised light from still-burning fires.

I lever myself out from the rocks and roots and stretch. My spine cracks and my leg muscles are sore but I've felt worse. What now? I've come this far without thinking about what's ahead, my direction or purpose, and I now realise I'm at least halfway back towards Northolt. Something is drawing me back there. Whether I choose it or not, I can't ignore the magnetic pull I feel deep in my bones, as though every atom of my physical being is twisting, aligning their electrons and positrons along preordained lines. I have to go north and I don't need a compass. I am a compass.

I stay out of the woodland as much as possible, keeping to clear ground where there isn't much fuel for any kind of a fire. All day and the day after I follow the pull northwards, feeling neither hungry nor thirsty, but drinking handfuls of water from burns whenever I come across one twisting down the hillside. The water is brown, full of earth and twigs and tastes like an ashtray. Despite all the burns having widened and deepened in recent years bearing the melt from the high-altitude snow beds, the water volume isn't damping the fires.

Finally, on the third day, I push through a dense patch of woodland, scraping my face and hands on dry branches, and emerge into the clearing where Northolt stands. The structure isn't as seamlessly invisible as it was before. Between the reflections of trees and rocks the mirrored exterior flickers with a bloody light that multiplies itself in glittering facets around the clearing. Whatever is happening to the wider area, to the world, is also happening here, now.

I tell myself I could turn around and leave but know I'm not going to do that. I scratch my neck where a trickle of blood has run down from a cut on my temple, the skin hot and grimy from travelling, the itch following the line of old scar tissue.

XV

I make my way inside through the bothy, the fireplace still stuck halfway where I left it weeks ago. The air on the other side is warm and damp. Emergency lighting throws a red cast over everything. As I enter into the network of corridors and work my way deeper, it's as though Northolt is alive, a giant animal embedded in the hillside, and I'm moving through its veins and arteries. I don't know if I'm the infection or the cure. The body or the antibody.

The same compass that drew me across the hills to Northolt now guides me like a homing beacon directly to the bear's lab. The bear is there as always, frosted inside his glass coffin, breathing slow, little lights blinking. He is the calm in the eye of the storm.

'Isobel?' Clyde pops up from behind the unit, wide eyed and jumpy looking. He stares at me, chewing his lip. With my shaved head and caked in blood and dirt from the journey, I must look like cause for concern. 'How did you get here?'

'The door was open.'

'But, I mean… You're back.' Is that emotion in Clyde's voice? Surely not. 'What happened to you?'

'Never mind me. Do you know what's happening out there?' It's possible that the last death throes of the human race could entirely pass Clyde by.

He makes a visible effort to pull himself together. 'Ah, yes, yes, all gone a bit pear shaped eh? And much faster than we'd projected. Bad timing, you could say. Ha!' There's a slightly hysterical edge to Clyde's voice and his gaze keeps sliding down to his left.

I walk around the glass coffin. Alex is sitting at a desk with a console set up. His head hangs forwards, chin almost touching his chest.

'What's going on here?'

His hair is wet and plastered to his brow. I push it back. Electrodes are taped to his temples and there's a drip in his arm. I shake his shoulder.

'Alex.'

Nothing.

'Alex! Wake up!'

Clyde is shifting from foot to foot beside me. 'That's really not a good—'

'Shut up, Clyde,' I snap but leave off trying to rouse Alex. 'What the fuck are you doing to him?'

'Nothing he didn't ask me to. We're attempting a temporal transfer. It was his idea.'

I notice the wires from Alex's electrodes trail over the desk and plug into a set of inputs on the base of the bear's unit. 'Don't tell me. It's perfectly safe, right?'

'No. This is definitely not safe.'

'So why are you doing it?'

'Believe me, I didn't want to. Alex insisted. Said we had to try one last time.'

'To do what?'

'The temporal transfer takes the human consciousness, actually more a copy of it but never mind, and places it within Snowball's cerebral-temporal field. It works, to an extent. We've successfully achieved the transfer before with other subjects. But accuracy is a problem. We can't control the exact point in time at which the human consciousness will emerge or whether it will be compatible with Snowball's innate animal consciousness. Especially in situations involving extreme responses. Fear, hunger, sex, all of these cause problems with control.'

A line of drool runs over Alex's lower lip and drips off the end of his chin. He moans. His mouth opens and closes, his lips flex and draw back from his teeth. He's trying to say something. 'Hhhhuuu... huh... hunng... rrrr.'

'Oh dear,' says Clyde, 'that's not good.'

'Can you stop it?'

Clyde starts fiddling with the controls on the console, tutting exasperatedly, jabbing harder at the buttons as Alex's guttural growls and moans grow increasingly desperate.

'Do something!'

Alex is starting to fit. His body twitches and foam gathers at the corners of his mouth as his teeth grind together. Clyde jerks the wires from the base unit. Alex's body goes rigid then slumps forwards. I catch him before he falls off the chair and push him back upright. His breathing is rapid, his eyes flutter then close again.

Clyde pushes me aside and takes Alex's pulse. 'Okay.' He peels the electrodes away from Alex's forehead. 'He might

take a few moments to come around. That's providing...'
He examines Alex's drip, rummages around for a new bag,
hangs it on the IV stand and starts the process of swapping
them over.

'Providing what?'

'There are risks. Sometimes there are residual traces in the
neocortex, a kind of negative feedback loop compromising
the spatial-temporal—'

'Clyde!'

He finishes changing the IV, drops the empty bag into a
bin and closes the lid with a clang before turning to face me.
'They don't always come back the same.'

While we wait for Alex to regain consciousness, or
whatever parts of it he still possesses, I press Clyde about
their previous attempts at temporal transference. He tells
me they tried it with several of the *Polar Horizon* crew.

'All completely voluntary, I promise,' says Clyde. 'But the
results weren't what we were hoping for. Nothing changed,
you see? Or rather, nothing important.'

'How do you know what's—'

'I mean nothing critical to the course of the survey. We
need to disrupt the survey timeline in such a way as to
change the outcome, resetting the chain of events it set in
motion.'

'So, if you can do that, everything would go back to how
it was before? And we wouldn't be here now?'

Clyde checks the IV tube for air bubbles. 'It's a bit more
complicated than that but, yes, that's about the size of it.'

'Why didn't you try this with me?'

'Your scans.'

'What's wrong with them?'

'Nothing at all. They were brilliant. The most three-dimensional we ever retrieved. We hoped, if we got enough of them, they'd mean we didn't need a human volunteer at all.'

'But I left before you managed to get enough.'

'As it turned out, there wouldn't have been time, even if you'd stayed.'

'We could do it now.'

'We're out of time. As I said.'

'No. I mean, this.' I point to the bear, the discarded electrodes. 'You could hook me up.'

Clyde scratches his ear and looks at Alex, as if hoping he'll take over, but he's still out. 'Okay. Full disclosure. You should know that your scans also indicated a high susceptibility to damage. It's very likely you wouldn't survive.'

Alex stirs and opens his eyes. He's groggy but seems to know where he is and who we are, as far as we can tell.

'What do you remember?' Clyde asks.

'There was a seal,' Alex murmurs, shakes his head, wipes at his mouth.

> • <

This isn't a life or death situation. It's not a choice; we have to take both. One is always nested within the other, separated only by the skin of time.

I am here, have been drawn to this point so that I won't be. I have to do this in order to not have to do this. If it works, there will be no need of any of it.

'You sure you want to do this?' asks Alex.

'Do I need to be sure?'

'No.'

'Well then.'

Snowball's cover slides all the way back. Clyde presses a button and there's a soft hum as the tilt mechanism engages, making it possible for him and Alex to heave and roll the bear onto his side for me. I have an idea of how this should be, of what will feel right, although I don't know where it comes from. I climb on the table and tuck my spine into Snowball's chest, lift his heavy foreleg and drape it over my shoulder. The crown of my head fits exactly into the crescent of his neck and the passage of his breath purrs over my skull.

It's already beginning, time and memory contracting and dilating, collapsing into each other and exploding out, all part of the same cycle, building momentum, gathering power.

Alex hands me the pages of my journal. I hold onto them tightly. My anchor. My release.

Clyde attaches the electrodes to my temples. Electricity surges and snaps. Nearby everything is already burning. Red light flickers at the doorway then advances into the room. The flames eat their way across the ceiling, crawl across the floor and up the walls.

We stay where we are, where we were, where we never were and will always be, curled together, spines nestled one within the other, floating on a frozen sea.

The pages of my journal catch fire and the words are unwritten, the story untold.

White flakes of ash swirl in the updraft, like snow.

I close my eyes and let go.

ACKNOWLEDGEMENTS

Always North started life as a short story, originally published in Gutter magazine in Spring 2011. Without that early act of faith in my initial experimentation, Always North, the novel, quite possibly wouldn't have made it any further.

This book has been on a long, strange journey but has finally found its true home with the wonderful folks at Unsung Stories. Their flagrant disregard for genre boundaries and publishing conventions makes the book world a more interesting place.

Thank you to the friends, family and fellow writers whose perseverance and support make everything possible. You know who you are.

THE ARRIVAL OF MISSIVES

BY ALIYA WHITELEY

From Aliya Whiteley, author of the critically-acclaimed *The Beauty*, comes a genre-defying story of fate, free-will and the choices we make in life.

In the aftermath of the Great War, Shirley Fearn dreams of challenging the conventions of rural England, where life is as predictable as the changing of the seasons.

The scarred veteran Mr. Tiller, left disfigured by an impossible accident on the battlefields of France, brings with him a message: part prophecy, part warning. Will it prevent her mastering her own destiny?

Get a free extract
www.unsungstories.co.uk/trymissives

Follow Aliya  @AliyaWhiteley

OR SCAN THE QR CODE